THE SOURCE OF DEATH

JAY MICHAEL NIGHT

SYNEDRIUM PUBLISHING

CONTENTS

NEW YORK CITY, 1999

"They've found us!" Mikey's mother yelled across their small apartment, holding a phone to her chest. "We can't let him be taken, Jake." She grabbed Mikey protectively and rushed toward the closet that held their luggage.

"Wait, wha—slow down, Angela. Who was on the phone?" His father asked, appearing from their only bedroom.

"It was Mogrin. We need to leave."

"What did he say?"

"The Verdaat know where we are, which means my people will too if they don't already. I won't let Mikey be used by either of them. The Accords won't last."

His mother started frantically packing while still trying to keep Mikey close. His father reached out and grabbed them both in a big hug.

"You know I won't let that happen. I have a friend with a cabin up in Watertown. I'll call him." Jake nodded reassuringly. He pulled out his phone and headed into the kitchen.

In Mikey's five years of life, he'd never seen his mother this shaken. "Mommy, who found us? Are you okay?"

"Yes, sweetie, there are some people that want to take you away from us. But we won't let that happen," she said.

"Why do they want me?"

"Because you are very special. One day mommy and daddy will tell you all about it."

Mikey didn't know how he was special but nodded as she kissed him on the head.

"Okay. It's all set. It's about a five-hour drive to Watertown from the city. If we leave in the next hour, we should still be able to get there before daylight," his dad informed them.

Soon after, they were on the road. Mikey was in the backseat trying to sleep, but his ears pricked up at the sounds of his parents' whispers.

"Did Mogrin say how they found us?"

"No. He overheard Magnus talking to a few elders who claimed to be coming for you and Mikey in the city. Your father terrifies me, Jake."

"After six thousand years, Magnus still terrifies me too."

It was the first time Mikey had ever heard his parents talk about their families, let alone his grandpa. He wondered why they would be scared of him. Grandpas weren't supposed to be scary.

"Also, Mogrin said he'd transfer funds into our account to hold us over. I don't know what we'd do without him."

"He has been a part of our family for over a century. Our people would not run without him. We've always been close."

Mikey wanted to stay quiet and listen in more, but his bladder wouldn't have it. "Daddy, I have to go potty."

"Okay, bud. I saw a sign up ahead; you can go there."

They pulled into a rest area surrounded by trees and parked in front of a tan brick building. A single streetlamp illuminated the empty lot.

"Alright, man-cub, let's go." His dad opened the back door, reaching out a hand. Mikey loved when he called him that. It was from his favorite movie, *The Jungle Book*.

"I'll stay here and guard the fort," his mother gave them two thumbs up as they walked to the bathroom. Mikey walked in and pointed at his chosen urinal. His dad laughed as Mikey pulled his pants all the way down.

"You don't have to pull them all the way, remember?"

Mikey never listened when he told him that, more chance for messes. "Why don't you ever have to go?"

"Um, daddy has a different body than normal people, so he doesn't have to go like you and Mommy do."

"Is it cause you only drink tomato juice?" Mikey asked, walking to the sink. The knobs were too high, so Mikey stuck his arms out to signal for help.

Laughing, his dad obliged, turning on the faucet and patting him on the head. "Yep, it's the only food I need. Luckily, you can have yummy regular food."

His dad's head suddenly jerked towards the door, then he turned off the water to listen. Mikey almost laughed as his father sniffed the air like a dog.

Is he playing a game?

"What the—why would they be here?" His dad looked confused.

A loud crash outside made Mikey jump. Then he heard his mother scream. "Stay here! Don't come out unless me or your mom come get you!" his father ordered before rushing out the door.

Something was definitely wrong. At the sound of glass shattering outside, Mikey dashed underneath the sink, pulling his knees to his chest. He covered his ears to block out the monstrous, inhuman growls and screams. The building shook as thunder rumbled outside. Then, almost as quickly as it began, everything went silent.

BOOM!

Mikey screeched as something pounded on the metal bathroom door. He was too scared to move as the banging continued. With each boom, the metal creaked and groaned in protest. He screamed as the door finally gave, ripping from the hinges to fly across the tiny bathroom with a deafening clash.

His expression morphed into horror as a grotesque creature stood in the doorway. Mikey could never have imagined a thing so terrifying in his worst nightmares. Black, leathery skin reflected off the dim bathroom light. The hulking monster was hunched over, accentuating its elongated arms. Its clawed hands seemed to drag across the floor.

The creature sniffed the air before cold, glowing eyes focused on Mikey. He froze as a massive limb lifted him by his clothes. The monster threw him over its shoulder, carrying him to the carnage outside.

Mikey searched frantically for any sign of his parents among the glass and rubble, though his view was limited. He cried out at the sight of his dad on the ground. Something was sticking out of his neck, his body still. Mikey was filled with emotions he didn't know what to do with.

He screamed and punched the creature's back as hard as he could. "Daddy. Daddy, get up! Get up!"

The creatures were everywhere, and the nightmare was getting worse. Mikey saw his family's burning car lying upside down on the grass. Then her, his mother; next to it, blood pooling underneath. Her arm was outstretched towards the bathroom as her lifeless eyes stared at him.

"No, Mommy. NO!" Warm leathery hands covered his mouth. A fury unlike any he'd ever known overcame Mikey as the air around him shifted. He began to feel stronger. Better. Energy welled inside him, so much so that Mikey thought he would explode. The monster holding him began to shake, then Mikey fell, hitting the ground face-first. But he didn't feel it. There was only the power and anger.

The creature's glowing eyes grew wide as its skin began to shrivel. It slumped to the dirt, shrinking until nothing was left but ash. All around him, the monsters collapsed, and the nearby plants wilted. Mikey stood there, screaming at the carnage the creatures had wrought. But the building pressure inside of him became too much. It exploded, hurling him backward into the woods. Then his world went dark. Everything within a hundred feet of where Mikey had been was blackened, shriveled, and dead.

CHAPTER 1

"Finally!" Mikey yelled at the small TV screen in his room while doing a little victory dance. A heavy blizzard had been passing through Buffalo the last three days, and the news had listed his new high school as closed for the day. It was three days too late, but Buffalo never closed for weather unless you had eighty feet of snow.

Mikey never minded snow or the cold; he always felt warm, even when it was freezing. The only thing that ever bothered him was being around other people. His whole childhood was spent being tossed from foster home to foster home. What was he supposed to do when he was radioactive, and every living thing around him would become sick, then die?

It varied, but as far as Mikey could tell, people would become agitated within an hour of being next to him. After a week, they'd feel like they were in the middle of a bad flu. After a month—well, Mikey never lasted more than a month.

Several families had accused him of poisoning them. They had gone to the hospital, but the doctors couldn't find anything wrong. Their bodies were just deteriorating. Environmental testers checked for heavy metals in the water, radon, and all the other things that might be causing it. Nothing was ever found.

But it hadn't stopped them from sending Mikey back to the children's home. Families heard about the kid secretly poisoning those he lived with, and the fostering stopped altogether. Even though they couldn't prove Mikey did anything wrong, he was kept isolated and locked away from the other kids and staff. Mikey couldn't blame them, though—he was cursed.

In his loneliness, Mikey often thought back on the monsters and what his mother had said that night. She had called him special. As if slowly killing anything near him was a gift. Instead, it made him so lonely sometimes he wanted to end it all. Mikey hated that part of himself and that he had no idea what had happened that night. But it made sense his parents kept him away from others his whole life. Mikey couldn't remember ever being around anybody other than his mom and dad.

He was told that deer hunters had found him wandering the woods the following day, crying about monsters. When police arrived at the scene, they found the wreckage of a terrible car accident; no bodies were recovered. The best explanation for the circle of death was a chemical spill or gas leak. Strangely, no records of Mikey or his parents ever existed.

Mikey glanced up at the drawings pinned up on his wall. The glowing eyes he would never forget. 'Night Prowlers,' he called them. Putting those eyes on paper had started his journey into art. Monsters and the macabre had become his way of combating the almost crippling anxiety of his everyday existence and coping with his lonely life. It was also another way to keep those memories alive.

The only friend Mikey had ever really had since his parent's murder had been his new foster father, Arthur Cafferty. He was a sixty-three-year-old mailman with mostly grey hair who always had a smile and wave for everyone. The adoption happened so quickly that Mikey was still amazed it had ever happened. After years of being locked away, he thought he'd never find a home.

He'd been walking to the children's home after school while Arthur was on his mail route. Some of his classmates had followed Mikey and cornered him in an alleyway, claiming he was cursing them with his monster drawings. They pushed him to the ground and took turns kicking and hitting him. It had been a typical routine throughout his life. People would instinctively figure out he was doing something to them, and they'd lash out. The punches and kicks never caused him any actual physical pain. It just cemented what Mikey knew already: he'd never belong.

He'd often curse his fate, being shortchanged in the superpowers department. If he was so 'special,' he should've at least gotten some webs to shoot out of his arms or the ability to read minds.

But during the attack, Mikey felt warm pressure around him. The kicks stopped as one of his classmates yelled, "Let's get out of here!" When Mikey opened his eyes and looked up, standing before him was an out-of-breath Arthur, staring at Mikey like he had seen a ghost. Instead of going about ignoring him like everyone else, Arthur stayed. He asked questions, and they chatted for an hour that day. Afterward, Arthur was always there on his route when Mikey walked home from school to make sure he was safe.

A short time later, he asked Mikey if he could foster him. The adoption was unorthodox due to Arthur's age. No one else had wanted to for years. Even the social workers at the children's home steered clear. Still, he had a stable job and was well-liked within the community. Arthur was required to foster Mikey for three months, but after, his adoption was approved. The incredible thing was, somehow, his radioactivity didn't seem to bother Arthur.

It had been two years since then. Arthur was offered a postmaster job in Buffalo that was too good an opportunity, so here they were.

Mikey had started his first week at a new high school. He begged to be home-schooled, but Arthur said being stuck alone with him as a 'youngin' wasn't the right way to bring up a teenager. Mikey needed to learn to interact with other kids and adults or at least see how everyone else does. He begrudgingly accepted Arthur's request, not wanting to cause a fuss. Going to high school was a small price for a real home.

Snapping himself out of his thoughts, Mikey glanced at the clock, which read six a.m. Arthur would be up. After delivering mail for over a decade, he had the early morning schedule mapped into his body. Walking downstairs, he saw Arthur was already making himself some coffee in the kitchen.

"Hey, bud. I just saw the news. Though I would've gathered from the dancing upstairs, you got your snow day."

"Yeah. At this rate, I thought they would make us shovel our way to school."

"Back in my day—"

"Yeah, yeah, you used to swim through the snow uphill both ways with no socks or shoes on. I know how hard you old fogeys had it 'back in the day.'"

At that, Arthur handed Mikey a mug, "Well, in celebration of your momentary freedom, I made you a delicious black coffee."

Mikey grabbed the cup and crinkled his nose questioningly until he caught the sweet aroma of hot cocoa. He looked up just in time to see Arthur's smirk disappear.

"Only seems right for the occasion."

"Thanks, Arthur!" Mikey beamed. It was the perfect way to start the snow day. "I'm about to whip up my famous strawberry frosted Pop-Tarts straight from the box if you want some. It has real fruit filling!"

Making fun of silly advertising claims was an inside joke between the two. Like when a cleaning product says something like, 'now with 33% more cleaning power.'

"Well, sign me up for a package, Chef Black."

Mikey walked over to the cupboard sipping on the cocoa, and grabbed the Pop-Tarty breakfast box of champions.

They sat at their small dining table and quietly ate breakfast. This was the wonderful thing about being with Arthur. They were content with just each other's company. In the living room, another news channel droned on. "This blizzard was a doozy, but it looks like everything will probably be back open tomorrow morning," the local weatherwoman announced.

Who starts school back on a Friday?

"So much for a snow day tomorrow too." Mikey slumped. He'd never told Arthur about his aura of death. Mikey didn't want to scare him away. But secondly, it didn't seem to affect Arthur anyway. It put certain constraints on their relationship with Mikey's aversion to being around other people.

"Look, I know it sucks, and you don't get along with other kids, but that isn't your fault...." Arthur paused, seeming to struggle with what to say.

Mikey was sure Arthur wanted him to be more sociable but didn't want to push.

"Just get through school, and after you graduate, you should focus on your art. See if you can become a cartoonist like you want. Who knows, this school might be different. The first couple of days have been fine, right?" Arthur tried to put a positive spin on the situation.

"Yeah, I've been able to pass by unseen, thankfully. But you know it is only a matter of time before someone decides to harass the quiet monster-art dork."

Arthur just sighed and nodded, a familiar torn look on his face.

Unfortunately, the snow day flew by. He and Arthur played board games, watched TV, then went out and shoveled the driveway.

Mikey worked on a ten-eyed tentacle monster drawing for the rest of the night before heading to bed. It looked like a grey and black octopus with six muscular legs. Its four-pronged beak, filled with serrated teeth, took up most of the creature's bulbous head.

What a looker.

Nodding in satisfaction at his newest abomination, Mikey tried to squash down his anxiety for the next day. He put away his art supplies and crawled into bed. "Here's to an uneventful Friday," he muttered.

CHAPTER 2

The following day Mikey walked downstairs to the smell of blueberry pancakes. "That smells great!

Is he finally breaking out that syrup from Smith's maple farm?

Arthur had taken Mikey for a tour last summer. It was so delicious Arthur actually bought a bottle. He joked the syrup should only be used on special occasions, like some high-brand scotch from the 1900s.

"I think you are in definite need of cheering up, so I broke out the syrup," Arthur grinned.

The pancakes had been a great start to the day and a good distraction until Mikey started his five-minute walk to the bus stop.

"Come on, Mikey, let's not poison anyone today," he chanted. The ritual knot of anxiety in his throat was growing by the minute. Mikey realized early on that being first in line for the bus was better. It gave a higher chance of getting an open seat towards the front. Also, the loud and obnoxious students always seemed to sit in the back.

Mikey usually put his backpack next to him to ward away anyone who wanted to sit beside him. It was a subtle enough message, and most people obliged.

He looked up from his thoughts and noticed quite a few more kids at the stop today than before. Mikey guessed their parents had wanted them to stay home during the blizzard.

Lucky.

His bus came into view down the street, and everyone lined up.

"Oh my gosh! Get in, get in! You must be freezing—it's fifteen degrees outside." Mikey heard as soon as the bus driver opened the door. He realized, looking around, that all the other kids were bundled up like they were climbing Mount Everest. All he had was a hoodie from his favorite anime and some jeans. His long, thick brown hair was up in a messy bun. The thought of putting on gloves or a beanie hadn't even come to mind.

Why don't I feel that cold? What a lame power.

"Oh yeah, I'm a little cold but not too bad," Mikey replied, trying not to draw attention. He hurried on and found an open seat closer to the front.

Score.

Mikey placed his backpack in its proper place of warding and let out a sigh of relief. But as the extra number of people got on the bus, a worrying thought occurred to him. This was one of the first stops, and the bus was already a quarter full. If it continued at this rate, he might have to share his seat out of necessity.

Mikey tried not to focus on the inevitable as the bus rolled on.

After a few stops, Mikey realized he was staring at his drawing of a Night Prowler, pencil tapping on the corner of the sketch pad. So far, he'd gotten through with the seat to himself, but Mikey's heart sank as they pulled up to the next stop. There were a lot of students waiting. The math didn't add up; he'd have to give up the spot.

At least the bus ride is only fifteen more minutes.

That shouldn't be enough time for anything to happen. Mikey mentally counted those walking on and the number of seats left when his attention was drawn to the girl walking toward him.

Mikey hadn't seen her the last few bus rides, and she wasn't dressed like a cold-weather explorer either. Her pink, ugly Christmas sweater was the first thing he noticed.

That sweater does not bring the word ugly to mind.

Her outfit was coupled with matching pink gloves and maroon-dyed hair in a neat ponytail. She had on black leggings and pink, furry boots.

Mikey tried not to stare. Her emerald-green eyes were scanning for a place to sit, and it suddenly dawned on him she would need to sit next to him.

Oh no. She's looking over here...oh no. Don't do it!

Mikey panicked and hoped his face was hiding the terror. Too soon, she was standing next to his seat.

"Uh...can I sit here? You're the only spot left this far back, and there's a line behind me." She gestured to his backpack.

"Oh, sorry. Yeah—here," Mikey fumbled to make space.

Mikey's most uncomfortable bus ride ever was made even worse by the fact that every time his eyes glanced over, she was staring at him. Then he'd have to push the anxious knot that formed back down his throat and pretend to focus on his drawing.

"Oh, a perfect picture of a Wendigo. Are you new to the Sect?" the girl said.

It took him a moment to realize she was the one who had spoken.

"Huh?" Was all Mikey's genius brain could think to say.

"The Wendigo," she tapped on his sketchbook. "Also, your Source feels...different. Almost like a constant...weak attack? It's really weird."

Wendigo? Is that what they were...

Mikey was fascinated by lore about monsters, creatures, and different cultures. He wanted to draw them for a living. But she mentioned them like they were real. Like he wasn't crazy. He'd also never heard of 'Source.'

It must be some new slang.

Mikey realized he was sitting silently and should probably respond.

"Um, it could be a Wendigo. It fits the general lore description for sure. And I'm sorry, what do you mean by Source? And—I'm not attacking you...I don't think."

She stared at him for a second before shaking her head like he was the one speaking gibberish. "Wait, you don't know about OS, do you? So, you're a Sap—but then how did you see a Wendigo? And even though it's not right, you are definitely using Source or something like it." She looked even more confused than Mikey.

Oz? Like 'Wizard of Oz?'

Before he could gather his thoughts together to respond, the bus screeched to a halt in front of their school.

"Um...Just forget everything I said, okay?" the girl jumped up quickly and was off the bus before it was their turn.

Mikey's shoe crunched on the dirt path, his mind reeling. He stumbled towards his first class, replaying their conversation over again. The girl obviously knew something he didn't about the Night Prowlers and maybe even Mikey's radioactivity.

Source, she called it...

He decided no matter how uncomfortable it would be, when he saw bus girl again, he'd talk to her and figure this all out.

The first half of Mikey's day passed by uneventfully. Typically though, he'd be able to focus on his classes. But for some reason, all his teachers seemed to sound like the one from *Charlie Brown*. The lunchtime bell rang, signaling the end of biology. Mikey followed the crowd toward the cafeteria. After rounding a corner, lost in thought—Mikey suddenly found himself on the ground.

"Argh! Watch where you're going, moron!"

A tall, tan student stood above him, angrily rubbing his forehead.

Mikey realized he had been looking down while walking and practically headbutted him.

"I—I'm sorry. I was looking down and didn't see you around the corner—"

"Just watch it next time." The guy turned to leave, but his eyes suddenly went wide like someone had slapped him. He cornered Mikey against the wall.

"What the hell are you doing? Are you attacking me with Source?" he growled just loud enough for only Mikey to hear.

"Source—I don't know what that is... I'm not doing anything." Mikey muttered. He was at a loss, another person talking about Source.

"That is against our order; you're gonna pay!" He stabbed a finger at Mikey's chest and then stormed away.

"What in the world is going on today?" Mikey looked up and sighed.

The rest of the day passed by in a blur. He hoped the 'you'll pay' guy would forget the whole thing in a couple of days.

Despite the craziness of the day in general, Mikey didn't want it to ruin his last class, and the only one he looked forward to at school, art.

The best word Mikey would use to describe his art teacher Mrs. Tursley was "off." But that's what Mikey liked about her. All artists were a little eccentric.

"Come, come, my future artists. My young Van Goghs. You Picassos in the making. Have a seat," Mrs. Tursley instructed as he entered the classroom. "Let's get this show on the easel." She let out a hearty laugh at her joke. Every day she made art puns only she found hilarious.

Like his last few classes with her, Mrs. Tursley looked disheveled. Her long red hair was frizzy, poofed out, and in disarray. There was always at least one paint smudge somewhere on her face, and she wore an apron that Mikey assumed was white at some point. It was covered in so many paint streaks there was no real way to tell. She wore large, round glasses that were always falling off her nose. Mikey guessed she was in her mid-thirties.

"Good afternoon Mrs. Tursley," Mikey smiled, scanning the room for an empty easel. He froze when his eyes locked onto a particular area of the classroom. Bus girl was chatting with another student he hadn't seen before.

She was not so subtly going back and forth from Mikey to the other student with her eyes as if to tell him, "that's who I was talking about." When they realized Mikey had seen them, the chatting stopped, and they watched him. Mikey's anxiety began to claw its way out. He smiled meekly at them and quickly found an open easel on the opposite side of the room. It was easier when people were just angry at him. It was much worse when Mikey had no idea what was happening.

"Alright, class, today we will be drawing an apple," Mrs. Tursley started once everyone was settled. A bright red apple appeared from the front pocket of her apron. A few groans erupted from the class, but she smiled like that was her expected reaction.

"Now, now," her grin widened, "there is going to be a twist. You must include this apple in your piece. But you can create anything you want using the apple as the focus. With any medium you please. Pencils, paint, pastels, etcetera, etcetera." She held the apple up for emphasis like it was the ambrosia of the gods. "We will be working on this project today and Monday, so keep your time in mind."

"BEGIN!" She twirled, placing the apple on a stool in the center of the class.

Mikey had already begun thinking of ideas, ultimately deciding to make a play on Adam and Eve. He imagined a giant green and black serpent encircling the apple with a woman's arm reaching for it. It was challenging to focus on the outline as Mikey continued to feel eyes on him. At every glance, the duo was looking at him with puzzled looks. He wondered if he was the only one who wasn't in on the secret. Despite his nerves, Mikey's resolve to confront bus girl about their earlier conversation grew.

The bell finally rang while Mikey finished putting his art supplies away.

He was working up the courage to talk to bus girl when Mrs. Tursley called, "Mr. Black, I'd like to talk to you for a second before you leave. Don't worry. You won't miss the bus."

A few kids in the class snickered, but Mikey was more upset he might miss his chance for answers.

"Of course." Mikey came to her desk. As the duo walked behind him to exit the class, their eyes were still on him. He heard the subtle rasps of whispers as soon as they walked through the door.

"So, I'm dying to know what idea you came up with. Fellow artist to fellow artist," Mrs. Tursley beamed. Mikey was relieved that was all it was about and explained his idea as quickly as possible. Mrs. Tursley had seen his sketchbook on the first day of class, and they'd talked about his wish to become a cartoonist.

He felt terrible because he'd generally love having this conversation, but bus girl could have answers. Also, the longer he was around Mrs. Tursley, the worse she would feel, and Mikey didn't want to jeopardize the one class he enjoyed the first week.

After a few minutes, Mikey looked at the clock on the wall, and Mrs. Tursley got the hint.

"Oop, I'm sorry. Your idea sounds great; I can't wait to see the finished piece. Go, go catch your bus and have a good weekend."

"Thanks. You too."

The art building was at the opposite end of the school across the track field. It was covered in snow, forcing the students to walk through the woods bordering the area with less accumulation. He hurried across, hoping the bus wouldn't leave without him.

Mikey detected a familiar sensation he couldn't quite place when he was almost through the woods. He turned towards it, only to hear a cracking sound before his body was hurled into a tree.

"That was too far, Thomas; you could've killed him," a voice shouted.

Mikey couldn't breathe. Panic filled him when the air wouldn't come.

Breathe!

Finally, with an audible gasp, sweet air rushed to his lungs. Mikey looked up to see the angry guy he accidentally headbutted at lunch a few feet away. Behind him was bus girl and friend.

"Stay out of this, Sabrina. He used his Source on me first," Thomas spat. "Our rules say I was free to defend myself from an unprovoked attack."

"He isn't aware he's doing it. And he doesn't even know about OS. Let's talk to Elder Cassandra about it first before this gets out of hand."

"Yeah, Tom, I was in art class with him. He didn't seem to have a clue what he was doing," the other student chimed in.

"I don't buy it, Marcus. I've never felt this before. It's not right. He's not normal."

Thomas came up to Mikey just as he was trying to stand. He sensed that same pressure as before, then an invisible force knocked him back down.

He didn't even touch me. Wha—what is happening?

Mikey was scared for the first time since his parents' murder.

Then Thomas was on top of him.

"Tell me who you are and what kind of freak Source you are using," Thomas demanded, sending another wave of energy at him.

His body pressed into the ground like an imaginary boulder was laid on Mikey. He wasn't sure whether it was the day's craziness or that he had just experienced the most physical pain of his life—but Mikey had finally had enough. Something inside of him reached out for the energy pressing him down.

And there were no words. Every cell in Mikey's body grew alive as the energy coursed through him.

This is heaven...

Life and strength filled him as the pain disappeared.

"Stop it," Thomas yelled, throwing another wave of energy.

This time, it did nothing. Mikey just wanted more. The pressure holding him down stopped as Thomas began punching him instead. Mikey saw panic in his eyes as each strike grew weaker. The blows stopped as Thomas tried to escape before collapsing to his knees a few steps away.

Mikey's vision blurred from the incredible sensation. He thought for a brief moment that there was yelling in the distance. It didn't matter, though. The energy was all there was.

Yesssssss, more! A voice whispered.

His eyes shot open to a voice screaming. It took Mikey a second to realize it was his own. *Cold,* his brain told him. Cold so profound it was as if his veins were injected with liquid nitrogen. The pain was unbearable; just as fast as it had come, it was gone.

"Mikey, are you okay? Mikey." A familiar voice brought him back to reality.

As his vision cleared, Mikey could make out Arthur kneeling next to him, a worried look on his face. Mikey remembered where he was. He turned his head. The students were on the ground, struggling to get up. They stared at him, their faces a mask of terror.

"Arthur? What happened?" Mikey tried to shake his head clear.

"Oh, thank goodness," Arthur wheezed. He was hunched over, hands on his knees, trying to catch his breath. He turned to the students as Marcus helped the other two stand, seemingly not as affected.

"Leave. Go back to Haven and tell no one of this." Arthur commanded.

Thomas looked like he was about to speak, but Sabrina and Marcus grabbed him and hurried off. Mikey was at a loss for words; the whole scene replayed in his mind.

"Let's go back to the car." Arthur helped Mikey up as soon as he caught his breath.

"Arthur... I—"

"Sorry, bud, just give me a minute. Are you all right, though?"

"Yeah, I think."

"Good, let's head to the truck."

Mikey stayed quiet as they both sat in Arthur's post truck.

"Dammit. I'm such an idiot," Arthur slammed his fist on the dashboard, breaking the silence. "I should have just home-schooled you like you wanted. Thank goodness I decided to pick you up from school today. You could have killed them!" Arthur shook his head. "I just wanted you to have some semblance of a normal life. It's what your mother wanted."

"You knew my   mom?" Mikey   practically   gasped. How could Arthur have known about her and not told him?

"I guess the cat is out of the bag," he sighed. "Yeah, I knew Angela quite well. I was one of her instructors in the Source."

"Bu—"

Arthur raised a hand.

"Just hold your questions until we're home. There is so much to tell you, and I have to figure out how to go about it. And I know those acolytes will spill the beans to Cassandra when they get to the Sect."

Mikey had never had a more challenging time staying quiet in his life.

CHAPTER 3

They both sat on their living room couch, and Arthur finally spoke.

"Before I say anything...I want to tell you I didn't want you to enter this world. Feeling a little lonely, but living a mostly normal life seemed to be better for you than the alternative."

"I have like twenty thousand questions, Arthur. But first, I have to ask, how did you know who I was?"

"That answer is—complicated. Listen, how about I tell you what I feel I should, then I'll answer your questions as best as possible?"

"Okay," Mikey agreed, but he wasn't sure he could hold back from asking questions.

"Now, this is going to all sound as crazy as can be. But I think you've seen crazy enough in your past and today, so you'll know what I'm saying is true."

Mikey nodded, with no idea where this was going.

"Well, I'll just come out right and say it then. Your dad was a vampire."

"A vamp—"

"I know, I know," Arthur held up a hand. "Just let me finish my thoughts before you ask any questions, okay?"

"Sorry." Mikey dug his nails into the palms of his hands as a reminder to listen.

"Most of the stuff you've seen in the movies is pure bologna," Arthur continued. "Vampires...well—I guess we are the only ones who call them vampires. They call themselves the Verdaat. Your dad was one of the first ones. I don't know how old, but at least a few thousand years, I'd wager."

Mikey's eyes practically burst out of their sockets. A memory of his father drinking from a glass filled with a red liquid came to mind. When he'd asked about it, his mother said it was tomato juice.

Mikey recalled the night his parents were attacked. They'd mentioned the Verdaat looking for him. His mom had called his grandfather "Magnus." Both of them said he was terrifying.

"Does Magnus mean anything to you? And do you know why my parents were killed?"

"Magnus...is the leader of the Verdaat and one of the most powerful beings in OS. There are rumors he is the first Verdaat. And I'm sorry. I don't know exactly why your parents were killed. But I know it had to do with you."

"Why me?"

"Because Mikey, you are half Verdaat and half human. A hybrid; the first one ever."

"I—what does that even mean? What kind of freak am I?"

"Not a freak, son," Arthur placed a hand on his shoulder. "You are something unheard of. I don't know exactly how, but you absorb the Source around you."

"The Source?" Mikey recalled the girl from the bus—Sabrina, saying his Source felt weird, that it attacked her.

"Source is...the energy of life. It's in all living things. There are a bunch of theories on where it came from. Chakra, chi, qi—whatever you wanna call it, the idea of it has been around for a long time."

Realization hit Mikey. A memory of one of the mothers who fostered him flashed in his mind.

"Get in there, you demon! I won't let you poison my family anymore!" She locked him in their basement after Joseph, her son with whom Mikey shared a room, became so sick he could barely walk.

My entire life, I've been literally sucking the life out of everyone around me...

It all made sense now. Emotions welled up inside. Mikey didn't know what to do with them. He didn't want this power; he didn't want any of it. Because of him, his parents were murdered by monsters. Whoever was behind it had wanted Mikey. The Wendigo had picked him up and tried to take him away, not kill him.

"Are you okay, bud?"

A drop on his arm made Mikey realize he was crying. "Yeah—I'm good. Just a lot of old memories popping up that I thought I'd forgotten. What's OS?" Mikey tried to focus on other questions.

"Before I continue, promise me you'll let me know if you need a break."

Mikey wiped his face and nodded.

"Good," Arthur continued. "Your mom was a Jaecar, an elder, to be exact. They are humans that can, and are trained, to use Source to hunt and kill the monsters of Otherside, or OS, that prey on people."

"My mom killed monsters?" Mikey's eyes went wide.

"She sure did; was darn good at it too. The Jaecar can harness their inner Source making their bodies faster and stronger than a normal person. Utilizing that energy lets them do many amazing things. Some can heal the body. Some—Arthur pointed to himself—can shield others or themselves. And, as you have felt first-hand, some can project it out like a weapon."

Mikey recalled the pain when Thomas hit him.

"I thought it was magic."

"Where do you think the term 'sorcerer' came from? They were the first people that could harness the Source thousands of years ago."

"Wait, you're a Jaecar?"

"Was. I—I'll tell you about that some other time." Arthur grimaced. There was a story there that pained Arthur greatly. Mikey knew that look.

"And OS," Mikey tried to change the subject, "is it like a different world or something?"

"Yes and no. It's kind of what we call anything that has to do with the supernatural. The creatures of Otherside have always been here. They were at the top of the food chain long ago until the first Sorcerers came. With our numbers increasing, those of OS were forced to change their tactics. They found ways to hide among us, undetected."

"How?"

"Depends," Arthur shrugged. "Some live in remote places. Others can blend in with humans like the vampires. I'm sure there are some we don't even know about. Many creatures of OS can use Source in ways we can't imagine."

"And they are all like—monsters?" Mikey shivered as he imagined the Night Prowlers lurking about.

"No, not all of them are bad. Goblins, faeries, yetis... and many others are generally okay. Some even work with us, like the gnomes."

Mikey realized his jaw was touching the floor when Arthur started laughing.

"You're joking...."

"Nope, they exist. And so do the bad ones," Arthur's face took on the same pained look as before.

"Are you okay?"

"Yeah, sorry. Bad memories."

"Been there," Mikey nodded in understanding.

Arthur's demeanor seemed to change for a moment as he stared out the front window. Then he stood up, turning to Mikey. "All right, I think I need a break. I'm sure you have other questions. But my stomach is eating itself. How about you go upstairs and shower while I order a pizza." Arthur motioned to the dirt on Mikey's clothes. "It should be here by the time you get done. I'll answer the questions you have after."

Mikey felt something odd about Arthur's behavior but shrugged it off.

He is probably just tired and hungry.

Besides, it would take a million years for Mikey to process everything he had just heard. Vampires, monster hunters, Source—a warm shower might clear his head.

"Yeah," he started walking upstairs, "that's a good idea. I'll be back down soon."

Arthur was right, Mikey thought, standing under the warm shower. This was just what he needed. After replaying the day's events over, Mikey knew deep down what Arthur had said was true. The pieces fit together. Plus, he had literally been thrown into the air by magic.

Mikey hopped out of the shower and started getting dressed when his ears pricked up from odd voices coming from downstairs. Quickly putting on clean clothes, he crept to the top of the stairs as quietly as possible. Arthur was still sitting on the couch, facing a woman he'd never seen before. Her back was turned, so Mikey couldn't quite make out her face.

He noticed two other people nearby. One was a dark-haired man standing by the front door like he was guarding it. The other was a blonde woman near the sliding glass door to their backyard.

"The boy will be coming with us. He is untrained and dangerous. Three of our acolytes almost died. You know it is only a matter of time before those bloodsuckers find out he's alive," the woman beside Arthur practically spat.

"Listen, Cassandra—" Arthur started.

"Do not use that familiar tone with me! I am an elder now, and you lost all right when you left Haven," she fumed.

Arthur looked more hurt than Mikey had ever seen him.

"That may have been too harsh." The woman softened slightly, "I do not know what it is like to have suffered a loss such as you've had. But there are many—me included—who feel abandoned by your decision."

"I'm sorry, I never meant—"

"Enough," the woman lifted her hand. "Let's not dwell on the past. I'm not without sympathy. Clearly, you care for the boy, but he will be safest at the Sect for now. His mother and I were very close, in a way."

Another person who knew my mom.

"I figured this would be the best route for the kid if the truth ever got out. But I didn't want this life for him. Neither did his parents, as you know," Arthur sighed.

"We often do not get to choose the life we lead; it chooses us," the woman replied. "I understand why you kept him uninformed and from us, but it was not the right choice. What if another incident like today happened and you weren't there? What if Saps were killed because the boy could not control his vampiric urges?"

"I—" Arthur started. He stopped, then nodded.

"Furthermore, Sabrina informed me that the boy seemed to relish using his powers. He cannot be allowed to roam free until they are under control," she stated.

Arthur continued nodding, then looked up. "Saps?" He raised an eyebrow.

Mikey was glad Arthur asked because he wanted to know what that meant too.

"Some of our youths have begun using the term for humans without the use of Source. It has...started to catch on. I believe it's short for sapiens."

Cassandra jerked her head towards the stairs, and Mikey instinctively ducked down.

"Undoubtedly, you have heard our conversation. Pack what belongings you need into a single bag and come down to say your goodbyes," the woman ordered. "I have spent enough time here as it is."

Mikey froze like someone caught him with a hand in the cookie jar after being told, 'not before dinner.'

This day just keeps getting weirder and weirder.

Now a strange woman who knew his mother shows up to offer a chance for him to control his powers.

I didn't even think that was possible.

But if it was, he could be around other people without fear. He could have a normal life—well as a normal life that a hybrid vampire could have. Besides, he thought, the Jaecar were his mother's people. They hunted monsters like the Night Prowlers and helped humanity. Mikey decided the opportunity was too big to pass up. And from Cassandra's tone, he didn't really have a choice.

"Well?" the woman called up after Mikey hadn't responded.

"Yes...elder." It seemed like the right thing to say.

"Ah, at least the boy learns quick," she smiled. "That will most certainly help you in the trials to come."

Mikey turned to do as instructed then a thought occurred to him.

"When you say, 'say goodbye,'...do you mean I won't see Arthur again?"

She turned completely towards the stairs, her expression dead-pan.

"That will be entirely up to you."

Okay...no pressure.

He did his best to squash the rising anxiety and focused on the task. Sifting through his dresser, he packed a week's worth of clothes and then went to his art supplies to figure out what to bring. Mikey headed towards his small closet and grabbed a black gym bag he sometimes used when Arthur took him camping. When that was finished, Mikey remembered to nab essential toiletry items before heading back downstairs.

At the bottom of the steps, Mikey got a good look at the woman for the first time. She was almost as tall as he was at around five foot eight. Her black hair was pinned up in a tight bun with what appeared to be two Chinese hair sticks poking out. When Mikey got closer, he realized they weren't sticks. They were tiny swords.

Are those real?

The reflection of a gold pin on her chest caught his eye. He'd never seen the symbol before.

She nodded at Mikey and motioned to Arthur. "Say your good-byes. Make it brief. You will see Arthur again if the training doesn't kill you." She signaled the other two Jaecar and left.

Before Mikey could speak, Arthur grabbed him in a hug.

"Look, son, I'm sorry for all of this, but there is nothing we can do about it now. Once you learn to control your gifts, you are not obligated to anyone but yourself."

"What do you mean?"

"They will want you to become one of them...but this is not a game. You know the reality of OS firsthand. You, your team, even your family could—" Arthur struggled to finish the sentence.

"I understand."

"No, you don't," he straightened. "The Jaecar hunt MONSTERS! A whole lot of them eat people. What they do is more important than anything on this Earth, but that doesn't mean you have to. Once you control your Source absorption, they'll pressure you to join them. I'm not telling you not to; I'm telling you to decide for yourself. Now you should go before we get all emotional," he sniffled. "Cassandra is not someone who should be kept waiting."

Arthur patted him on the back and opened the front door. A black SUV was waiting on the curb outside, engine running.

The reality of the situation seemed to hit Mikey at that moment. He would be leaving his home. The only home he'd ever had since he was five. And if he didn't control his—specialness, he wouldn't be coming back.

Swallowing the knot forming in his throat, Mikey tried to think of what to say. Arthur meant more to him than anyone. He was family.

All Mikey could think to do was give him another big hug. "I'll see you soon," he promised.

"Of course you will."

Determined, Mikey got into the SUV. He took one last look at his home as the vehicle began its journey to the Sect. He was truly about to enter Otherside.

CHAPTER 4

During the ride, Mikey wondered where a secret monster-hunter organization would keep its headquarters. But kept the thought to himself.

I'll let it be a surprise.

The drive had been mostly silent until Elder Cassandra finally spoke. He was sitting in the backseat with Cassandra. The other two Jaecar were in the front.

"When we arrive, you are to be seen by Elder Neema. She is one of the best Healers Haven has ever had. You will do as she asks and give her the utmost respect," the elder glared until he nodded.

"I didn't get a chance to ask Arthur, what is Haven?"

"It is the name of our order, the English Translation. Many still call us by 'Portum' around the world."

"Got it."

"After," she continued. "You will be taken to an isolated room for the night, and tomorrow you will start your training. Your aptitude for the Source will be determined over the next few months. If you show promise, you might be given the opportunity to become a Jaecar."

Arthur's warning flashed through his mind.

"If you cannot control your...vampiric nature, or you threaten one of our Sect, you will be stopped by any means necessary."

Mikey's throat suddenly felt very dry. She gave the impression that her threats weren't made idly.

"How will I be trained?"

"Part of that will be determined by your exam with Elder Neema. If you were not aware, you are quite an unusual case."

"Arthur gave me the gist."

"Wonderful. Getting back to your original question," the elder continued. "Acolytes normally begin training at the age of twelve. The Jaecar have been around for thousands of years and branch from hundreds of different families throughout the world."

"So, I take it I'm pretty far behind?"

"Very. But occasionally, a human will be discovered with the capacity and ability to harness the Source. Like them, you will learn about OS, battle tactics, and teamwork. Your mind and body will be reforged into those of a Jaecar. Of course, that is only if you join us. For now, we will focus on control."

She made it sound like Army boot camp or something. Then again, Mikey thought, how else would you form elite, monster-hunting soldiers?

"I am confident we can help you learn to use abilities to save others, not harm them. Though, as I said, we have never seen anyone like you before," Elder Cassandra said.

Here was his chance to turn this curse into something more and figure out what happened that night his parents were killed.

Whatever it takes.

"Ah, here we are," she said as the car pulled into the parking lot of what appeared to be a dilapidated factory.

The headlights of the SUV highlighted a sign above a door. It was dark, but Mikey could make out the words 'Hostess,' 'Wonder,' and 'Bakery Thriftshop.'" He realized they were at the old, abandoned Wonder Bread factory. Mikey remembered from his first day in history class that Buffalo was full of abandoned factories. It used to be one of the leaders in manufacturing during the early 1900s and again after WWII. By the 1970s, modernization and economic pitfalls shut down many factories and plants. This led to a graveyard of abandoned buildings throughout the city. He and Arthur had passed by it on the freeway a few times.

Having the Sect here made sense to Mikey, except for one issue.

"How do you keep this a secret? I'm sure there are tons of ghost hunters and generally curious people who come here. How do they not find the Sect?"

"That—" she grinned, "is something you will soon find out."

Mikey's door opened, and the male Jaecar motioned for him to step out. The two guards were carrying flashlights illuminating the way while they walked toward the factory entrance. Mikey could make out a pink awning and pink rails leading to a single door. The guards opened it and gestured for him and the elder to walk in.

Mikey was unsure what would happen as he walked through. Was the doorway really a portal that would send him to another dimension? He didn't realize he was holding his breath until stepping through. Mikey's brow furrowed at the garbage and rubble littering the floor. Several walls had crumbled, and no magical land was in sight.

Well, this is creepy.

As if reading his mind, Elder Cassandra looked back with a smirk.

Are they messing with me?

"I love what you've done with the place. I see the Jaecar didn't want to waste their funds on decorating." Mikey joked more for him than anyone else.

"Have patience," Elder Cassandra assured without missing a step.

The guards led the way towards the leftmost corner of the building at the back. They'd reached an endpoint, and the guards stopped and stood to either side of the elder. Mikey did his best not to trip and impale himself on one of the scattered broken beer bottles.

"Wait here and enter ten seconds after me," Elder Cassandra instructed.

She walked forward several feet until she stood in front of a cracked, crumbling wall. Cassandra lifted her arm, pressing a device on her wrist.

The air shifted as the wall in front of the elder began to ripple; it was like a lake someone had just dropped a pebble into. A deep hum emanated from the—*portal?*

No, there's no way that's a portal...

"Try not to tense your muscles when you go through. It helps," the elder explained before walking through and vanishing.

"Oh. My. God. There IS a portal!" Mikey yelled, wide-eyed.

The male Jaecar snorted at his outburst, startling Mikey. It was the first time he had heard a peep from either of them.

Panicking slightly at the idea of walking through, Mikey turned to him and joked, "Do I have to say abracadabra?"

"Does this look like Hogwarts to you?" Mikey thought he saw the corner of his lips turn up. "Go."

How can you tell someone not to tense up before they walk through a portal?

He walked up to it as his entire body, shockingly, tensed up.

As Mikey stepped up to the shimmer, the horrors of what would happen if it closed while he was halfway through flashed through his mind.

You're sick, Mikey. Stop it.

He glanced back at the guard. The man stared at him with annoyance before motioning towards the portal.

Swallowing the growing knot in his throat, Mikey hopped in.

All the things Mikey expected to happen never did. He was in the
factory one moment, then the next, he was on some sort of raised
platform in a plain white room. There was no rushing sensation.
None of his atoms felt like they were being ripped apart and re-
assembled. Mikey gasped, realizing he had been holding his breath
again. He scanned the room and saw several platforms like the one
he was standing on. The wall before him had an elaborate digital
schedule that changed rapidly.

The top row of one calendar area had the labels 'Por
1' through 'Por 5'. There were red and green lights, alternating flash-
es for each one but never simultaneously for a single portal.

Elder Cassandra was standing to the side with a giant grin. It was
the first time he'd seen her really smile. She motioned for him to
step off.

"You made it seem like it was going to hurt or something." Mikey
was still in shock from the fact that he had teleported.

"Yes, even we have jokes. There is a rule not to speak of the
experience to new acolytes. It is much more fun to make it a mystery,
right?" She chuckled.

Mikey could see the humor in it if you weren't on the receiving
end. But he smiled. He had just gone through a portal to a secret
organization's hideout inside an abandoned factory.

"Yeah, I guess it is," he realized.

"Come. Let's go see Elder Neema." She pressed the device on her
wrist, and the rippling portal again solidified into a solid wall.

Both guards had already come through; this time, they walked
behind as Elder Cassandra led the way. They walked through several small hallways until before them was a large room the size

of a warehouse with various hallways and adjoining rooms. Mike glanced up at the ceilings

It must be at least thirty feet high.

The room would fit two hundred people easily. It was divided into different sections that were teeming with activity.

In one area, hundreds of various kinds of weapons were hung against the wall. A few Jaecar appeared to be deciding which ones to choose. One girl picked up a sickle-like silver weapon before tossing it back and forth between each hand. She repeated the same test with several others.

The opposite end was filled with tables and chairs. At least a dozen people were reading books and taking notes; Mikey guessed it was a study area.

As Cassandra led them past one of the rooms, Mikey peeked through the square window on the door to see several students not much older than him trying to knock down targets that popped up with their Source. He watched their powers with awe. Rather quickly, the students began sitting out, clearly too exhausted to continue. Soon, they'd all tapped out until a lone student remained. The Jaecar knocked down a few more targets, and Mikey noticed blood coming down his arms. The Source user turned triumphantly to the others before locking his eyes on Mikey's. It was Thomas. He sneered at Mikey before turning back to the group.

The sound of foot tapping brought Mikey back to the present. He turned to a glowering Elder Cassandra.

Mikey tried to look as apologetic as possible and continued to follow.

"This room is called the TC or Training Center," she motioned around them. "You will spend much of your time here if you get to that point."

As Elder Cassandra walked through the TC, Mikey noticed all the eyes staring at them. Any Jaecar nearby stopped and bowed their head to Cassandra while acknowledging her with an 'elder.'

Was I too familiar with her?

He could hear not-so-subtle whispers from the students around them as they walked through.

"Who is that with the Sect leader?"

"There is something wrong with his Source."

"Is he from another Sect?"

They left the TC and headed down another series of hallways, passing a few more Jaecar looking at Mikey with puzzlement. When they noticed Elder Cassandra, however, they bowed and continued on.

After walking for a few more minutes, they arrived at what Mikey assumed was Elder Neema's clinic. The entrance had two glass doors, and above was a silver emblem of the Rod of Asclepius. It was a rod with a single snake coiling around it. Asclepius was the Greek god of healing. Mikey had researched many ancient gods from different civilizations. When he watched *Hercules* with Arthur and saw Medusa for the first time, it took him down a long road of learning about the various Greek gods and monsters.

They headed inside, and to Mikey's astonishment, it appeared to be a regular doctor's office. He again expected the Healer for a secret organization of monster hunters to have potions on the wall and jars of creatures on shelves with some foul scent in the air.

Instead, it was a typical waiting room. The walls were white, with neutral floral paintings scattered throughout. Wood chairs with blue cushions were evenly spaced and centered around a matching wood table. A reception area was straight across the entrance doors and next to it was a set of double doors that Mikey assumed went to the treatment rooms.

I need to stop letting my imagination run wild. But as the Wonder Bread factory portal came to mind, Mikey thought perhaps he wasn't too far off.

There was a guy already sitting on one of the blue-cushioned chairs. Mikey winced as he looked him over. It seemed like someone had smashed him in the face with a frying pan. His left eye was swollen almost completely shut, and the area around his nose was severely bruised. He also had a cloth covering what appeared to be a long gash on his right arm.

The injured Jaecar stood as soon as he saw Elder Cassandra. "Elder," he nodded.

"Ah, acolyte Jason. I see you've gone a little overboard with your training yet again," she chastised.

"I'm sorry, elder. But you know what they say. No pain, no gain," he shrugged, grinning. "And you know Luke is practically frothing at the mouth to get as much practice as possible."

She arched an eyebrow at him, "Indeed."

A boy who looked the same age as Mikey walked through the doors next to the reception area, and all eyes turned to him.

"Hello, Sect leader," he bowed. "Elder Neema is ready. We'll take him back for examination and ensure he gets to his room."

Mikey felt like the actively bleeding student needed more attention than he did.

"Um, maybe you should take care of him—" Mikey gestured to Jason, "he seems like he needs more urgent care than me."

"Oh, don't you worry, I'll get him fixed right up!" the boy exclaimed. Mikey was a little put off by how excited he sounded about it.

"Good. With that, I will take my leave. Do as you are told, and we might expect great things from you," the elder said.

"Thank you. I will do my best," Mikey bowed.

Seemingly satisfied with his answer, she nodded and left.

The boy waited for Cassandra to leave before sticking out his hand, "I am acolyte Lucian. Apprentice to Elder Neema, but you can call me Luke."

"Nice to meet you. My name is Michael, but everyone calls me Mikey," he replied.

Luke inclined his head and gestured toward the door he was holding open. "If you will follow me, please. I want to get started on Jason."

At the mention of his name, Mikey turned back to Jason, who used the hand holding the bloody rag and gave him a thumbs up. Mikey saw how big the gash was and cringed. Jason must've noticed his concern and waved him off. "I'll be fine. Happens all the time," he assured.

With that, Mikey followed Luke into the clinic.

The first thing Mikey noticed was the smell in the hallway. It smelled like lavender and a hint of another scent that Mikey thought was...*honey?* He hadn't been in many hospitals or health clinics, but he was sure no one ever described them as smelling of lavender and honey.

Looking around, he noticed they were in a hallway with the same white walls, and at least a dozen numbered doors. Mikey noticed some medical posters taped to them in between two empty gurneys. He glanced at one that depicted a human form with what looked like veins running through it. The sign had the words 'Meridians' at the top of it. Mikey thought it was a poster about the circulatory system until he realized the veins were green.

"Man, I wish Jason would've let his arm get a little more severed," Luke said out of the blue.

It took a second for Mikey to process what he thought he had heard. "Wait, did you just say you want him to have a severed arm?"

"Yeah, I mean, it doesn't have to be all the way off, but I've never put a severed arm back together. I bet I could do it!" Luke's eyes burned with a sudden fiery determination.

"Okay..." Mikey was unsure how to respond.

"We are short on Healers; I need to get much better, much faster. What better way than in real-time?" Luke asked.

That made more sense. Ultimately, Luke just wanted to improve so he could help. Mikey could respect that.

"So you know," Luke turned to Mikey, "in training, maybe, could you try and get a little more roughed up? I promise I'll take care of it."

Nope. He's definitely crazy.

"Sh—Sure," Mikey offered.

"Great," Luke beamed and started walking again. Mikey followed him into the back of the hallway, where he stopped at the door labeled 204.

"I have to go patch up an unfortunately NOT severed limb. Elder Neema is waiting for you inside," Luke sighed.

Mikey paused at the door, a tightness brewing in his chest. He had no idea what the 'examination' entailed or what answers he would find. Elder Cassandra said Neema was one of the best Healers Haven had ever had in thousands of years. So, if anyone could tell Mikey what was wrong with him, it would be her.

As long as I don't have to drop my pants and cough, right? He tried to make a joke to settle his nerves.

With a deep breath, Mikey walked in.

CHAPTER 5

As Mikey walked into the smoky examination room, the oldest woman he'd ever seen was in front of him. She was standing over a counter and lighting what looked like incense. The tiny elder couldn't have been more than five feet tall with long, snow-white hair draped down to the floor. Wrinkles covered every inch of her face. He had the impression a strong breeze might knock her over.

"I'm sure you thought this clinic would be filled with magical potions... maybe some shrunken heads in jars?" The elder chuckled. Her voice was raspy but strong.

"Well, I didn't know what to expect, really...." Mikey shrugged. "It smells nice in here."

"The smell of lavender and honey helps me focus my Source, which in your case is extra important," she said to Mikey, still focused on the incense.

Once lit, she motioned for him to sit on the examination bed. It was one of those beds that came standard in all doctor's offices. It even had that crinkly white baking sheet strip going down the middle of it.

She moves surprisingly well for a mummy.

"Now child, I am Elder Neema. You most likely don't remember me, but I was the Healer who assisted your mother in giving birth to you," she smiled warmly. "A shame what happened to her and that I have not gotten a chance to examine you until now."

"Did everyone know my mother?" Arthur and Elder Cassandra knew her; now, one of the best Healers in thousands of years was the doctor who delivered him as a baby.

"Not everyone, I'm sure. Your mother was a very skilled Jaecar, and she became even more famous when all of OS discovered the peculiar circumstances of her pregnancy with you. Most of the elders in the United States at least are aware of her name and the accident.

"I often treated her wounds back in her youth," she looked past him as if reminiscing.

"My mom lived in Buffalo?" Mikey asked. He knew practically nothing about his mother's past. He only remembered her chest-nut-brown hair, kind brown eyes, and how she always fussed over him.

"No. I don't think that she did," Neema replied. "But I have not always lived at this Sect. I was born in Buffalo and went to medical school here in 1905. I have lived all over the world in many different countries, learning all I could about the healing arts. Many Sects have been my home throughout my life.

"It is only now after I have trained two" —Neema grimaced and shook her head as if to clear away unpleasant thoughts—"healers of my caliber to be at the SHOP, was I was given leave to come home."

Mikey did the math in his head. If she went to medical school when she was at least twenty years old in 1905...that meant she was at least 117 years old!

Elder Neema laughed, watching the apparent calculations going on in Mikey's head and the realization as his eyes went wide.

"Yes, the Source can allow us to do many extraordinary things. It allows me to heal my body and control my cells to regenerate to their maximum potential. I am 121 years old. I don't know how much longer I have in this world, but I will live as long as a human being is physically capable," she shared.

"Wow, that's amazing," Mikey gasped.

"Not as amazing as you will be, I think," she winked.

"Also, you mentioned SHOP?" Mikey inquired.

"Oh, I apologize. There will be many acronyms for you to learn here. Just like governments and armies worldwide, we have our shorthand. SHOP stands for Sect Headquarters of Portum. It is located on the other side of the country.

Let's get on with it," she clapped her hands. "The curiosity is killing me. I will use my Source to enter your body to analyze it and your meridians. I can learn more once you have formed your core, but I am certain this will still reveal much."

How much is this gonna hurt?

As if sensing his thoughts, the old woman smiled. Her small face disappeared in the wrinkles. "Do not worry. None of this will hurt. Though it may feel a bit odd. Above all, make sure to keep calm. From what I was told from today's events, your emotions play a role in your Source vampirism. I can shield myself from your current absorption level, but I doubt I'd be able to stop you if you lost control."

"Wait, you can shield yourself from me?" Mikey didn't realize that was possible. Thinking back, he realized that was what Arthur must have been doing the entire time.

"Yes. To put it into perspective—your current Source absorption is like a gentle breeze. I can put a window up, and it will not go through. However, if you were to lose yourself as you did back at the school, it could turn into a tornado. So, relax and close your eyes. That's it...now focus on your breathing."

Mikey nodded while taking deep breaths, trying to calm himself.

Two small, slightly clammy hands grasped the sides of his head.

Definitely strong for a 121-year-old.

Neema wasn't kidding when she said it would feel odd. At first, Mikey felt that familiar pressure he now knew was the Source gently wrap around his body. A sensation of tiny tendrils went from the outer layer of his skin to deep inside his body, breaking into smaller and smaller branches the further they went. Mikey's muscles clenched from the odd feeling of invasion.

"Relax, child. It is not painful like I said, right?" she whispered calmly.

At her voice, Mikey relaxed. She was right; it didn't hurt. It was just weird. He refocused on breathing as the tendrils softly poked and prodded in examination. A few minutes passed in silence before Neema spoke.

"Incredible. Two separate sets of meridians anastomosed together, both vampiric and human!"

"What do you mean?" Mikey kept himself still, eyes closed.

"Shhh, I need to focus," Neema whispered.

Mikey was getting used to constantly hearing words and terms that might as well have been another language. He continued to focus on staying calm and breathing. The tendrils began to recede after what felt like hours but were only around ten minutes in reality. Soon they were out of his body, and the pressure was gone.

He opened his eyes to the elder holding onto the bed for support, breathing heavily.

"I just need a minute, child. This body doesn't have the stamina it used to," she wheezed. "Here, help me to sit."

Mikey grabbed her offered arm, easing the old Healer into a chair like those in the waiting room. After Mikey thought she'd sufficiently caught her breath, he couldn't hold his questions in any longer.

"Elder Neema...you mentioned meridians a bunch of times, and I even saw a poster outside with green veins that said meridians. From how you talked about them, I figure they have something to do with using the Source?"

"That is correct. Meridians are like the vessels in your body that Source moves through. They can't be seen, only felt. At least by humans. They are connected to everything in your body that makes it run and keeps it alive: nerves, the brain, your organs, everything." she explained.

"When you examined me, I heard you say I had two different sets that...anatomized?" Mikey couldn't quite remember that word she said. He hadn't heard it before and his memory was only perfect with things he saw.

"Anastomose. It is a common term for blood vessels joining together from different branches. And yes, you have two different sets of meridians. I have never seen such a thing. One vampiric set and one normal set that we all have. This new meridian is what allows you to absorb the Source around you. But it joins with your human one creating something miraculous," she shook her head in amazement.

"Why would it be miraculous? All I do is hurt everyone around me," Mikey asked.

"Think about it, child. Normal Jaecar can only use the Source that is inside them. After years of training their bodies and minds, they can increase the precision and control of their inner Source. But that is their limit!

"Source is what drives all living things. It is the energy of life. What do you think happens to a Jaecar if they use all the Source in their bodies?" the elder asked.

It didn't take Mikey long to think of an answer.

"They die?"

"Exactly!" she beamed. Neema was wracked by a coughing fit, and Mikey jumped to her side.

"No, no. I'm fine. It just took a lot out of me," Neema raised a hand to reassure him. "These old bones aren't what they used to be. Anyways...where were we? Oh yes. With you, there is no such limitation. You can continue to absorb the Source around you. If something living is nearby, you can absorb its Source and use it like a Jaecar," she asserted.

"I don't know how I feel about gaining power by killing things around me," he confessed. Mikey couldn't even fathom the morality of that.

"I'm glad that was your first concern. But what if you had mastery over it? Hmm?" The elder cocked an eyebrow. "What if you could take just enough that the living thing was only tired, and a good sleep would see it back in tip-top shape? Though I don't know if you would say the same thing if you were facing down a Bugbear or a Wendigo that had just consumed an innocent child. That is the very reason why we exist," she said.

Mikey hadn't thought of that. What if he could use his abilities to stop monsters like the one that killed his parents? What if he could prevent a child from having the life he had? It might be what he was meant to do. Mikey hadn't cared about his own life much after his parents died. All of it was spent trying not to hurt those around him until he met Arthur.

"Do you think I could control it?" Mikey couldn't hide the hope in his voice.

"Honestly, I don't see why not. Why wouldn't you be able to control the Source coming into your body and leaving it? But first, you need to control your Source vampirism. It is dangerous to those who cannot shield themselves."

"Agreed," Mikey nodded.

"I'm guessing that total blockage of your absorption will be very uncomfortable for you to maintain for long. Much like the vampires, where your second meridian comes from, you NEED to absorb Source," she stated.

But I'll be able to control it.

"Now I need to let these old bones rest," Neema stood up on wobbly knees. "We will speak again after you have learned to at least stop your Source vampirism and formed your core. You will learn what your core is when you have accomplished the first feat."

"Okay. Thank you."

"It will be a dangerous task. Not only for yourself but for the Jaecar training you," Neema warned. "Stay calm and have confidence in yourself."

She pressed a button on the wall and spoke into it. Mikey realized it was an intercom.

"Lucian, please come and take Mikey here to his room. I was told it would be one of the isolation rooms on the West Side."

She turned to Mikey and added, "I look forward to seeing your progress."

Luke came into the room. He gave Elder Neema a worried glance but motioned for Mikey to follow. When they left the clinic, Luke turned the opposite way they had come, and Mikey committed the layout to memory. His visual memory had been eerily perfect his entire life.

I wonder which side of the family that comes from?

"So, did the elder figure out what is going on with you?" Luke inquired. He looked slightly ashamed for prying, but it was obvious he was more curious about the whole interaction.

"Apparently, I'm a half vampire, half Jaecar hybrid, first of my kind," Mikey laughed as the words came out. He should have felt like he had entered *Alice in Wonderland*, but strangely he felt good. This was the first time everything made sense, and he had an explanation.

"Wait, so it's true? You ARE the lost hybrid kid?" he gasped.

"So I've been told," Mikey answered.

"Is that why your Source feels so weird?"

"Yep. Apparently, it is Source vampirism which everyone likes to call it. I have two different meridians; one like you and one for absorbing the Source around me," Mikey explained.

Luke stopped dead in his tracks before opening his mouth so wide that Mikey imagined his tongue rolling onto the floor like in cartoons.

"Wait, did you just say you have TWO DIFFERENT MERIDIANS?" Luke yelled.

Mikey was thankful the hallway they were in was deserted. He didn't want to go around being the freak of the Sect and just wanted to focus on controlling his powers.

"You have to let me inside you!" Luke blurted.

"Uhhh—"

"I mean my Source—so I can examine you. I'd learn so much!" the Healer corrected.

"Maybe some other time..." Mikey trailed off. But Luke just jumped to the next thought.

"This is crazy. Like what does that mean? You can keep using your Source indefinitely as long as you absorb more?" he guessed.

"Pretty much nailed it. At least that's what Elder Neema thinks," Mikey shrugged.

"Wow, what a life hack. Literally," Luke said, resuming his walk down the hallway. They walked in blissful silence for another minute until they came upon a room with three grey doors, one on each wall. Several chairs and a console table sat squarely in the middle. Along one of the walls was a lone shelf filled with several books. Luke directed them to the front of the left-most door and stopped.

"Its easy to guess why they want you to be in isolation. I could sense you when we first met, trying to take a little of my Source. Luckily, I'm close to keeping up my minor shield at all times," Luke puffed out his chest a little. "It's one of the requirements to becoming a Jaecar."

"It sort of just does it automatically. I don't know how to control it. That is the first thing they want me to do. And I will," Mikey declared.

Luke nodded.

"I'm rooting for you. With full control of your powers, you'd really help us out here. Monster attacks have been increasing the last couple of years, and we're unsure exactly why," Luke sighed.

"No one told me anything about that. What do you mean attacks?" Mikey asked.

"Over six-hundred-thousand people go missing every year in the U.S. A lot of the time, it's a creature or creatures from OS. The natural food for many of them is us. But there has been an increase in sightings in the last couple of years. Hunting parties have been coming back saying they are encountering more and more monsters, especially Wendies." Luke answered.

"What are Wendies?"

"Oh, Wendigos. I call them Wendies to make them less terrifying. Nasty creatures. Somewhat intelligent but have a BIG appetite. They are fast and strong, with large claws, normally alone. A hunting party, or omada, can easily take care of one. It can be dangerous when they turn into a pack, which sometimes happens," Luke explained.

Mikey shuddered to think of people being eaten by the Night Prowlers. It gave him even more reason to become strong so another family wouldn't have to endure what he did.

The thought occurred to him that his father was one of those monsters from OS. But Mikey knew that wasn't true, at least for him. His dad loved him and always made him feel safe. He used to watch *The Jungle Book* with Mikey over and over and even called him man-cub.

"You okay, man?" Luke asked.

Mikey realized how awkward he must look standing quietly, lost in his thoughts.

"Yeah, sorry. Gotten a lot of information today. Just trying to process it all," Mikey said.

"Understandable. Alright, here is your room. Blankets and sheets are on the bed for you. Someone will come in the morning to take you to breakfast in the cafeteria and then training afterward. Have a good night, and good luck tomorrow."

"Thanks, Luke. I appreciate it," Mikey stuck out his hand.

"No problem," Luke grabbed Mikey's hand, a mischievous grin on his face. "Remember our little promise from before. With your vampiric half, I bet you could recover no problem from a severed arm. You'd be the perfect person to practice on."

With that, he turned and left.

Yep, crazy.

Mikey shook his head as Luke walked off, but he couldn't help but smile.

The room had a full mattress on brown metal springs, two pillows, white sheets, and a big green blanket. It reminded Mikey of some of the barracks in military movies he watched. The room was bare except for a few pieces of furniture. A small nightstand with a black lamp rested next to the bed in the center. A grey, four-drawer dresser sat in the corner across from the bed. The walls were bare except for a small mirror on the opposite side and a black yoga mat rolled up in a corner. Mikey was grateful for the small brown desk in the corner with some pens and blank paper. He could draw sitting on the bed, but there was no comparison to the comfort of a desk.

Using the monotony of putting on the sheets and pillowcases, Mikey's mind replayed the day's events. His dad was an ancient vampire. His mom was a powerful monster hunter that belonged to a secret organization of people like her. He'd almost killed his classmates, who also happened to be monster hunters in training.

And I enjoyed it...

Mikey pushed that thought away and focused on the fact that he finally had an explanation for his radioactivity.

Everything led here, in a secret portal building inside an abandoned Wonder Bread facility or wherever they were. Mikey knew they weren't joking about keeping him there if he didn't learn to control his powers. Elder Cassandra meant every word. Mikey had no idea what normal was for a teenager in this new world. Still, he'd always wanted to have some friends and be around people without constant anxiety. This was his opportunity.

And I'm not going to let it go to waste.

There were so many things throughout Mikey's life that he couldn't control; his Source vampirism, his family situation, and how people reacted to him. Instead, he always tried to focus on the things he could control: his own feelings and emotions. Mikey realized early on that if he hated others for the way they acted because of him, then he'd hate everyone. The alternative was to empathize with their point of view. Something was happening to them when Mikey was around. Something bad. Should he fault them for being angry or scared?

But that was then, and this is now. Mikey's mother harnessed the Source and used it for good. She, his father, and Arthur had always believed in him. So, Mikey decided to try to make friends here while doing everything in his power to become stronger. The alternative was to give up, stay stuck in this building, and never learn about his parents or what he was capable of.

And that isn't an option.

CHAPTER 6

Mikey awoke to a knocking sound. Like a slow zombie, he groaned and lumbered to the door. He was surprised to see a face he recognized from yesterday. It was Marcus, his classmate in art. In his hands were a pair of dark-grey sweatpants and a shirt; the same outfit Marcus wore.

"Uh...I was tasked with taking you to the cafeteria for breakfast and then to training with Elder Ryan," Marcus stated, visibly uncomfortable. "Oh, here." Marcus offered the clothes in his hands. "This is our training uniform. I guessed your size, but I think it'll fit. We can get you more later today."

Mikey took the clothes and thanked him.

How do you say 'Hey? Sorry I almost killed you, your brother, and your friend by absorbing your life energy.'

They stood awkwardly in the doorway for a few seconds until Mikey decided now was the time to be different, follow Arthur's advice, and be more assertive. It seemed Marcus didn't hate him. Not like Thomas. Maybe they could be friends.

"Look, I don't know how to say I'm sorry for what I did, but I really am—" Mikey started.

"It's okay; Elder Cassandra told us who you were and what happened," Marcus interrupted. "I'm Marcus Sante," he smiled.

"Mikey Black," he replied, relief flooding him. Marcus didn't hate him.

"I can't say the same for my brother, though," he finished. "Ever since we lost our oldest brother Simon, Thomas hasn't been the same. He was an amazing Healer, Simon, trained by Neema herself." Marcus tried to hide the pain on his face and continued. "Since then, Thomas has been on a kick to be the baddest, strongest Jaecar in all of Haven. I think it comes from a good place, but he's very...combative."

Mikey thought back to the comment from Neema when she said she trained two Healers of her caliber. One of them must have been Simon. It must be tough for the Jaecar, Mikey thought.

How can you get used to losing the ones you love?

"I'm so sorry. This world is completely new to me. Up until yesterday, I thought my parents were killed by monsters that no one else knew existed and that I was radioactive and hurt everyone around me," Mikey responded.

He had a limited amount of experience talking with kids his age. Still, since Marcus gave up personal details about himself, Mikey felt it was only right he did too.

"Man, that's rough. I can't even imagine learning about all this now. And with your Source sucker problem? Jeesh."

"Yeah...thanks."

"The Sante family can be traced back to some of the first Jaecar, so we've known about OS our whole lives," Marcus sympathized.

"Oh crap," Marcus looked at his watch. "We gotta hurry up and get to the cafeteria. He wants us back here in an hour to start your training. And trust me, Elder Ryan is not someone you want to make wait," he shuddered.

"Okay, give me a sec. I'll be right out," Mikey promised. Marcus nodded as he shut the door to change.

Afterward, Mikey was led back towards a familiar entryway that opened out into four hallways. If they had gone straight ahead, that would lead back to the clinic and the TC. Instead, Marcus turned left. They walked past another large hallway with several doors along the side before reaching the cafeteria at the far end.

"Get as much as you want," Marcus explained, "keep in mind, we will be training right after. So, I'd recommend something light."

When Mikey grabbed the tray and got up to the food line, he realized it was pretty much a buffet with everything you could want in a breakfast. Sausage, bacon, pancakes, waffles—you name it, and it was there. Mikey realized he had never had the pizza last night or any dinner. Oddly, he hadn't felt hungry until now.

Was it all the Source I consumed last night?

He instantly felt bad that he essentially 'fed' on his fellow classmates.

But that's what I'm here to fix.

Considering what Marcus had said, Mikey asked hopefully, "Got any Pop-Tarts?"

"Oh yeah, they're over there," Marcus pointed to a separate counter.

He headed towards an area with microwaves and toasters. Mikey quickly realized this area was more to his liking. It had different dry cereals, oatmeal with a bunch of topping options, and different kinds of milk. Various slices of bread and assorted muffins were on a tray, and the holy grail—several boxes of different flavors of Pop-Tarts. Mikey opted for the frosted wild berry with 'natural flavoring.'

With his wholesome and healthy breakfast of pure sugar in hand, Mikey looked out into the cafeteria and felt like he was back in school again. Everyone around him was sitting with friends, talking.

Mikey's instincts kicked in, and he looked for an empty table as far away from everyone as possible.

Maybe I'll just go back to my room and eat?

He had memorized the way back. But before he could decide, his thoughts were interrupted.

"Mikey, over here," Marcus called out.

Mikey turned towards the voice to see Marcus sitting across from Sabrina, aka bus girl. Marcus was waving him over. Sudden dread filled every pore of his body at the prospect of sitting and having lunch with people, let alone people his age.

What if I say something stupid? What if Sabrina doesn't forgive me like Marcus did? What if I hurt them by accident?

As if Marcus could sense his growing angst, he called out, "We'll be fine, man. Just sit." Feeling awkward just standing there with all eyes turned on him at Marcus's outburst, Mikey walked over to them. He sat next to Marcus, nodding towards Sabrina. "Hi...uh... I'm Mikey Black," he stammered. Mikey figured it was best to keep it short.

Less chance of stupid coming out of my mouth.

"Yeah, I know. I'm Sabrina Adelmund. My mom—er Elder Cassandra, told me about the crazy situation. How about we skip the whole apology thing and start fresh?" Sabrina offered.

"Oh, I should have guessed Elder Cassandra was your mother." *They have the same emerald eyes.* "That sounds great. Sorry, I'm not used to sitting around people. I always felt like I'd hurt them," Mikey blurted.

"Well, Marky here is an up-and-coming Shielder, so you don't have to worry too much about him. As for me, you're taking in such a small amount it won't bother me for a while. But I'm close to having my minor shield perfected. So no worries," Sabrina stated.

Marcus gave her an annoyed look, "I hate when you call me Marky."

"And that's why I have to call you Marky every chance I get," she smirked.

Mikey couldn't help but smile at their antics. He figured they had known each other for a long time by how at ease they seemed. At the word Shielder, Mikey thought of Arthur.

"My foster parent Arthur is a Shielder; I don't know exactly what it means other than they use the Source to shield themselves or others. Honestly, I don't know much about anything other than what I've learned in the last day."

"Did you say your foster parent was a Shielder named Arthur? Does his last name happen to be Cafferty?" Oddly, at the mention of Arthur, Marcus's eyes lit up.

"Yeah, that's him. Why?" Mikey said.

"SHUT. UP. Are you telling me your foster dad is THE Arthur Cafferty? Considered the best Shielder in all of Haven for the last hundred years? You have to introduce me! I bet I could learn so much. I mean, I know he quit being a Jaecar and left Haven because his daughter died, but his knowledge and control must be out of this world," Marcus rambled on excitedly.

At the mention of the loss of his daughter, the pieces from the other night came together.

That's why Arthur left Haven and why talking about the Jaecar brought him so much pain.

He felt terrible Arthur carried that burden.

"Marcus, I don't think he knew about Elder Arthur's daughter," Sabrina guessed.

Marcus stopped and saw the look on Mikey's face.

"Oh... I'm sorry. I thought you would know. It's just like me to put my foot in my mouth. I just got super excited...he is—like a legend among the Shielders," Marcus apologized.

"No, it wasn't you. That just put a lot of pieces to the puzzle together for me. Some of the things he's said before and the pain I've seen on his face. I was just lost in my thoughts. I do that a lot," Mikey admitted.

"That makes sense," Sabrina commented. "You have spent your whole life pretty much by yourself, so you don't hurt anyone. It sounds very lonely. Of course, you spent a lot of time in your own head."

Huh?

Mikey was so surprised by Sabrina's words that he was at a loss of what to say—no one had ever tried to be in his shoes before. Especially a beautiful girl he just met who just happens to be a monster-hunter acolyte. A knot began forming in his throat as the memories of crippling loneliness bubbled up. He didn't want to let his sadness show, so Mikey pushed it down and attempted to change the subject to something positive.

"I tried not to focus on that part. I just wanted to know what was wrong with me. Never in a million years would I have guessed the truth, but I'm glad I know now and can do something about it. And Marcus," Mikey added, "if I can ever control myself and they let me out of here, I'll be sure to introduce you to Arthur."

"Crap, that reminds me. We have to make it in time for elder Ryan." Marcus took a few quick bites of his bagel and cream cheese before cleaning up.

"You are training with him? I thought you were just showing him around?" Sabrina questioned.

"Apparently, elder Ryan wanted me involved in his training for some reason. I guess I'll find out when we get there. Catch you later, Brina," Marcus smirked.

"Nope, not the same as Marky; it'll never catch on," she quipped. "Go, though. We'll talk later." Sabrina turned to Mikey as he was getting up. "And good luck to you!" she smiled warmly.

"Thanks for letting me sit with you both. It was nice." Mikey's face felt hot.

"Well, I'll be busy with my training, but maybe we can all meet at the cafeteria for dinner if Marcus is okay with it. My mom is staying late doing Sect business. Let's say around five?" Sabrina offered. "And don't tell her I called her mom. As you can imagine, she is pretty strict about titles when we aren't home."

"My lips are sealed," Mikey assured her. "That would be great, though. Hopefully, see you then."

They walked to throw away their garbage and headed back to Mikey's assigned room. As they walked, Mikey's anxiety began to rear its ugly head. He didn't know what his training would be like but wondered if Marcus had any idea.

"Hey, I know you said you don't know why they want you involved, but do you have any idea what this training is going to be?" Mikey asked.

"Nope. I guess it will have something to do with shielding because why else would I be there? Elder Ryan is one of the best Movers and overall controllers of the Source, so I'm sure that's why he was chosen. I've never heard of training to stop someone from absorbing Source around them, though," he shrugged. "By the way, how do you do that anyway?" Marcus probed.

"Elder Neema examined me and said I have two different meridians. One that absorbs Source, she calls it Source vampirism, and then a normal one like you. They will never let me leave if I don't learn to control it. So, I'm going to no matter what," Mikey swore.

Marcus stopped and stared at Mikey briefly before shaking his head and continuing down the hallway. "I don't even know how to process someone having two meridians. Based on what happened at school, if you get that under control...I bet you could become a Superman-level Jaecar."

"Heh. I guess we'll find out soon," Mikey shrugged.

They returned to the main entrance where his room was, and Marcus went through the center door adjacent to Mikey's. Inside was an ample, open space with dark blue, matted floors like in a karate dojo. There was a small, white folding table near the door. The back of the room had a six-inch-thick concrete countertop that ran across the entire wall length—which was also concrete. Both had gashes, craters, and chips as if someone had been practicing their grenade throws and machine gun aim with it.

The sight of the concrete wall and counter heightened Mikey's anxiety even further.

"Uh, what is all this about," he asked Marcus, nodding toward the wall. "It looks like a shooting range over there."

"That's nothing. This is the isolation area. Jaecar who have trouble controlling themselves or want to try a new technique come here where they don't have to worry about hurting someone else. We usually repair the concrete once it gets too bad. It looks like it is about due," Marcus answered.

"I just hope that isn't what I'm going to look like by the end of this," Mikey said.

"Na, you'll be fine. Only a handful of people have exploded from training."

Mikey's eyes widened until he noticed the smirk forming at the corners of Marcus's lips.

"Sorry, too easy," Marcus teased.

Shaking his head and smiling, Mikey turned to look back at the carnage on the wall. He couldn't imagine a creature surviving against that kind of power.

The monsters of OS must be something else.

"Good. You are both here," a deep, unfamiliar voice called behind them.

Mikey turned to see a tall, black man with short hair standing at the room's entrance. He tried not to stare at the three large scars that ran from the side of the man's left cheek to his ear. A small part of his lower ear was missing. In the man's arms were several books. He was wearing the same training pants as Mikey and Marcus, except the elder's had a gold stripe on the outside going down each leg. Mikey assumed it had something to do with distinguishing between levels of Jaecar. His theory was confirmed when he noticed a blonde-haired woman behind him with a blue stripe down her pants. She couldn't have been more than a few years older than him. Elder Ryan introduced her as Jaecar Michelle.

Michelle gave a slight nod in their direction, "Hello."

"She's a Shielder, too," Marcus leaned in and whispered to Mikey. "Doesn't talk much."

"These," Elder Ryan lifted the books, "will be for you to study when you have ANY free time," the Elder emphasized. "Don't ask, 'Oh, how many pages should I read,' or 'What should I focus on.' All of it should be memorized as soon as possible. The information contained within these books could save your life or the life of another, and you are already behind everyone else.

"You are supposed to go back to school in two days. If you cannot stop your Source vampirism, you will not be going back. Every day you fail is another day your old life slips away from you." Mikey tried not to flinch away as the elder's gaze bore into him.

"I am Elder Ryan. " He motioned to the wall, "Most of that hand-iwork is mine. I am the head instructor for Source control at this Sect and have been tasked with helping you control your...unique situation."

"I'm Mikey Black. Thank you for your help, Elder," he greeted.

"Whether you feel I helped or not remains to be seen," Elder Ryan replied. He sat the books down on the white table and walked towards the center of the room. Michelle leaned against the wall near the door.

"Marcus has heard all this, but a refresher never hurt anyone. Mikey, you must pay attention and try to grasp the concepts we discuss," the Elder said.

Mikey nodded.

"Now, do you have any idea of what the Source is?

"I was told that it is life energy," Mikey answered.

"That is the simplest way we can define it. In this universe, the law of conservation states that energy cannot be created or destroyed. If so, then where did the original energy come from?"

Elder Ryan looked solely at Mikey as he asked the question and motioned for him to think of an answer.

"I don't know...maybe the Big Bang?" Mikey offered.

The Elder nodded.

"Could be. Some might also say it came from God or a supreme power. The honest answer is no one truly knows. But we call it the Source. It gave rise to our universe, the primal energy inside every living creature.

"Some of our older texts suggest perhaps the creatures of Oth-erside were formed when the Source of our world was new; much denser and wilder," he continued. "That these creatures were our natural predators and humans were not at the top of the food chain. Of course, that was until the first sorcerers came to be."

The Elder turned towards the concrete wall and stuck out his right arm. He made a show of curling his pointer finger under his thumb as if he was going to flick someone. Mikey felt a small gathering of Source around the Elder. It continued to form and condense around his finger until Mikey felt like he could almost see it. Like the waves of heat that come off the ground in the desert but condensed into a ball.

The Elder flicked out his finger, and a crack echoed across the small room as dust and rubble obscured the impact. When it cleared, a newly formed crater the size of a person's head was plain to see.

"Wow..." Mikey uttered.

Elder Ryan smiled, clearly pleased with his display.

"The Source is a tool. Not magic. It can only do what we will it to do. A knife does not cut an onion; we cut the onion using the knife. Think about this and use it in your own mastery. A chef will utilize a knife much better than your average person. A dull knife in the chef's hand will still be more effective than a sharp knife in the average person's. To be the best, you need both power AND efficiency of your Source," Elder Ryan explained.

He gestured towards the wall, "To do that, I used minimal Source and a lot of control and efficiency. I could have just used a large amount of Source and blasted off most of that wall. Can you tell me why that would be a huge mistake?" The Elder asked.

Mikey thought about it for a minute until he came up with two reasons.

"I would think that it could be dangerous to the people around you, not just the monster, and if you use all your Source, you could die," Mikey answered.

"Excellent. Protecting your fellow Jaecar is another aspect you must always be aware of. To your next point, expending a large blast of Source wouldn't kill me. It would leave me with very little reserves and increase the likelihood of being monster food," Ryan clarified.

"The further away your Source is from you, the more energy it takes to control and the less control you'll have. A Source bullet is the epitome of control and power for Movers. It takes more energy to lift and throw a creature down and much less to fire a Source bullet through them. You must shield yourself from the backblast while shaping and projecting a small amount of concentrated Source forward at high speeds. If it turns out your main archetype is Mover, this is a lofty goal to aim for. The same principles apply to the others, though. You can read about the different archetypes in the texts I've brought."

"Now," Elder Ryan clapped his hands, "If Jaecar Michelle will join us, I will explain my plan to help you at least stop your draining of Source."

Michelle walked towards him as the Elder gestured to his left.

"I thought acolyte Marcus could use this opportunity for shield training. Marcus, I want you to practice shielding yourself from Mikey for as long as possible. His Source vampirism is the perfect opportunity to practice basic shielding for acolytes safely. Before attempting it with others, I wanted to use this opportunity for a test run.

"Mikey, can you feel the Source when it is used around you?" Elder Ryan asked.

"Uh—yeah. It feels like...a pressure," Mikey shared.

"Good, that will make this much easier to start with," the Elder nodded. "Now, much like your brain tells your heart to pump, your nerves to fire, and generally runs everything, you will use it to control the Source and your meridians."

The Elder sat in front of Mikey, and Michelle did the same on his right side. Marcus was already seated to the left of him.

"I am going to use Source on you with increasing force. I want you to focus on that Source and bring it into yourself," the Elder instructed. He held up a hand when Mikey looked like he was about to protest. "Don't worry. That is why I have Michelle here. She is an Adept with a focus on shielding."

Marcus looked surprised by that information.

"She will be able to shut off your meridians briefly," Elder Ryan continued. "I don't expect it will be easy, and I don't expect it to feel pleasant. Mikey, I want you to focus on where the Source is going into your body and picture yourself closing it off completely. It helps if you use your imagination and visualize it happening. For example, I envision my hand as a gun when I fire a Source bullet," the Elder explained.

"If you lose control and begin absorbing more Source than I give you, I will knock you unconscious. Michelle here will completely shield your meridians, cutting off their flow instantly. This is a lot like trying to restart the heart with a shock from a defibrillator. We will repeat this until you can shut off your vampiric meridians at will or any of us give from physical exhaustion."

Mikey recalled when he lost control the day before. There was nothing but the feeling...then suddenly, it was freezing cold when Arthur showed up. Mikey realized Arthur must have cut him off from his meridians and knocked him out. It had felt terrible, but at least it made Mikey feel they would be safe. The unconscious part was what worried him. His eyes went to the concrete wall. After seeing what the Elder could do to it, Mikey shuddered to think of what he could do to his head.

"Any questions?" Elder Ryan finished.

Mikey raised his hand, "Just one. When you say unconscious...."

"I mean, I am going to hit you very hard to knock you out," the Elder interrupted. "This is a life-or-death matter, not a game. Everyone here is putting their lives at risk to help you. I am not going to do—" he pointed to the wall--"*that* to you. It should be just enough to knock you out. Besides, you are half vampire; I'm sure you will heal quickly. The alternative is we do nothing, and you stay here for the rest of your life until you control it. Is that what you want?"

Mikey reminded himself of what the real goal was. There was nothing more important than controlling his powers. He felt silly worrying about a bit of pain when people were risking their lives to help him. Even Jason at the clinic had multiple wounds and acted like it was nothing. Everyone here was struggling to get stronger, and Mikey worried about being knocked out.

"No, do what you have to do," Mikey declared.

"Good, let's begin."

Closing his eyes, Mikey could feel the Source press onto him. It wasn't holding him down like when Thomas attacked him at school. The energy was more like a gentle pressure around his entire body. Like he was in between two air mattresses. Elder Ryan's Source slowly started fading as Mikey felt invigorated.

"I just gave you some of my Source. Feel in your body where you are absorbing it," Ryan instructed. "I am going to throw more at you now. Marcus, continue to shield yourself."

Mikey nodded as another wave of Source pressed down onto him, this time much stronger. His body absorbed the energy quicker as Mikey tried to focus on where it was going, but the sensation became too much. Every cell of his body felt alive. It was pure ecstasy. He briefly thought of his left hand, but the euphoria won out. His worries, hunger, and everything negative in his life just began to float away.

Through the blissful fog, Mikey might've heard his name and 'stop' followed by 'Michelle,' but none of that mattered.

COLD! His body screamed.

It was immediately followed by a loud crunch that came from the side of his head. And then nothing.

CHAPTER 7

When Mikey came to, his head felt like Humpty Dumpty after the great fall. He tried to open his eyes but quickly closed them as tiny needles pierced his skull from the lights on the ceiling.

"Aaagh," he managed to blurt out.

"Good. You were only out for a few minutes," Mikey heard the deep voice of the Elder. "That method seems to be effective for restarting your meridians. Let's take a few more minutes to catch our breath, and we will try again."

A minute later, Mikey peeked one eye half open to see the Elder and Michelle talking in the corner. They both looked a little tired, but overall okay. He glanced at Marcus next to him. Marcus was sitting with his hands behind him, staring at the ceiling. Sweat dripped across his forehead, and he was breathing heavily.

"Sorry," Mikey whispered.

"Dude, you looked like you enjoyed that too much. Maybe keep those faces for alone time," Marcus wheezed.

"I can't explain it. It's the best feeling in the world. Better than food, better than any—thing," Mikey emphasized the last word so Marcus would get the hint. "The whole world disappears, and all I can feel is...amazing."

"Well, while you were off in pleasure town, we were trying to stop you from sucking the life out of us, literally. Though Elder Ryan was right, this is great training." Marcus tried to sound upbeat. But Mikey could tell it had taken a lot out of him.

Why do I keep losing control?

"Sorry, Elder Ryan, Jaecar Michelle," Mikey called out. "I... can't stop it. It feels too good."

"Do not apologize. Do better," Elder Ryan demanded. "The vampires feel ecstasy when they feed on fresh human blood, yet many choose to never do so again. One of those vampires was your father. Do not give in to the feeling. Mind over body is not just an expression. DO IT."

Mikey nodded. He was more than his heritage. Hearing about his father gave him the push needed to overcome his guilt. If his father could control himself, so could he. There were no other options.

"Were you able to figure out where the Source was being absorbed from?" the Elder asked.

"Before, uh...I lost myself," Mikey blushed, "it felt like it was being absorbed in my left hand."

"Excellent, that is more progress than I'd hoped from our first try. Normally your meridians will coalesce into one or two locations. Training teaches us to condense the Source further and form it into a core. Think of it like the sun. We gather the Source from our body, much like the sun's gravity, and pull it into our core. From there, we guide it to do what we wish. But for now, I want you to focus on where the Source is absorbed and try to imagine closing it off."

"Okay. Ready when you are."

"Ready, he says," Marcus propped himself back up, "after a delicious meal of OUR Source."

"Marcus, are you too tired to continue?" Elder Ryan asked. Mikey thought he saw a smile form at the corner of his lips.

"No, Elder Ryan, I can keep going. Just had to bust his chops one last time," he grinned at Mikey. "This really is good shield training. I'm sure Jaecar Michelle will agree."

"Yes. We were just discussing that very subject. Whether we can utilize it or not will depend on what happens here. Now let's try again."

They each took their respective positions, and once again, Mikey felt the Source surround him. It felt like a small draft of air flowing across your skin that made your hairs stand up, except it was going to his left hand. Like before, it slowly disappeared, but Mikey was confident he was right about where the Source was being absorbed.

Ignoring the rising euphoria and the fact his hand was pulling in the Source with increasing speed, Mikey focused on the feeling as the next tier of pressure hit him. He imagined his palm and his fingertips as doorways that were slightly open. But as more Source was pressed onto him, the doors were nudged open further and further.

"Remember to use your imagination to help you form the meridians in your head. Your body will respond to your mind," Elder Ryan instructed. His voice seemed strained.

Mikey realized he was on the right track with the doorways. The pleasure continued to creep at the edges of his control while he pictured the doors slamming shut. But they wouldn't close. The energy rushing through was just too much. Mikey felt like he was in a small closet at the bottom of a lake, and the only thing keeping the water back was a single door being pushed open from the other side. Except, in this case, the pressure was overwhelming, and the water rushing through gave you the most incredible feeling of your life.

Mikey tried with all the might and control he could muster, but it was no use. The Source kept pouring in. Mikey was about to lose himself for the second time when the euphoria suddenly shifted to pain. Nausea overwhelmed him, and Mikey began to shake. He wretched up the morning's breakfast as the ground and ceiling seemed to switch places. It was becoming too much; everything was too much.

"Something's wrong. I don't feel good," Mikey heaved.

"What is it. What are you feeling?" Ryan asked as the pressure around Mikey vanished.

"I don't know...it feels...like I've had too much." Mikey felt like his body was swelling.

"I think his body has absorbed too much Source, and he doesn't know how to get rid of it yet," Elder Ryan suggested. "Michelle."

At that, Mikey felt the familiar ice in his veins as his body jolted from Michelle's meridian shield. The agony of the cold was a little more bearable this time. It was lifted almost as quickly as it came. Immediately, Mikey began to feel a bit better other than lingering nausea.

At least he didn't knock me unconscious.

"Okay—I think—I have to—call it quits—for today," Marcus declared through heavy breaths.

"I think that will be for the best," Elder Ryan agreed. He stood up, helping Michelle to her feet. Mikey and Marcus followed suit.

"It didn't occur to me that you could absorb too much Source. And without a way to release it, the results could have been disastrous. This was my fault," Elder Ryan said.

Mikey felt like a failure. Everyone was exhausted, and Marcus's joke almost came true. Who knows what would have happened if the energy exploded.

The Elder must have seen the look on Mikey's face because he followed with, "Do not look so glum. We made a lot of progress and identified where you will form your core. We will continue tomorrow with more caution. I suggest you begin reading the books provided."

"I'm sorry, I was so close; it was just too much Source coming in. I couldn't push the doors closed," Mikey shared.

Elder Ryan snorted, "What did I say about saying sorry? Don't apologize to me. Figure out what you could have done better and do it. How long it takes does not matter. Always strive for progress. The fact that you said 'doors' shows you are on the right track. How do you feel?"

"I felt terrible before Michelle shielded me, but now I just feel a little nauseous," Mikey answered. "Thank you," he turned to Michelle.

"It was my duty," she bowed. Mikey noticed her almost unnaturally deep-blue eyes. The Jaecar looked exhausted, but she was hiding it well. Mikey realized he was staring at her a bit too long before a familiar voice grunted behind him.

"It wasn't all for nothing, I suppose," Marcus winked at Mikey. "I did learn how to strengthen my shield more with Mikey trying to rip it away from me with his super sucker vampire powers. So, can I come for training tomorrow as well Elder Ryan?" Marcus asked.

"That's fine. I'm glad this proved helpful to your shielding Marcus. See you both tomorrow, same time," Elder Ryan answered.

Mikey and Marcus followed them both out and headed for Mikey's room next door. Once inside, Marcus sighed, plopping down on the floor next to Mikey's bed.

"Man, that was exhausting. I'm definitely going to need a nap. And you'll probably need a cold shower after staring at Michelle," Marcus joked, prodding Mikey with his elbow.

"It wasn't like that; she is very pretty, though." Mikey thought back to Michelle and a question popped into his head. "How old do you have to be to become a Jaecar?"

With that question, Marcus's expression became more serious. "There is no age, really. The youngest in a while has been sixteen. It depends on how good you are, both physically and mentally. Control of your Source and obtaining all the knowledge needed to be a Jaecar are the basics. Most important is to be mentally tough and not freak out when things get real. Michelle's sister was in my brother's group when they disappeared. They were all good friends who trained together," Marcus revealed. "One of the books Elder Ryan gave you is called *Omada Taktiki* or 'group tactics,' it will explain a lot there. Omadas are big things for a Jaecar."

"I'm sorry for all of you. What happened...to your brother?" Mikey asked. He realized it might have been inappropriate to bring up bad memories for Marcus. "You don't have to answer if it's too painful."

"No, it's okay," Marcus exhaled. "Better you find out from me. Simon was a phenomenal Healer and on the verge of becoming an Elder. He was personally trained by Neema for almost a decade.

"His group was powerful. There was a report near Kingston, New York, of an increasing number of missing people. They were sent to investigate if it was from OS and were never heard from again."

"I'm so sorry."

"The worst part of it all," Marcus shook his head, "is that they just...disappeared. Several omadas were sent to investigate afterward, but they turned up nothing. No signs of a struggle, nothing.

"It was assumed they were killed and eaten, or they abandoned Haven and ran off together. But I know for a fact that wasn't true. Simon loved being a Jaecar and would never have left his friends and family."

Mikey put his hand on Marcus's shoulder. Even though he saw his parents lying there that night, there was a small hope that they might still be alive because their bodies were never recovered. Over the years, that slowly faded. But Marcus's brother had only been missing for a year.

"I still have some crazy hope that he is alive somewhere and will come back," Marcus finished as if reading Mikey's thoughts.

"Yeah, hopefully," Mikey tried to sound optimistic. "Thanks for telling me. I know what it's like to feel that way. Even though I remember seeing my parents' bodies, they were never recovered."

They sat together for a while until the silence was interrupted by a gurgle from Marcus's stomach. "Okay. First some lunch, and then a nap," he declared. "You coming?"

The thought of food added to the nausea Mikey still felt. "Na, I'm too nauseous. Even though I didn't eat, I feel oddly full," Mikey shrugged. "I also want to get started on the books they brought. But I still want to have dinner with you and Sabrina later if that's cool?"

"Of course. And you're welcome for the free meal, but don't ever ask me to spoon-feed you," Marcus laughed. "Oh, and the bathroom and shower are in the room next to the one we were just in. Do you remember how we got to the cafeteria?"

"Yeah. I've memorized all the places we've been so far," Mikey affirmed.

"I guess we can chalk that gift up to your dad's side of the family. I've heard vampires have a perfect memory," Marcus said. "Any who, back at the main hallway to the cafeteria, the first door on the left is clean clothes, towels, etcetera. The door on the right is for dirty. It's all labeled and everything, so it's dummy-proof. I'm sure it's something an up-and-coming super Jaecar can handle," he chuckled, giving Mikey a thumbs up.

Mikey laughed. Even though it had only been a day, Mikey felt he could be himself around Marcus. It was nice to have someone his age he could joke with who didn't look at him like he carried the plague.

"I'd give you my number, but unfortunately, it's torture at the Sect for acolytes because our phones don't work in here. Stupid portal," Marcus sighed, standing up. "They have special computers and stuff the gnomes made for Jaecar and the elders, but acolytes," Marcus put his hands up and made air quotes— "'must focus on becoming Jaecar, not internet stars.'"

Must be a touchy subject among the acolytes.

"So, if you need anything, just ask someone."

"Where do you clean the dirty clothes?" Mikey learned to wash his own clothes at an early age. He didn't want to be a burden to anyone.

"Oh no, the Brownies take care of that. It's their thing; they love it. It's like they have OCD for cleaning," Marcus explained. "Don't try and look for them. Just drop it off and leave. And if you do happen to see one, pretend you didn't. They don't like being noticed. And everyone will despise you if it gets out you started a Brownie protest."

It took Mikey a second to remember one of the books he had read years ago about common mythological creatures. Brownies were tiny fairies in British and Irish folklore. They didn't like to be seen and snuck around tidying and cleaning the owner's house.

"Are you talking about those little Irish fairies that clean houses and stuff?" Mikey wanted to verify.

"Yeah, we got a bunch of them around here. I don't know how many. But if we leave them bread and milk and don't bother them, they keep the Sect neat and tidy," Marcus confirmed. "My bet is they live in the walls." Marcus made a show of knocking on the wall next to the door.

"That reminds me, I take it you've never seen a gnome before?" Marcus asked.

"No, but I've heard them mentioned a couple times."

"There are a few here in the Sect. I just wanted to tell you so you didn't get freaked out if you saw one," Marcus explained.

"What do they look li—"

"You'll know one when you see one," Marcus interrupted. "They are friendly but always absorbed in whatever project they're working on. The gnomes invented the portal technology, which was a lifesaver in keeping the Sect locations a secret.

"There is a rumor," Marcus pretended to put his hand to his mouth as if whispering— "that the gnomes invented the internet."

Mikey couldn't stifle a laugh. He imagined little men with white beards and pointy red hats using computers to develop one of the most revolutionary technologies ever created.

"I'll make sure not to tell ALL the people I know about the gnomes that invented the internet," Mikey smirked. "Also, in all serious-ness...thanks...for being there today and hanging out," Mikey stam-mered. He wasn't the best at expressing his emotions, but he was glad Marcus was there.

"Anytime, man. See you tonight."

"See ya."

Finding himself alone, Mikey glanced at the nightstand's alarm clock. It was 12:30 in the afternoon. With a few hours to kill until dinner, he decided to go and take a shower. Mikey was grateful that Marcus hadn't forgotten to tell him where the clean clothes were. He secretly hoped he'd encounter a Brownie.

It wasn't difficult to find his way back to the main hallway to the cafeteria. Mikey planned on getting enough clean training clothes for a few days and would drop off today's dirty clothes on the way to dinner.

Quite a few people were walking about, which generally wouldn't bother Mikey, except everyone stared at him when they walked by.

With short interactions, Mikey usually blended in. It seemed the word had gotten out about the lost hybrid kid.

More whispers echoed around him as he walked through the Sect. Mikey turned to several angry glares when he heard someone in a small group say, "I can't believe they let a vampire in here."

Others just seemed curious, and Mikey tried to nod and say 'Hi' to them. He felt like one of those lost children that everyone knew about that ended up being raised by wolves in the woods and now was returning to society.

There wasn't much he could do about it except learn what everyone else already knew, so he didn't seem as much like an outsider. Mikey rounded the corner to the cafeteria hallway and saw what could only be described as—a gnome.

The gnome was walking away from the cafeteria, munching on a cookie. In his other hand was a small tablet. He was either speaking to himself or someone on the other line. Mikey could hear him talk so fast he began to wonder if gnomes needed to breathe. He was about two feet tall with a neat, black, pointy beard that went down to the middle of his chest. The gnome's pants were small and green, and he wore a black sweater.

Mikey's attention was drawn to the top of his head. It was full of messy curly black hair, but the shape of his head was elongated, going straight up and rounded at the top. It reminded Mikey of *Coneheads*, except not as tall or pointy.

That's why they are always depicted wearing pointy hats!

As he got closer, Mikey heard the gnome more clearly. "Nonothatwillnotworkatall. Howcanyouevensuggestsuchathing, thexenonparticlesaretoounstable!" Mikey could hear similar fast-talking gibberish from the tablet he was holding and knew it was another gnome on the other line. Mikey must've looked odd standing in the hallway just watching the gnome because it looked up from the screen at him.

"Hi..." Mikey stammered with a wave.

"Hellogoodbye," the gnome replied. He continued walking down the one main hallway Mikey hadn't been down.

Maybe it's the command center for the elders and Cassandra?

Mikey wasn't sure if he'd ever get used to this crazy new world he had now become a part of.

A real gnome!

Also, one of life's greatest mysteries had been answered: why gnomes wear tall, pointy hats.

"That's Zobit. He's one of the more personable gnomes," Mikey heard a familiar voice behind him. Turning, he saw Luke walking towards him from the cafeteria with several small white paper bags.

Mikey was glad to see a familiar face. "He talks so fast you can barely understand him."

"Word to the wise, don't EVER ask a gnome about what they are working on. If they think you are interested, they will talk your ear off. You'll never get them to shut up about it. Keep it simple," Luke advised.

"Haha. Noted. So...news travels fast here," Mikey motioned to everyone staring as they walked by.

"It's practically impossible to keep you a secret. Everyone can feel you stealing their Source. Plus, your mom was a famous Jaecar, your dad is an Elder vampire, and you are the first-ever offspring of the two. And—" Luke eye's shifted downwards as he kicked at an imaginary pebble—"maybe Thomas is also going around talking about the vampire spawn who tried to kill him."

"Of course he is," Mikey sighed. "You know I didn't mean to do that. He thought I was attacking him, so he Source-punched me in the chest after school, and my body just took over," Mikey explained.

"Yeah, I know. I pestered Elder Neema about you until she told me the story. Thomas has been different since he lost Simon. It's been hard on us all, but especially him. Any progress controlling it?" Luke asked.

"Not as much as I'd hoped, I absorbed too much Source, and with no way to get rid of it, I got super sick. Elder Ryan basically said I could have exploded and killed everyone," Mikey lamented.

"Ouch. Rough start," Luke tried to sound sympathetic, but his face looked hopeful. "I'm sure you'll get there. And you know, if not, I'll be happy to patch you up!" Luke grinned, a crazy glint in his eye. "Cookie?" Luke offered one of the bags, letting him look inside.

That looks like a chocolate chip...

Mikey's sweet tooth got the best of him. He wasn't hungry now, but who knows if he would be while studying. "Sure, thanks," Mikey grinned.

"I got to get back to the clinic, but I'll see you around." Luke waved. "Good luck. If you do explode, make sure to come get me!"

"Uh, deal," Mikey laughed as he waved back.

Feeling better after talking with Luke and witnessing his first gnome, Mikey followed Marcus's instructions to the clean-clothes room. It was plain with the same white walls that decorated the rest of the Sect. There was a white folding table across from a wall filled with cubbies. Each cubby had clothing that was labeled by size and sex. Underneath the cubbies was a small, indented area with different bins filled with clothes. Mikey assumed they were clean clothes that had yet to be put away.

There were signs on each non-cubby wall that read, 'Do not make a mess or bother the Brownies.' Mikey walked to the men's section, which was furthest from the door. As he found the shirts in his size, Mikey noticed movement near the bins from the corner of his eye.

Remembering not to stare and using his peripheral vision, Mikey could make out a tiny woman with curly auburn hair. The little woman couldn't have been more than eight inches tall. Despite her small stature, the faerie had a stocky frame and pale skin. She wore a loose, plain brown shirt with heavily patched red-brown pants. Mikey couldn't get a good look at her face.

As she peeked behind a bin to look at him, Mikey pretended not to notice and grabbed the shirts. The pants were in the lower cubbies, so he kneeled and pretended to look at the sizes. The Brownie ducked away as he got close but slowly peeked her head out again. Mikey realized she was looking at the cookie bag.

Ah, a woman after my own heart. He smiled.

In the folktales, Brownies loved bread and milk.

But what is a cookie other than much better bread in every way?

Mikey thought it was probably more challenging for her to get cookies than him, so he decided to try and make a friend. He placed the cookie bag near her on the other side of the bin. She ducked away again as his hand came within a foot of the fairy. He grabbed the pants and stood up, stretching and trying to appear nonchalant. "Well, I'll just leave this delicious chocolate chip cookie here. Maybe someone will enjoy it." Mikey saw her head peek out on the other side of the bin, and the bag disappeared behind it. He laughed and walked out, smiling ear to ear.

It didn't take long for him to get back to his room and head to the shower. The warm water was phenomenal.

There is nothing like a nice warm shower to wash away the day's stresses.

Mikey briefly wondered how they got water through a Portal to wherever they were, but he just shrugged and was grateful to have any at all.

When Mikey returned to his room, he changed into his regular clothes. There were plenty of others walking around with normal clothes on, so he figured you only had to wear training clothes only when training. Glancing at the clock on the nightstand, Mikey was glad to see it was only 1:00 p.m. He had a few hours left to study before dinner.

Thank goodness I'm half vampire.

Mikey stared at the eight books stacked on the desk with hundreds of pages each. He didn't read particularly fast, but it would all be memorized once read. Starting easy seemed like the best thing to do, so Mikey grabbed the shortest book titled: *Source Archetypes of the Jaecar* and began reading.

CHAPTER 8

Lord Magnus

"Lord Magnus, our informant at Haven brought me some very interesting news. Yakub's son has been found," Mogrin bowed. "He is currently at a Sect in Buffalo, attempting to control his abilities, and will remain there until he does."

"Interesting indeed. I had thought the boy was killed in the blast at the scene. After the failed kidnapping, you reported he was nowhere to be found; likely dead," Magnus raised an eyebrow. The Verdaat Lord was sitting at a large oak desk encompassing a large portion of an already grand study. The walls were lined with shelves holding thousands of books filled with ancient historical artifacts. Some were in glass cases, sensitive to the passage of time. Others, like the sword Excalibur that hung on the wall behind Magnus, were impervious.

"I only reported to you what was found at the scene. The boy was nowhere to be found. Every living creature, including the...kidnappers, was killed and drained of all their Source. When your brethren arrived shortly after the incident, they stated the child most likely died from the blast. I would never deceive you, my Lord," the goblin swore.

"Is there any word on how his powers have manifested?" Magnus questioned.

"Nothing definitive, my Lord. Only what we expected from the bodies we examined at the rest stop. The boy can absorb the Source of those around him without...feeding. It is assumed because of his mother, he will be able to become a Source user."

"Then perhaps it is better he was discovered by the humans. Only they could train him in the use of Source. Having that kind of untrained power unleashed again could be dangerous. We will monitor him for the time being. Send in Victoria when we are done here," the Lord ordered. "Has our new Healer made any progress?"

"Not yet, Lord Magnus. He states that it is difficult to determine how to fix it without knowing exactly where the code came from and what was done. But the human claims he has made progress and needs more time. I do not see any reason to doubt his word. Our hostage seems to be enough leverage. I will inform you of any progress."

"Tell our Healer that once we acquire the child's blood, if he cannot produce results, he and his companion will be given The Gift."

"At once, my Lord. I will send in Victoria," Mogrin bowed and quickly left.

The boy lives! Magnus cheered in silence.

It had been many years since he'd felt much at all. But now, there was renewed hope for his people on the horizon. When Magnus was changed by his first love, the Verdaat Lord spent several hundred years trying to make more of his kind. After everyone he had known and loved died, Magnus realized living alone and without purpose for eternity was a road that would lead to madness.

He had found that a human could be turned if given his blood. Thousands perished in the process; most weren't strong enough to accept The Gift. But to Magnus, it was a small price to grow his family. The worthy would survive. They'd be elevated just as he was.

Some humans didn't die outright. They would change into monstrous dogs, the failures he called them. Their bodies would break down and eventually perish. But they still had their uses from time to time. Most of the Failures could be ordered to carry out basic tasks. Wendigos, the humans called them.

Magnus had thought blood was the only way to make more of his kind. That was until the first female he turned became with child. A miracle, he had declared. A chance for his species to reproduce and take their rightful place as rulers. His hopes were dashed when the baby was born still. That day, the tiny body of his lifeless child had been forever burned into his memory. After thousands of years, only three of his children out of dozens had survived. Their women could only have one child; if it did not make it, there would never be another chance. It weighed heavily on them and Magnus.

For thousands of years, he searched for a way to stop it...to no avail. No Healer and none of the creatures of the Tenefae could find a solution. Though Magnus suspected the dark faeries pretended to be ignorant. They had no love for him or his people. Magnus decided using The Gift was the only effective way to grow his family. A few thousand human lives to find one worthy of becoming Verdaat was a trivial price to pay. But the sorcerers had been breeding like rabbits while his people dwindled. Every time he attempted to create more, the Source users would come.

The cost of an outright battle with the sorcerers and their allies would be too great. He even signed that ridiculous treaty—The Accords—a hundred years ago to prevent another war. It had taken everything Magnus had at the signing not to rip out their leader's throat and drain him dry. His people were hunted simply because some get overzealous and sloppy with their dinner. And because of the treaty, he must turn a blind eye when it does. If Magnus solved the infertility of his people, the Verdaat would flourish. The Source users wouldn't stand a chance; they'd be put in their rightful place.

When Yakub ran off with that woman and stories spread that she was pregnant, Magnus was skeptical. His people occasionally sleep with humans, and some even risk The Gift to spend eternity with them. But never had a pregnancy occurred between a human and Verdaat. But when the child was confirmed to be real, Magnus thought it would surely perish.

When he was again proven wrong, the Verdaat Lord hoped for the first time in thousands of years that maybe... just maybe, the child could be the key.

But Yakub would not see reason. He did not want 'his family' involved in the salvation of their species. Yakub wished to live with the woman and raise the child as she would. Magnus denied his request, rightfully so. The boy's birth was bigger than petty wishes. It could change the world.

"Our children should grow up together," he'd try to appeal to Yakub. Instead of accepting his generosity, Yakub went into hiding. Moving from place to place. When his second turned defied him after six thousand years together... it hurt Magnus deeply. He wouldn't have killed the child; he was a Verdaat, maybe more. The Verdaat Lord might have even spared the boy's mother once the cure was found. It had taken all Magnus's resources to find them. Even the goblin network had failed. When the unfortunate incident occurred ten years ago, and the child was thought dead, Magnus lost what little hope he had left.

That was until their new Healer was acquired. A man who had been trained by one of the sorcerers often compared to his first love.

A great Healer. So far, it had borne little fruit. But these things take time, and Magnus had nothing but time. Now, with the boy's blood, Magnus was confident the Healer would find the cure.

And not a moment too soon. Another threat may be looming. For centuries Magnus had heard whispers from the Tenefae about beings of darkness that consumed all life in their path before vanishing. But none had ever brought him any proof. Eventually, Magnus shrugged it off as propaganda by the sorcerers, 'tales to frighten us.' But the stirrings have increased lately. He'd even heard the Clarafae were getting uneasy. And he never heard much from the faeries of light.

All the more reason our family needs to grow.

"Hello, father. I'm sorry for the wait. I was sparring with Brittania," Victoria announced, bringing Magnus back to the present. She was his third natural child and youngest.

Magnus looked up at her and was reminded of her mother. She had been an Egyptian ruler of great renown but had lost a crucial battle in a town that was, at the time, called Actium. Magnus knew she would be killed and felt it was a waste. With little option, he offered her a chance at The Gift. She accepted and lived. And after two thousand years, she became with child seventeen years ago.

"Yes, little one. We have just been given wonderful news. Yakub's child still lives! He is learning to master his powers with the sorcerers in Buffalo."

"That is great news, father. What do you need me for?" Victoria asked.

"You will befriend the boy. Learn his gifts and when instructed, bring him to me. But, keep him safe. Yakub's son is one of our own, and the fate of our people and the world might depend on him."

"Do you know his name? Or what he looks like?" Victoria inquired.

"His name is Mikey Black. Yakub had told me once. As to his appearance, Mogrin will provide you with all you need. Any more questions?"

"No, father, I will do as you ask," Victoria bowed.

"Good. Do not disappoint me."

The large double doors closed behind his daughter with a thud.

CHAPTER 9

Viki

What did he mean by 'fate of the world'?

Her father wasn't one to overdramatize. *Whatever*—she shrugged—*It's just another freaking mission.*

Victoria, or Viki, as she preferred to be called, had only been to Buffalo once to see Niagara Falls. But that experience wouldn't help much in finding Mikey. Viki hoped Mogrin had more information. Her father was always like that. Giving no info, just orders; expecting you to figure it out.

Rumors about the locations of the Sorcerers' hideouts were plentiful in their circles. Still, no Verdaat had ever found or been inside one.

"Until now, I guess," Viki chuckled aloud. Mikey was technically one of their own, but he got to live as a regular kid. Viki started to get annoyed just thinking about it.

Being the seventeen-year-old daughter of an 8,000-year-old vampire in the modern world wasn't easy. Magnus demanded absolute obedience. And he had the strength to back it up.

As a child, she wasn't allowed to go to school with humans. Instead, Viki was given the best tutors the world could offer. Her family was wealthy beyond imagination, so her father had flown them in. By age ten, Viki had essentially graduated from college and spoke twelve languages. There was no choice in the matter, though. If her father said she would learn something, she would, one way or another. Her life was a hell of doing what he said or facing punishment. After one week locked in a dark cell, she learned quickly. During all this, Viki wasn't only to train her mind. Magnus and the other ancients personally instructed her in combat. She spent years beaten to a pulp until she could hold her own against all but the ancients.

when she became a teenager, Viki often snuck out to explore the world outside their Albany estate. Her mother or Brittania were the ones who usually found her and brought her back. Once, while exploring, she met two human children. Due to the rarity of Verdaat kids, Viki had never interacted with anyone her own age and was rightfully curious. Sneaking around the human town, Viki heard loud sounds from a small black box and saw two girls painting their toenails on a front porch. She learned later that it was rock music playing from a 'Boombox.'

Curiosity got the better of her, and she was spotted by the pair. But to Viki's surprise, the human girls invited her to join them. That was the first time she'd ever had her toenails painted. The next time Viki snuck out to see them, they invited her to watch movies. Her favorite was called *Hercules.* It was a cartoon with everything; gods, devils, and even singing.

Magnus was not a fan of this new generation of humans or anything that wasn't Verdaat. Her father would have been furious if he had known. Viki kept her feet hidden from him until the polish had worn off. She remembered how the sisters complimented her olive skin and silky, dark-brown hair. They had wanted to braid it—and she wanted them to—but Viki wouldn't have been able to hide it.

For years, Viki, her mother, and Brittania begged Magnus to give her some freedom. And when she was fifteen, he finally consented.

"There is no threat to you now in our world or the humans," he had told her. "A few years means nothing. You may travel as you please, but know I am watching. When you are summoned, you will come."

It was the best day of her life.

She visited her mother's land in Egypt. Viki flew to Ireland and had tea with Helena, the dark fairy queen. So far, her favorite adventure was when she'd gone to Suriname—the most forested country in the world—to see the Forest Dragons. They blended in so well that it took Viki two weeks to find one. All she wanted to do was see more and learn more.

But during her travels, Magnus had ordered her home to help capture that Healer. That ordeal renewed Magnus's obsession with finding a cure for their fertility. Viki also wanted her people to thrive but felt her father only wanted to rule over everything. She didn't have any love for the humans in particular, but she certainly didn't hate them or want them to suffer.

Now—Viki sighed—*I have to find some boy in a city of hundreds of thousands of people.* She would do as he asked, though. No one defied her father. No one really could. She headed toward the entrance of the estate where Mogrin would be working.

"Ah, Victo—Viki," Mogrin corrected. He stepped away from his small square desk. "I hope the meeting went well. May I help you?"

She appreciated that he was trying. Her father refused to call her Viki and gave her a look that said, 'If you continue this foolishness, you will be punished,' so she let it go. Other than her mother and Brittania, Mogrin was the only other person that seemed to actually care for her.

He was a three-and-a-half-foot-tall goblin with grey skin, large lavender eyes, and pointy ears. Usually, goblins were thin, gangly creatures. But being the assistant to the most powerful being in the world had some perks. Mogrin was a little on the heavy side and wore a custom blue-grey suit with a white undershirt and black checkered tie.

"Father wants me to go to Buffalo to find the boy and become his friend. Then I am to wait for orders to bring him here," Viki informed. "Is there any way you can help me?"

"His foster father is a great shielding sorcerer named Arthur Cafferty. He is in a suburb called Lancaster. I will text you the address when our informant provides it. I am sure if and when the boy can control his gifts, he will want to return home," Mogrin speculated. "I will arrange funds and travel for you immediately, my lady. Is tomorrow soon enough?"

"Yeah. That should be fine. Thank you, Mogrin," Viki replied.

"Think nothing of it," he bowed, then returned to his desk.

Viki went to her room to start packing. "Let's get this over with," she sighed allowed.

But maybe he'll be like the other half-breed I know...

CHAPTER 10

Mikey

Mikey was able to finish the book before dinner. He learned there were five archetypes among the Jaecar with varying rarity. There were the Movers, who could use the Source to project it outward as a weapon. Shielders harnessed their Source to armor themselves or others from damage. Healers directed the Source into the body, helping it to regenerate or rot. Adepts were able to use more than one archetype. And the rarest of all, Elementals.

Using the Source, Elementals could force the atoms in the air to move at incredible speeds and ignite. Likewise, the heat could be stripped from the air to create ice. The book mentioned nine Jaecar Elementals in all their history could create changes in the atmosphere to produce lightning.

Mikey was awed by the things the Jaecar could do.

No wonder they were called Sorcerers.

He imagined a Jaecar hurling a fireball at the Wendigos in one of his drawings. If his parents hadn't been ambushed, Mikey knew they would have stood a chance against them.

Shaking the thought away, he headed down to the cafeteria and was happy to see the Sect was emptier. It was the weekend, so Mikey guessed after training, most of the Jaecar went home, and only essential personnel stayed overnight. Looking around, he saw only a few tables had people. He spotted Sabrina by herself in the corner.

Why did I want to get here early?

This time his habit of being early would force him to sit alone with her. Ignoring the stares from the other tables, he walked over to see she was reading a book.

Sabrina glanced up as he came closer.

I think they can all tell I'm here because they can feel my Source drain...

"Hey. Glad you could make it," she smiled. "Have a seat. I figured I'd wait for you two to get here before I got dinner."

"As you know, I've got a lot going on. But I cleared my schedule to make it," Mikey joked. "Whatcha reading?"

"Just a book about a leg armor relic I secretly hope to find one day. It's kind of a little obsession of mine. I'm always looking for books in the archives about relics to see if I can find a clue where it is."

"Um...what are relics?" It was yet another term he hadn't heard before.

"Duh, of course you wouldn't know." Sabrina made a show of flicking herself on the forehead. "Relics are ancient artifacts made by the dwarves before they disappeared—I guess you don't know about dwarves either...."

"I know the dwarves in like video games and stories."

"Okay. Essentially the same. They were an ancient race of OS that was supposedly wiped out thousands of years ago. They kind of just vanished, but most people think they died out after a big battle between the Jaecar and the not-so-kind creatures of OS," she explained. "They were the only race that could use runes to create Source-forged weapons and armor. Sometimes they made items for Jaecar."

"Have you ever seen one?"

"My mom has one. They look like two small daggers. She keeps them in her hair or two small slots she has built into her armor."

"I've seen those," Mikey remembered. "I thought they looked oddly fancy for Chinese hairpins."

"If you ever watched her use them, you would never think of Chinese hairpins again," she stated. "It took years to find them, according to her."

Seems like a long time to search for two small swords... Now Mikey really wanted to see them in action.

"A relic could help a Jaecar in different ways," Sabrina continued. "Some can boost the user's power dramatically. Others give them focus. It all depends. Most relics were specifically made for a Jaecar based on their core or archetype. My cores are in my legs."

"How do they work?" Mikey could see how someone would spend twenty years trying to find one if it could make you that much stronger.

"No clue." Sabrina shrugged. "No one does anymore. We'd all have relics if we knew how to replicate them."

"Okay. So, there is only a certain number in the world. And what—people go on a quest to find them?"

"Sometimes a wielder will pass down their relic to a family member if a user is born that fit. But most of them have been lost. So yeah, with only journal entries or historical accounts as a reference, many Jaecar go on quests for them. Usually, they come back emp-ty-handed.

"That's gotta be rough," Mikey whistled. "To spend all that time and not find one...."

"Regardless, one day, I'm going to get my hands on this leg armor," Sabrina puffed out her chest.

She showed him a sketch from the book. The relic looked like a medieval shin guard. Three separate metal plates joined vertically to cover the entire front of the leg below the knee. The plates were etched with Celtic-like symbols. Metal straps were clasped together at the calf to secure the armor.

"Those look awesome! I'm sure you'll find them someday," Mikey encouraged. "I wonder if they have a relic for vampire hybrid."

He was mostly joking but considered how cool it would be to have a unique armor piece or weapon designed just for him.

"Probably not," she chuckled. "But you should be able to use a relic if you found the right one."

"I'll add it to the growing list of all the wants and things I need to learn. Did Marcus get in touch with you after training this morning?"

"Yeah. I saw him briefly after lunch. He said he would rest for a bit and then talk to Thomas. Speaking of training, how did it go?" Sabrina asked.

"Made some progress. Found out where my core will be formed. But because I didn't have an outlet for what I was absorbing, I got sick. Elder Ryan said it could have been dangerous if I had released all the energy by accident. He wants to continue tomorrow but with more caution. I don't know what I'm going to do if I can't get it under control."

Mikey's shoulders slumped just thinking of the whole ordeal again.

"You will," Sabrina smiled warmly. "Sometimes it can take people months to figure out where their core will form. One step at a time. This is all new; it's not going to come all at once."

"Thanks." Despite everything that had happened the last few days, Mikey was grateful she chose to sit next to him on the bus. He might have lived out the rest of his life, never knowing the truth.

"There's Marcus." Sabrina gestured to the cafeteria entrance.

He turned to see Marcus walking towards them, looking flushed.

"Hey, Marky. You look a little flustered. Everything okay?" Sabrina tried to sound upbeat.

"I'm fine," Marcus glowered. "Just had a lovely talk with my darling brother about the rumors he's been spreading about you," he looked to Mikey. "I don't know what has gotten into him, but he's so hostile towards you it makes no sense. I tried to invite him to hang with us...." Marcus trailed off.

"And?" Sabrina asked.

From Marcus's tone, Mikey knew he probably didn't have anything nice to say.

"He said he had too much training to do. And that he'd never associate with a 'filthy vampire,'" Marcus finished.

Mikey felt Thomas's attitude was due to something deeper than accidentally bumping into him at school.

Is it really because I'm half vampire? He attacked me first before the whole almost-killing-him thing.

"I'm used to having people not like me for no reason," Mikey faked a smile to try and lighten the mood. "Hopefully, after a while, he'll get over it. I can't help what I am, only who I will be. I'm just grateful you tried to stick up for me."

"Of course. It's not your fault," Marcus sighed. "He's just—not himself anymore."

Mikey saw how conflicted both Sabrina and Marcus were about the whole situation. He wished there was something he could do.

The somber mood was interrupted by a perfectly timed, obnoxiously loud gurgle from Marcus's stomach. Sabrina burst out laughing, causing the other two to join in.

"I think your stomach talks almost as much as you do," Sabrina wiped at her eye.

"He is pretty chatty today. Time to get some grub. I'm obviously starving." Marcus stood up and headed for the food.

"Me too. I was waiting for everyone to get here first. I saw them take out a couple of pizzas as I walked in," Sabrina followed.

Mikey still wasn't hungry from this morning's training, but since when did you have to be hungry to enjoy pizza? He joined the duo to grab a slice of pepperoni and one of those chocolate chip cookies he had gifted earlier. Mikey made a mental note to drop off another for his little friend the next time he needed clothes. The rest of the night passed quickly as Mikey enjoyed dinner with two friends for the first time in his life.

They all agreed to have breakfast tomorrow before Mikey's round two of training. Sabrina wished them good luck and said she would head to the library to finish reading and wait up for her mother. Marcus was going to—in his words— 'coma' from the five slices of pizza he had. Mikey decided reading up on his new life might help make him feel less like an outcast.

Maybe a little sketching if I lose steam.

The trio enjoyed breakfast together the following day, and Sabrina gave some more encouraging words to Mikey, furthering his crush. When he and Marcus were walking back to meet Elder Ryan for training, he had to ask about her.

"Are you and Sabrina...a thing?" Mikey figured being direct was the best way to go about it.

"Sabrina and me? Together?" Marcus's face crinkled. "No, no. I'm gay. She used to date Thomas, though, before we lost Simon," he clarified.

"Oh, okay."

Yes. The corners of Mikey's mouth turned up even though he was a little concerned to hear she and Thomas used to be a thing.

"It doesn't bother you I'm gay, right? Doesn't happen often, but some people get weird about it, especially guys."

"Honestly, I don't care who you like. You've been a great friend to me. I don't know how I could have gotten through all this the last couple of days without you and Sabrina," Mikey voiced. "Does everyone know, though? I don't want to accidentally say something."

"Yeah. I mean, I don't go around announcing it just like you don't go telling everyone you're straight. But everyone knows."

"Cool." Mikey shrugged.

They began walking again, and Mikey thought he noticed more pep in Marcus's step.

"Soooooooo, you like Sabrina," Marcus blurted a few seconds later.

Mikey's face blushed. "Of course I do. I mean...who wouldn't—"

"Relax. I think it could definitely be a possibility down the road. She's still torn up from Thomas—which would be a different ball game to deal with—but I don't think she hates you." Marcus winked.

"Awesome. Not being hated is a great first start," Mikey laughed. "I just want to get to know her more. She seems like a good person."

"She is. We've been BFFs our whole lives practically. She has a lot of pressure on her shoulders and takes Sect stuff very seriously. But she's a softie at heart," Marcus shared. "Let's work on controlling your vampyness before we start this 'Beauty and the Beast' love story."

"Right. I know what I have to do to stop it. But doing it is a different story." Mikey's forehead creased. He had no idea how he could get those doors closed. So much was riding on this.

"You'll get it," Marcus assured.

They reached the training room and took their usual seats on the floor to wait for the Elder and Michelle. Soon, the door opened, and Elder Ryan and Michelle entered.

"Good morning. I trust you began your studies last night?" Ryan looked expectantly at Mikey.

"Yes. I finished the book on archetypes. And most of another." Mikey hoped that was enough.

"Excellent," he nodded approvingly. "Are you ready to begin? This time we will monitor you more closely. As soon as you begin to feel ill, let me know. We'll immediately stop. Do not push yourself in this way. Instead, focus on 'closing the doors,' as you put it yesterday." The Elder took his place in front of Mikey, and Michelle sat beside him, nodding to the two of them.

"Hello Jaecar Michelle. Thank you for helping me today as well." Mikey clasped his hands together in thanks.

"You're welcome." She nodded slightly.

"All right. Let us begin."

As the familiar pressure enveloped him, Mikey brought his focus to the Source entering his left hand. He formed the doors again in his mind and tried to push them closed with everything he had. But, to his frustration, he couldn't. It ended much the same as yesterday; Mikey woke up with a throb in the side of his head and everyone around him out of breath.

"I'm sor—" Mikey started to say until he saw the Elder's glare. "I mean to say, I don't have the strength to close it off. Even slightly open at their natural state." Mikey tried to convey that it wasn't a matter of willpower, he simply didn't have the ability. "You can tell someone to do 100 pushups in two minutes. But if they've never done pushups before, they won't be able to do them no matter how much they try."

"Then we have to think of another way for you to strengthen yourself. It could be that you've kept them open for so long the strength to close them has atrophied—so to speak. Any ideas?" Elder Ryan invited.

When Elder Ryan said atrophied, Mikey knew that was the perfect word to describe it. Then an idea began to form in his mind. Mikey had once watched a movie where a man woke up from a coma and could barely use his legs. The doctors had him hoisted up and slowly started to put weight on them. Over time the man was able to walk. The only way to make it even easier to shut his meridians off...*is to start from closed.*

"Your comment gave me an idea, Elder Ryan." Mikey's eyes lit up. "If the doors to my meridians are atrophied, we have to slowly strengthen them—starting from scratch." He turned to Michelle as realization dawned on her face.

"Ah. I see your plan now. That might work," Elder Ryan confirmed.

"I hate to interrupt, but what is the plan?" Marcus's brow furrowed.

"I want Jaecar Michelle to close off my meridians. I will try to hold them shut as long as I can. Hopefully, I'll be able to open and close them a bit from there. Eventually—after a ton of practice—I think I'll be able to close them off when they are completely open," Mikey explained.

"That's actually a good idea," Marcus admitted. "Bummer. I kind of enjoyed watching you get bopped unconscious."

Mikey couldn't help but laugh. A grunt from Elder Ryan brought them back to focus.

"Michelle," the Elder motioned for her to begin.

Mikey braced for the onslaught of pain. Instantly, his body felt like it was thrown into the arctic ocean. The cold permeated through every inch of his body. Gritting his teeth, Mikey pushed the agony to the corner of his mind and focused on his left hand.

It's itchy.

He concentrated on the new sensation and brought it to the forefront, envisioning the doors again. This time, they were completely closed.

I—I did it? Oh my god. I did it! Elation filled him. Even more to Mikey's surprise, he could keep them that way.

"Okay, you can stop shielding. I've got it under control." Mikey affirmed to Michelle.

In a heartbeat, it felt like someone he'd been leaning on vanished. Mikey was so caught off guard that he almost let the doors open before catching himself.

Physically, he felt terrible. But that paled in comparison to the excitement of what he'd done.

I'm really stopping it!

And Mikey felt then he'd be able to control it entirely someday.

"Wonderful." Ryan clapped his hands together. "I don't feel you absorbing any Source at all."

"Nice dude!" Marcus slapped him on the back.

"I couldn't have done it without you all." Mikey smiled warmly at them, getting the same in return. Michelle only nodded, but Mikey thought he saw a brief smile. He was still in shock from the whole ordeal.

The rest of the morning and part of the afternoon was spent strengthening Mikey's control until he could shut off his meridians from his default level of absorption.

However, the longer he went without absorbing Source, the more the itch in his hand got worse. By the end of the afternoon, Mikey wanted to scratch the skin off or just take the whole hand altogether.

"Let them open. You can have some of my Source," Elder Ryan offered.

Mikey nodded gratefully; the relief he felt was instant.

"As we suspected, keeping your vampiric meridians closed takes a toll. Hopefully, it will be less difficult with time," the Elder stated. "Continue to improve your control."

"I will," Mikey assured. "But what's next? What happens tomorrow?"

"I will inform elder Cassandra of your progress and recommend you be allowed to leave the Sect and attend your regular schooling. We will also let Arthur know. It has not been decided yet, but the elders will discuss the option of you becoming an acolyte...if that is what you wish," Elder Ryan answered.

"I, uh... I'm not sure," Mikey confessed. "Until I was born, this was my mother's world. She wanted to use her gifts to protect people. And strangely, I've felt I belong more in this world than anywhere else."

Mikey looked at Marcus. Did he want to give this all up? Marcus smiled warmly, giving him a thumbs up.

This is where I belong.

There was no going back at this point. He was in too deep. Mikey also suspected this was the only way he'd get answers about why his parents were killed.

And I want to know what I'm really capable of.

"Yes. I want to become an acolyte," Mikey declared.

"I will make this known at the meeting," Elder Ryan nodded. "We think it best that you take extra caution until you can properly defend yourself. The Verdaat will surely find out about you as well as other creatures from OS. I don't think they'd dare attack out in the open or at a school. But be mindful of your surroundings," the Elder advised.

"Duly noted. But how do I go to school and become an acolyte?" Mikey puzzled. "How do you hunt monsters and stay a high school student?"

"Normally, we go home Sunday night for school the next day," Marcus chimed in. "We train at night on the weekdays whenever possible and all day on the weekends. At least the ones who want to become a Jaecar before they reach thirty," Marcus chuckled. "I told you before, the youngest Jaecar was sixteen years old. Most graduate high school and some even college before becoming a Jaecar. Right now, our focus is mastering our Source, learning the knowledge, and combat skills."

"Indeed," Ryan nodded. "To become a Jaecar, you must have a primary mastery of your Source. This is determined by a Tribunal consisting of both group and individual tests. If passed, you will become a Jaecar after a ceremonial hunt with an elder and your omada. Then you will gain access to Haven funds and be assigned to go on hunts.

"How does that work?"

"We have teams and technology in place that scan for any information about unusual deaths and other odd occurrences. If it's flagged, we send an omada to investigate and eliminate the threat if there is one. These jobs are to be completed with the utmost secrecy. There is a delicate balance right now between the creatures of OS and humans. If either side was made fully aware of the other, there would be bloodshed. And I'm not sure the humans would win," Elder Ryan shared.

"Don't we have like—guns and stuff?" Mikey wondered.

"Guns are too noisy to use and the creatures of OS move so fast it would be just as easy to accidentally shoot your omada. Also, many monsters wouldn't be harmed by bullets in the slightest," the Elder explained.

"Okay...and how long do you go on jobs. Are there like... breaks?" Mikey couldn't pass up this opportunity to ask Elder Ryan all the questions he'd been holding in.

"Usually, an omada will work three to four months at a time and then take that same amount of time off. Jobs pay very well, but no one is technically forced to do them, but that is why we became Jaecar. And if we are called upon by the high council, we must come. No matter what."

"And when can you take the Tribunal?" Mikey continued.

"Technically, it can be taken at any time. However, you need a group or omada willing to take the test with you. The minimum number is three. We do not go on hunts alone except in dire circumstances. Forming bonds with your fellow acolytes and learning to work as a team is crucial to Jaecar. During the Tribunal, if one of you fails, you all fail. That is why we pick our omada carefully. We hold a tribunal every 6 months; the last was held a month ago," the Elder explained. "If you do not have other groups to compete against, you will have to challenge an elder with your omada instead. So, most wait until the official Tribunal."

That gives me five months if I wanted to try and take it, Mikey thought.

As if sensing what Mikey was thinking, Elder Ryan cautioned, "Don't get ahead of yourself. You have a long way to go before you're ready for a tribunal. It is not to be taken lightly. Focus on becoming stronger, and your time will come."

"I don't know, elder Ryan. After spending time with Mikey here, trying to stop him from vamping my Source...I feel like I've gotten much stronger at shielding in just a few days. I can pretty much keep a basic shield up at all times," Marcus boasted.

"That is excellent. Don't let it go to your head. Continue to improve. Now that Mikey can control his absorption, I would like to have the other acolytes come next weekend and focus on developing their basic shield. If that is all right with you," the Elder turned to Mikey.

"Yeah. I'm okay with that. Glad to help."

"Great. I'll go inform Cassandra and the others. Be at the porter room at 6:30 a.m. tomorrow, and someone will take you to school. Once approved as an acolyte, you will receive a porter watch. There are three locations in Buffalo that the gnomes have calibrated to this Sect. Once you receive your watch, you will be instructed on these locations and how to safely port here."

As if finished with all he would say, the Elder nodded at them and headed for the door. Michelle went to follow but hesitated. She turned to Mikey and said, "Congratulations. I was glad to help." She smiled a little, this time for real, then left behind the Elder.

"Dude, you did it," Marcus beamed. "Obviously, I was essential in this process, but no need to thank me. I'm not here for the praise." Marcus pretended to wave away some imaginary group of fans.

"Honestly, having you here really did help me. Thanks again."

They left the training area and headed back to Mikey's room.

"So, I gotta head home, but are you sure you're good?" Marcus asked. "We will save you a seat at lunch tomorrow."

"Sounds great. I'm fantastic. I can finally be around people like normal," Mikey grinned. "Have a good night, Marcus. See you tomorrow."

Mikey decided to head to the cafeteria and get some dinner. He'd barely had any Source today, and his stomach protesting. Sunday must not have been a busy dinner night for the Sect because no one was sitting when he got there. Two other people were getting dinner, but they didn't even pay attention to him, and Mikey had to force himself not to jump up and cheer. Before coming in, he'd shut off his vampiric meridians. It confirmed what Mikey thought; his Source drain was why everyone noticed him in the Sect.

The dinner for Sunday was macaroni and cheese, fries, and hamburgers. It was just about the best dinner for a growing teenage daywalker. Mikey decided to top it off with a couple of cookies and one for his new tiny red-headed friend. After dinner, he headed for the clean laundry room. Mikey placed a cookie a little bit further behind the bin than before.

There. Hopefully, she'll find it.

Back in his room, Mikey walked up to the side of the bed before letting himself fall face-first onto the mattress. So much had changed in the last two days; Mikey felt like he could drown. The best part was, other than Thomas, it had all been amazing. He had friends for the first time in his life, could now safely be around people, and was on his way to becoming a Jaecar like his mother. Mikey wished his parents could be here on this journey with him, but at least he had Arthur, Marcus, and Sabrina.

That reminds me. I can't wait to tell Arthur everything tomorrow!

He decided he was too amped up to study and chose to draw instead. Mikey recalled Elder Neema mentioning a creature called a bugbear. With that in mind, he sketched an ogre with a bear-shaped face covered in dark-brown fur. The creature's mouth was filled with oversized teeth jutting out of the sides. It had one large club in its left hand and an axe in the other. By the time Mikey finished the outline, he had begun to do the sleepy head bob, letting him know it was time for bed. He set his alarm for six a.m. And for once in his life, he looked forward to school.

CHAPTER II

At 6:15am, Mikey headed down to the portal room to ensure he was on time. He picked up some Pop-Tarts for breakfast and an extra pack in case he got hungry at school. Keeping his meridians closed was exhausting. The Sect was much more alive than he thought it would be this early morning. Several Jaecar walked through the halls in light, black armor with various weapons gleaming from scabbards, pockets, and straps. He ignored the expected stares and whispers as he walked through the hallways past the TC.

When he got to the porter room, Mikey was surprised to see the same Jaecar that drove him to the Sect with Elder Cassandra.

"Hi...again. Thanks for taking me to school," Mikey was unsure what to call him.

"No problem, kid. Being a taxi driver for high schoolers is my dream come true," he said, his voice laced with sarcasm.

"Sorry," Mikey tried to look apologetic.

"Don't sweat it. I'm just messing with you," he smirked.

Mikey saw the man wearing the same black armor outfit as when they had first met. He noticed a blue pin on the guy's chest with the same symbol Elder Cassandra had on at his house. It was one line straight down with another line intersecting it diagonally. At the end of the diagonal line was a triangle. It almost looked like a stickman firing a bow.

"Does that symbol mean you are a Jaecar?" Mikey pointed.

"Yep. It's the symbol of the hunter Orion. Jaecar get a blue pin while the elders get gold,' he answered. "Most of us know who is who, but it helps distinguish for the acolytes."

"It will definitely be helpful for me," Mikey agreed. "Anyway, I'm Mikey Black. Thanks again for driving me," he stuck out his hand. Mikey had his driver's license, but money was tight with the new move and only Arthur's salary. But they were saving to get him a car.

"I'm Jaecar Chase," he smiled, returning the handshake. "You can call me Chase when no one is around. I was never one for all that title crap. You live together; you die together. Anyone who chooses this life has my respect."

"Nice to meet you," Mikey replied. He instantly liked the man.

"Let's get you to school. It's kind of sad I can't mess with you anymore about the portal, though. Make sure to jump through with both feet like last time," he teased.

Chase pressed a button on his wrist, and the shimmer appeared on the platform. The Jaecar motioned for Mikey to go first. As he stepped through, Mikey expected to be in the Wonder Bread factory like before. Instead, he was in a cramped stone room. The rising sun shone through a tiny window a few feet above Mikey's head. Next to the window was a large wooden door. Mikey opened it with no other visible way out and found himself standing in what looked like a park. He stepped back, turned to look at the room he was in, and realized it was the small stone lighthouse at Como Lake Park in Lancaster. Arthur had taken him there a few times to walk, and he remembered seeing a couple taking wedding photos in front of it.

Must be one of the three locations the porters work on.

His school was only ten minutes away from there.

Chase came out soon after with a big grin on his face. "Did I get you with the new location?"

"It wasn't as crazy as a portal appearing in front of me for the first time...but yeah, you got me." Mikey laughed.

Chase led the way to the parking lot, and Mikey saw the same SUV that had taken him to the Sect, which felt like ages ago. They chatted during the drive, and Mikey's eyes went wide when Chase showed him his left hand was a prosthetic. He described how his omada went to investigate reports of missing people along the Oregon coast. It turned out a harpy nest was in the nearby cliffs. A harpy hid in the shadows and dove for his wife's head. Chase had given his hand instead. His wife's name was Shelly, and she was the other Jaecar at his house that night. Haven offered them the job of guarding the new Sect leader for Buffalo years ago, and it 'sounded like a good gig,' so here they were.

Mikey told him about his childhood, his radioactivity, and finding out who he really was the night they came to his house. He liked Chase, but when he showed Mikey his prosthetic hand, it hit home how dangerous this life was. Marcus's brother, Arthur's daughter, and his own parents came to mind. This wasn't some fantasy story or video game; this was reality. If he was going to enter this world, Mikey had to accept that he could die, or worse, his friends.

Chase must have noticed a difference in the mood because he tried to change the subject. "Look, kid, I didn't mean to bum you out about my hand."

"No. You didn't bum me out. I was just thinking about how real all of this is. That you guys go out there and risk your lives to save people all the time, and no one knows," Mikey lamented.

"Sounds like bummed out to me," Chase snickered. "Let me put it this way. We wiped out that harpy nest and avenged all those lives taken. We also prevented more from being lost. If you asked me would I take it all back if I could keep my hand and live my life as some bank teller or something... I'd tell you hell no. The only thing I would change is wishing I would've been faster and stopped those flying bastards from getting my hand in the first place. But I sleep great at night knowing what I'm a part of. I don't regret it for a second."

"Thanks." Mikey appreciated the Jaecar's intentions.

"It's just the truth. If we don't do it, helpless people suffer. I'd rather us than them, right?" Chase asked.

He looked at Mikey like the question was some sort of test. If given the option, would Mikey rather sacrifice himself for other people? For his friends or Arthur, he was sure he would. But for people he had never met? Mikey thought back to the night his parents were killed and imagined instead, they were perfect strangers. Mikey instantly realized that if he could have stopped those monsters and protected those other people, he would. Mikey never wanted another person to go through those horrors. He understood the point of Chase's question and was grateful for it.

"Right," Mikey answered.

"I knew all those horrible things everyone was saying about you weren't true," Chase said with a straight face.

"What horrible thi—" Mikey started to ask until it dawned on him. "Got me again," Mikey shook his head.

"That's okay. Eventually, you won't be such an easy target," Chase laughed. It was infectious, and Mikey couldn't help but laugh himself. By the time they pulled up to the school entrance, he was feeling better about their conversation. Mikey thanked him for the ride again and for putting things in perspective.

"I hope this taxi thing won't be a common occurrence. See you around," Chase waved, pulling out of the parking lot.

Mikey turned to his high school and took in a deep breath. Just a week ago, the thought of coming here would have filled him with dread. But after this weekend, with the real threat of never coming again, he was so happy to see the high school. Shaking his head at the absurdity of everything, Mikey closed his meridians and headed to his first class.

Even though his day went by as it always had, to Mikey, it was a new dawn. He was no longer nervous about hurting the people around him. Keeping his vampiric meridians closed made the itch in his hand worse and the hunger for Source greater, but Mikey didn't care. He occasionally opened the doors a little just to relieve some of the discomfort, but closed them before anyone would start to feel bad. It was more than Mikey could have asked for.

The first half of the day seemed to drag on, and Mikey knew it was because he was looking forward to lunch. It's a universal truth that whenever you wanted something to come quickly, it would take forever, and vice versa. He watched the clock on the wall above a poster of different mathematical formulas until the bell finally rang. Mikey practically jumped out of the chair. Not only was he starving, but he was also excited to see Marcus and Sabrina.

The lunch line had yet to reach epic proportions, so Mikey got in. He would find Marcus and Sabrina after sustenance. When he got to the sneeze guards at the end of the line, Mikey saw lunch was chicken wings and tater tots. But his head turned at a sudden flick on the back of his head. He was pleased to see it was Sabrina.

"Hey, you. I heard from Marcus today that you were able to control it," she beamed. "That's amazing! And in only two days. I thought you'd at least have to miss a week or something."

"Thanks for the vote of confidence," Mikey chuckled.

"I said you WOULD do it. Just didn't think that fast. I knew it would happen," she declared. "Me and Marcus are sitting over there."Sa brina pointed to a table in the corner of the cafeteria where Marcus was waving. "Sit with us when you get your food," she waved before heading back to the table.

Just seeing her made Mikey feel lighter. He headed over after successfully convincing the lunch lady to give him extra tots. Mikey took the seat next to Marcus. It was a toss-up between sitting next to Sabrina or being able to look at her beautiful eyes; the eyes won.

"Hey, dude. You get here, okay?" Marcus asked.

"Yeah. Jaecar Chase gave me a ride. The porter took us to the lighthouse in Como Lake Park," Mikey answered.

"We use that one sometimes if we stay late or overnight at the Sect. It's the closest one to the school," Marcus shared.

"I forgot to ask yesterday, but how do you get around? I can't imagine Chase driving around young acolytes from school," Mikey wondered.

"Well, I've got a car. It's an old beat-up grey Dodge Neon, but it's mine. Thomas has one too. As far as the younger acolytes go, they have a strict schedule after school, and the Sect has busses pick them up. Haven has deep pockets. But they only use their money for Sect business," Marcus answered.

"Not everyone from Jaecar families are fighters. A lot of them keep everything going and have other jobs in business; we call them supporters. Even though they don't do the actual fighting, Haven makes sure they are considered one of us and treated with respect," Sabrina chimed in.

"Huh. I guess that makes sense," Mikey nodded.

He couldn't imagine every single Jaecar being able to sacrifice their hands or watching one of their loved ones be attacked. It also explained all the equipment, food, and supplies. He appreciated the organization even more for having a culture of respect for the ones that help behind the scenes.

"If Marcus and Thomas have cars...with your mom being the Sect leader, it seems like she could get you a car too, Sabrina. How come you ride the bus?" Mikey wondered.

Crap, was that too personal?

"My mom doesn't want me driving around by myself; she's...."

"Controlling," Marcus finished for her.

Sabrina rolled her eyes at him.

"So, you are allowed to train to fight monsters that eat people but not drive a car," Mikey thought aloud. Cassandra seemed like a rational person, and that didn't make sense.

"It's not that. I may have been driving too fast right after I got my license and totaled my car," Sabrina admitted, sinking into her shoulders. "My mom won't let me drive until I'm eighteen." Her face flushed. "Besides, there is a perfect little café off my bus stop. I like to go there after school and unwind before dealing with all the Sect stuff."

Mikey thought she looked even cuter when she was embarrassed.

Sabrina reminded him that he needed to text Arthur about riding the bus home today to be with a friend and that he was excited to see him. Whatever the circumstances, Mikey was happy she ended up sitting next to him that day.

"Great, now the monster can blend in with the rest of us," a voice behind them hissed. "My brother has odd tastes in the first place," he glared at Marcus, "but I expected better from you, Sabrina," he spat. They all turned to see Thomas walking by, holding a lunch tray.

"I'm a big girl. I can make my own decisions Thomas," she retorted.

"Clearly, not good ones," Thomas looked at Mikey in disgust. "You might have fooled them, bloodsucker, but you will never be one of us."

"Uh, I think the term if anything, would be 'Source Sucker,'" Marcus quipped.

"Look, I have no idea what beef you have with me. I'm sorry for your brother and what happened last week, but I didn't know what I was doing or anything about all this," Mikey tried to ease the tension.

Thomas threw his tray on the ground and lunged at Mikey. Sabrina and Marcus jumped up in time to get in between them.

"Tom, stop! You are out of control, man," Marcus tried to reason with him.

Thomas pushed through them and shoved Mikey into the wall. "If you ever mention Simon again..." his face was a mask of rage, "no one will be able to keep you safe," Thomas swore.

Mikey had no idea why Thomas had so much hatred toward him. Did he hate the vampire side of him that much because Simon died during a monster hunt? There was nothing Mikey could do about that, and Thomas didn't seem rational enough to talk it out.

"My, my, what an energetic group of young students we have here," a smiling Mrs. Tursley walked up. "Surely, we don't want a trip to the principal's office. Hmm?" There was an edge to her tone that was somehow more menacing than sweet.

Thomas stood there clenching his fists, then growled in frustration and stormed off.

"Now, what happened to make that boy so angry?" Mrs. Tursley asked, pushing her glasses back up on the bridge of her paint-smudged nose.

"I apologize, Mrs. Tursley," Marcus started. "We lost our older brother a year ago, and Thomas—he's that mass of raging hormones that stormed off—is still really shaken up about it. Mikey tried to give his condolences, and in just bringing it up, Thomas got angry," he explained.

"Oh, well... I'm sorry for you both. Mikey, I think it best you stay away from that boy for the time being. Let him cool off," Mrs. Tursley suggested.

"I'm planning on it," Mikey assured her.

"I'm just glad nothing serious came of it. I'll see you all this afternoon. I'm looking forward to your finished pieces," their teacher grinned, this time sweetly. She looked at the mess on the floor. "Um..."

"I'll clean it up. Don't worry, Mrs. Tursley," Marcus said.

"Thank you," she sighed. She gave them a final smile before heading down toward the teacher's section.

"I'm sorry. I hate that I'm getting in between your brother and Sabrina," Mikey said.

"He's doing that all himself," Sabrina snorted.

"Let's just forget about it. Can't let Tommy Temper Tantrum ruin our lunch," Marcus tried to lighten the mood. He began picking up the food on the floor and putting it on the tray; then Mikey and Sabrina got down and helped.

The rest of lunch passed by much more cheerfully. Mikey exchanged phone numbers and promised to introduce Marcus and Sabrina to Arthur soon. He was looking forward to talking with Arthur alone and taking a break from the Sect for a day. Marcus offered to take Mikey with them to the Sect after school the next day to study and start his core training.

When his favorite class finally came, Mikey found his friends sitting in the same spot they were in last week. However, instead of whispering secretively, they both pointed to an empty easel beside Sabrina. Mikey tried to push down his rapidly rising pulse as he got his drawing out from across the room where they stored them last Friday.

When Sabrina went to get her piece, Marcus winked at him. Then he glanced at Mikey's painting before a mischievous grin appeared. He motioned for Mikey to lean in and whispered, "Tell Sabrina you need to use her arm as a reference for grabbing the apple." He chuckled but turned straight-faced as Sabrina came back.

"What was that about?" she asked.

"Oh, I uh, was telling Marcus that I feel like the arm in my piece doesn't look right and that, um...copying an actual woman's arm, like—your arm, would help make it look more realistic," Mikey stammered. It took everything in him to not start laughing. Marcus was behind where she couldn't see, giving Mikey a thumbs up, nodding in exaggeration.

Mikey thought he saw Sabrina's face turn a little redder.

"Yeah... I'm okay with that. If it'll help your piece," Sabrina said, definitely blushing. "What do I have to do?"

"You don't really have to do anything. I have a good memory. So I just need to have you hold," Mikey went to grab her arm to position it as the artist in him took over. When he saw Sabrina's eyes go wide, Mikey realized how close he was.

"Sorry, I was just going to hold your arm in the right position and open your hand up, so it looked like you were reaching for an apple. Once I see it, I can paint it," Mikey tried to explain. He felt like he must have been as red as Sabrina because he swore his face had a pulse.

"No, it's fine," she murmured, putting her arm out.

Mikey grabbed it and began placing it in the proper position. He tried to appear as professional as possible despite the sudden difficulty swallowing and breathing. Sabrina felt warm and soft and smelled like raspberry vanilla. He took her hand and opened her fingers in the perfect pose for grabbing an apple before committing it to memory.

"Okay, got it. It'll be much more realistic now," Mikey thanked her. *Marcus is a genius.*

"No problem, let me see it when you are done," Sabrina smiled.

Mrs. Tursley walked around the classroom, examining everyone's pieces. "Now, class, I know it has been two whole days since you began these pieces, but you know what they say, absence makes the art grow fonder. Ha. Ha. Ha." She produced the apple again from her paint-stained apron, making another show of placing it on the stool in the center of the room.

"Remember, today is the last day to finish. I will examine them after class and give you a grade tomorrow. Points will be determined by creativity and how you showcased the apple. Begin!"

Using Sabrina's arm would actually make Mikey's 'Serpent and Eve' piece look much more realistic. He was excited to have her be a part of his art. Mikey resketched the arm to replicate Sabrina's, then started painting it in.

As he was finishing up, Mikey glanced over to Sabrina's piece. She drew several different types of candy apples. There were some dipped in chocolate and caramel. Others had coatings in coconut and other candies.

"It's all I could think of," Sabrina shrugged.

Mikey realized he wasn't being subtle about looking at her art. "No, it's perfect. Sweets are the greatest gift to humankind," he joked. "The only way to make fruit good is to cover it in candy. I love it."

"Thanks," she laughed.

"Mine's a work of art too, you know," Marcus interrupted. "Behold," he gestured to his piece.

A single apple was on the ground, surrounded by fallen leaves with a worm crawling through it. Mikey thought it was relatively simple but well done.

"Sign me up for your art gallery opening Marky," Sabrina raised her hand.

"I don't know how that worm is eating the apple if it isn't covered in chocolate. Poor worm," Mikey teased. "Really, though, it's good."

"See Brina! Maybe I will open that art gallery," Marcus huffed, pretending to be offended.

"I told you, 'Brina' will never catch on. Give it up, Marky," she sighed, shaking her head. "Neither of us can compare to our young Van Gogh over here," Sabrina gestured to Mikey. "That looks amazing," she approved.

"Definitely a great-looking arm," Marcus elbowed Mikey.

Sabrina gave him a deadpan stare. But she couldn't hide the smirk. Mikey's painting had a serpent with alternating dark green and black spots wrapped around a perfectly depicted bright red apple, almost protectively. Sabrina's arm was reaching out of the side to grab the apple.

"Alright, time's up, artists. Leave your paintings on the easels," Mrs. Tursley instructed. She began walking around the room again, inspecting the work around her. "I will grade them tonight, and we will start a new project tomorrow." When she got to Mikey, her eyes went wide. She leaned in so only he could hear. "Splendid. True talent," she beamed. "Now, class, I want you to walk around the room and see what some of your classmates have created. NO judgments! This class is about exploring the inner artist inside of you all and getting out of your comfort tone. Ha. Ha. Ha."

The three of them walked around the room, examining the other students' work. One had drawn a small neighborhood that was being destroyed by raining apples. Sabrina's drawing was his favorite, but he really liked one painting with an apple dressed as Mr. Potato Head. It was silly and clever.

Mikey was surprised by how many interesting ideas and how much talent the class had. Several of the students commented on his painting, making him blush. That got him a nudge from both Sabrina and Marcus.

The bell rang and the trio headed across the field together. Marcus left for his car while he and Sabrina walked to the bus. When they sat together, Mikey felt like his chest would explode. It felt worse than the first time because Sabrina wasn't just a stranger anymore.

But after they spent the first few minutes of their bus ride talking about ways to bug Marcus, Mikey realized how comfortable he was with Sabrina. He asked her if she had found any more clues to the relic she wanted. Sabrina told him the book she was reading mentioned the relic was last with someone named Tahoma a long time ago."

They talked about the café she was going to when she got off at her stop, and to Mikey's surprise, she asked him to go with her sometime. He happily agreed. Sabrina wished Mikey a good time with Arthur and said she would see him tomorrow and try to help form his core when she could. It was the best bus ride he'd ever had.

Riding the high of the day, Mikey got off, his face full of smiles. Arthur was there to greet him. "Hey bud, long time no see."

Mikey walked up and gave him a big hug. Even though it was only a few days, so much had happened that it felt like a lifetime. "Looks like you survived without my famous culinary skills," Mikey laughed.

"It was tough. I could barely work the toaster without you," Arthur joined in. They started walking to their tiny red brick home, happy to be in each other's company again. "Oh, I thought I'd order out for dinner to celebrate controlling your...power, and it hit me after you left that I never got us that pizza. Pick whatever you want," Arthur offered.

"Let's do Chinese," Mikey answered. "But we have to get those powdered donuts."

"Deal," Arthur nodded as they walked into the house.

"I also can't really control my vampiric meridian yet. I can only open it a little and close it," Mikey told him.

"Vampiric meridian. You mean your meridian came from your dad?" Arthur looked puzzled.

"There is so much to tell you," Mikey realized. "I have two meridians. One 'vampiric meridian' from my dad and a normal one like you have." Mikey expected Arthur's reaction because he'd seen it a few times already.

"Two meridians—I... that's... amazing," Arthur stammered.

Mikey filled him in on the exam with Elder Neema, the training with Elder Ryan, and all that happened with his new friends and Thomas. When Mikey mentioned Zobit, Arthur said he'd met the gnome once to repair his porter watch.

Arthur couldn't believe Mikey's story about the Brownie fairy. "I always assumed they must talk to someone sometime... but I've never heard of one coming out on purpose. She must have a sweet tooth worse than you," Arthur teased.

The conversation was lighthearted until Mikey mentioned Arthur's daughter and what he'd learned. After several minutes of silence, Arthur sighed before telling Mikey about Emma. She was an Adept at Mover and Shielder. Her team was sent to investigate a slew of mangled bodies found in the woods at Big Brook Forest in Oneida, New York.

They were ambushed by a group of Bugbears. They had attacked their Healer and main Shielder first. Arthur explained that a Bugbear is a giant, humanoid monster about the size of a small elephant. And despite their size, they are skilled at blending into their surroundings.

"They have tough skin, and their wounds heal quickly. They'll also rip out a tree from the ground and use it as a club. Needless to say, Bugbears are one of the most dangerous creatures of OS," he told Mikey.

Arthur explained that Emma had stayed behind to allow her party to escape telling them she'd be right behind them. But she never made it back.

"I went to that forest with my old omada, and we tore those monsters limb from limb," Arthur snarled. Mikey had never seen him so angry and hurt. "But that didn't bring her back. Nothing could." Arthur clenched his fists.

"After my wife died in a hit and run many years before, Emma was all I had left. And I let her be a part of this world. She never should have become a Jaecar." Arthur's eyes welled up with tears, and Mikey put his arm around him.

"I know that's why you didn't want to tell me about all this," Mikey comforted. "I know my parents wanted me to be able to decide for myself too. It's what good parents do. Do you think if you gave Emma a choice to be a Jaecar or something else, she would choose something else?"

Arthur looked up and grabbed a tissue from the box on top of the end table behind the couch. "No, Mikey, she would have chosen to be a Jaecar, but if she didn't have the choice, she might still be here."

"She might, and maybe everyone in the omada that went would have died because Emma wouldn't have been there to save them," Mikey stated.

"I know, I know...." Arthur trailed off. He got up and walked to the kitchen, opening a cupboard. "You want some cocoa with your sugar donuts?"

"Yes, please," Mikey replied eagerly.

Arthur returned a couple of minutes later with two mugs and a white paper bag. It was almost see-through with grease stains on the outside. He handed the mug to Mikey and offered the bag filled with small, round sugar-covered balls of heaven.

"Thanks," Arthur said after a while.

"Mmhm," Mikey replied, a cocoa-soaked donut in his mouth.

Their dessert was interrupted by a knock at the door.

"Again?" Arthur grumbled, getting up to answer.

Elder Cassandra stood in the doorway holding a porter watch and a bronze pin of Orion, the symbol of the Jaecar.

"The Council of Elders has determined that you be allowed to become an acolyte. Do you accept?" She asked, even more businesslike than usual.

This was happening faster than Mikey expected. Elder Ryan made it seem like it would take more deliberation than a day. But he had already made up his mind before. This is what he wanted.

"Yes!" It came out louder than Mikey had intended.

"Congratulations. Welcome to Haven. As the Sect Leader, I am here to give you a porter watch. Not only does it tell time, which you can adjust with this knob here" —Cassandra pointed to the standard dial sticking out of the side— "but it will also detect when you are near a porter zone. There are two lights above the number twelve. Green on the left. Red on the right." The Elder pointed at each one.

"When you approach a porter area, the light will turn green. When it's green, you press the button underneath the number six, and the portal will open. Press the button again while it is green, and it will close. The light will turn red if you are too close to the porter area or a platform isn't available. You must be at least five feet away when you open it, or...bad things could happen. Do not press the button when the light is red. Jaecar Chase informed me you know of two of the three local porter locations; the 3rd is under the Buffalo Skyway overpass, near the Naval Park.

"And here," she handed the pin to Mikey, "is your official acolyte pin. We really only use these for acolytes if you are traveling to a different Sect where they don't know you. Any questions?" The Elder asked.

"What happens if I press the button below the six and I'm not in a porter area?" Mikey wondered. He didn't want to accidentally press the button and hurt himself or someone else.

"Nothing will happen. It is only dangerous if the light is red," Cassandra answered matter-of-factly. "If that is all, I have urgent business at the Sect. I will inform them of your decision," she inclined her head. "Welcome, Mikey. As I said before, I expect great things from you." She hurried into a familiar-looking black SUV.

After Elder Cassandra left, he and Arthur talked a little more about Mikey's decision, Haven, and Arthur even opened up with some stories about Emma. He said Mikey reminded him of her and that despite a difficult upbringing, she and Mikey always chose to do the right thing.

"Reminds me of a certain mailman I know," Mikey stated. "A man who would care for and adopt a lonely kid he didn't even know. I can't imagine what I would have done without you, Arthur."

"You helped me as much as I helped you, bud, trust me," Arthur sniffled. "Now, enough about that. How about you invite your friends over for dinner Friday? I know you will be busy for a while training and forming your core. I'm sure the Sect wants you to be supervised in case something goes wrong. But that doesn't mean we can't set time aside to have fun."

"I'll ask them tomorrow and let you know, but I'm sure they'd be fine with it if they're free," Mikey figured.

"All right, get some rest. It's not easy forming your core, but Elder Ryan is the man for the job. You are in good hands."

They said their goodnights, and Mikey headed upstairs to brush his teeth and prepare for his first day as an official acolyte for Haven.

CHAPTER 12

As the day began. Mikey started to get nervous about his training and hoped he'd be able to harness his Source like a Jaecar. The one bright spot in the day was the ride to school. As the bus driver pulled up to Sabrina's stop, Mikey smiled and waved when she got on and scanned for him. He still put his backpack to block off people sitting there, but now, it was to save a spot for her.

Everything had changed so quickly in his life. Mikey sat with Marcus and Sabrina for lunch. In art class, Mrs. Tursley had given him a perfect score on his 'Serpent and Eve' piece. Their new assignment for the rest of the week was to create an art piece representing what 'joy' was to them using any medium.

Mikey decided to draw an art workstation and, taking a cue from Sabrina, it was going to be surrounded by his favorite desserts. He was going to include a mailbox stuffed with mail to represent Arthur, the leg armor to represent Sabrina, and the symbol for Haven, which would sit in the background of it all. For his parents, Mikey decided to draw a worn leather book with 'The Jungle Book' written on the cover. Mikey realized he didn't know what Marcus was into, so he decided to ask him on their way to the Sect.

"Video games," Sabrina answered for Marcus in the passenger seat of his grey Dodge Neon. "Marcus is always playing video games on his computer when he's not training."

"Yeah, either that or Ryan Reynolds. And thanks, Sabrina; I don't know how I could've answered a question about myself without you," Marcus rolled his eyes.

"Noted. Thanks," Mikey chuckled.

"Why are you driving out here instead of the Como Lake spot?" Mikey wondered since the lighthouse was closer.

"Too many people right now," Marcus answered. "We only use the porters where someone might see if it's an emergency. Early in the morning, no one is there, and if they did see some people leave the lighthouse, they'd just think, 'those people snuck in,' or 'the door was unlocked, and they spent the night for a dare.' But if someone saw people go in and not out, it could cause issues."

"Gotcha," Mikey understood.

Instead of driving to the front, where he had come in with Elder Cassandra, Marcus pulled into a small area further away with several other cars and a bus already parked. The space was covered by several trees, so you couldn't see them unless you knew where to look. Mikey followed them to the factory entrance, and when they walked up to the portal area, the green light above Mikey's new watch turned green.

"You get the honors, acolyte," Sabrina teased.

Marcus made a show of bowing and gestured for him to proceed.

To satisfy his curiosity, Mikey walked over to the wall to see what would happen. Sure enough, the watch flashed red when he got too close. "Your mom came last night and said if you pressed it when the button was red, something bad would happen. What did she mean?" Mikey questioned.

"You might get part of your body cut off. I don't understand the portals much, but it's something about a space within a space," Sabrina answered. "So, if you are in the zone where it appears, the part of you that is too close might be ripped into the space before it stabilizes."

"Ouch," Mikey instinctively jumped back until the light turned green again. Following Elder Cassandra's instructions, he pressed the button under the number six. The portal shimmered, and a familiar hum filled the air. Mikey didn't hesitate this time as he suddenly appeared on one of the white platforms in the portal room. Marcus and Sabrina followed shortly after.

"Elder Ryan told me yesterday he wanted to instruct you on forming your core and have you practice in the isolation training room again. You know, for safety," Marcus teased. "I have some shield training to do, but I'll come to check how it's going in a bit," he promised.

"I have to do the same thing," Sabrina said. "Good luck!"

"Thanks. Happy training," Mikey waved them off.

He headed through the TC, then to the other end of the compound to change into clean training clothes. Mikey decided he would return to leave another chocolatey present for his little friend. With a fresh pair of clothes, he headed to the isolation training room. Elder Ryan was already there waiting.

"Welcome, acolyte. I'm glad you decided to join our order. Being a Jaecar is a fantastical yet grave responsibility. The training is grueling. Your mental and physical fortitude will be tested to its limits. But before all of that, you must form your core. Open your meridians and feel the Source coming in. Then, use that Source to locate that same energy inside of yourself and gather it into your hand; using your mind to direct it."

"Okay, I'll give it a shot," Mikey said. He opened the doors to his left hand and felt the Source from Elder Ryan. Following its flow into his body, Mikey searched for the same energy within himself. An odd feeling passed through him when he'd found it, like pulling a thorn from your back you didn't realize was causing an ache.

Finding it had been the easy part. But pulling it towards his left hand was like trying to drag a boulder while swimming upstream. When he got the Source to his left hand to condense it, the energy disappeared, and Mikey was left exhausted.

"Is it...supposed to be...this tiring?" Mikey croaked between breaths.

"Mentally, yes. Physically...no," the elder's brow furrowed. "Describe what is happening."

"I've found my Source, but pulling it to my left-hand takes all my energy. Then when I finally get it there...it just disappears," Mikey explained.

"I've never heard of that happening before. It is certainly difficult to condense your Source, and it takes intense concentration, especially at first. But you shouldn't be physically exhausted," Elder Ryan stated, rubbing the stubble on his chin. "This is to be expected, though. You are an unusual case, after all. At least it seems you are getting the hang of moving your Source. I wanted to make sure nothing dangerous happened while you attempted it. Keep trying, but don't overdo it. I apologize, but I must attend to other matters; I will check on your progress a bit later," he said, heading out of the room.

Mikey took a few minutes to rest before trying again; unfortunately, with the same results. His body was resisting every attempt to pull Source towards his left hand. Marcus and Sabrina had come to check on him after a couple of hours, but Mikey hadn't made any headway.

They gave him encouraging words, and Marcus stayed with him to practice shield training and—thankfully— to help give him some Source so he could go at it a little longer. Before he forgot, Mikey asked them about coming over Friday for dinner and was elated when they both said yes.

"Really Mikey, you are making incredible progress. Keep at it. I gotta head out and help Elder Cassandra with some admin paperwork, but I'll see you tomorrow. Have a good night," Sabrina said before she left."

"Thanks, see ya. Have a good night," Mikey replied.

By the time Elder Ryan came to check on him, Mikey had been at it for four hours with no improvement. He felt like he had run a marathon.

"Do not be discouraged. The fact it has only taken you a day to locate your Source and move it within your body is an amazing feat. Often acolytes take weeks—sometimes months to do so," the elder encouraged. "Continue to practice. Eventually, it will come."

Despite his and Sabrina's kind words, Mikey didn't feel like he had made progress. Admittedly, he might've also been a little grumpy because of how exhausting the training was. When Mikey finally called it for the night, he felt like eating an entire large pizza. He changed out of his dirty training clothes before he and Marcus headed for the cafeteria to get a snack. Mikey made sure to grab an extra cookie.

"Wait a sec, I'll be right back," Mikey told Marcus. He walked into the clean clothes room and dropped off another cookie in the same spot as last time, chuckling at the thought of his fairy friend trying to eat a cookie almost half her size.

"What was that all about?" Marcus asked when Mikey came out of the room without the cookie bag.

"Oh, I just made a little Brownie friend last weekend. She might have a bigger sweet tooth than me," he grinned. "I followed your advice and pretended I didn't see her, but she came out and was eyeballing my cookie. So, I left one for her. Now it's kind of a tradition for me."

"I've never heard of a Brownie purposely showing themselves," Marcus said.

"Yeah, Arthur said the same thing," Mikey shrugged.

"The faerie whisperer," Marcus waved his fingers at Mikey.

They headed back to the portal room, and Marcus dropped Mikey off. By the time they pulled up to his driveway, Mikey was fighting for his eyes to stay open.

"Thanks for the ride, man. Same fun tomorrow?" Mikey asked with more pep than he felt.

"Of course. Looking forward to talking with Arthur Friday. I have a lot of questions," Marcus grinned. "And don't beat yourself up about today. You'll get there. Seriously, you are progressing super-fast."

"That helps. I guess I've grown impatient in my old age," Mikey joked. "I just didn't know I'd be this physically exhausted."

"That's not normal, but neither are you," Marcus shrugged. When Mikey frowned a little, he added, "I meant it in a good way. Who knows what you'll be capable of."

"I know. I just wish I had an instruction manual to all this or something."

"This is more of a 'you learn it yourself' kind of thing. You'll get there," Marcus encouraged. "See you tomorrow."

"Later."

Mikey dragged himself inside and mustered the strength to chat with Arthur briefly. It was the same story with him as well. 'Give it time' and 'you are progressing fast' seemed to be the story of the day. Mikey hoped it was true and fell asleep almost as soon as his head hit the pillow.

The next day in art class, Mikey added a big gaming rig with dual monitors to his art piece outline. He finished the sketch of things that encompassed 'joy' and would paint it over the next couple of days. Marcus gave the three of them a ride to the Sect after school.

When Mikey entered the isolation training room, he was determined to make some sort of progress. Unfortunately, determination doesn't always equal success. Throughout the night, no matter what he did, Mikey couldn't get his Source to condense in his left hand. All he managed was to build up a little more Source than yesterday. Still, as soon as Mikey did, the energy disappeared. Elder Ryan popped in early that evening to say he was confident the training wasn't dangerous for him or others and to continue to focus on forming the core of energy. For most of the night, Sabrina and Marcus had stayed with him. They alternated giving support and some Source, but he just couldn't do it.

Feeling defeated, Mikey gave up after a few more hours. He lay on the mat looking up at the ceiling, drenched in sweat and breathless.

"It seems like you have to use your own Source to move it where your core is," Sabrina looked puzzled. "I've never heard of that before. Maybe it's a side effect because you can absorb Source around you, that it takes much more to condense it?" she suggested. "But that doesn't answer the question as to why it disappears..."

"I don't know," Mikey croaked.

"Well, now is as good a time as any to tell you both. I forgot I have a family birthday party tomorrow for one of my cousins. So I won't be able to take you to the Sect," Marcus apologized.

Mikey decided he would just ask Arthur to let him borrow the car until Sabrina gave a much better suggestion.

"How about you come with me to my café after school? We can hang out for a bit, and my mom will take us to the Sect afterward?" Sabrina offered. "You know...if you want to."

"No—yeah. That sounds great. I'd love to. Must be a great spot if you like going there so much," Mikey recovered.

"Awesome," she beamed. "My mom comes around six thirty...so you won't have as much time to train if that's okay."

"No problem, I'm not making much headway anyways." It would have taken a natural disaster to prevent Mikey from spending time with her. Plus, he did want to see the café where she spent her free time. And as much as he did want to keep training, what he was doing was getting nowhere. Maybe an idea would come to him like before.

Sabrina headed home, and Marcus drove Mikey back to his house. It was almost 9:30 by the time he walked through the door with barely enough energy to brush his teeth before bed. Arthur was understanding and said they could talk tomorrow. Mikey wished he had time to draw, but at least there was his art project tomorrow.

If only my core forming came as easy to me as art did.

At least it wasn't all a disappointment today, he thought back to Sabrina.

Don't overthink it, Mikey. It doesn't matter if it's a date or not.

Just the fact that she asked to spend time with him at her favorite place was enough. His last thought before succumbing to exhaustion was a hope that he wouldn't say something stupid tomorrow.

CHAPTER 13

The bus ride with Sabrina that morning felt extra special. Because Mikey knew later that day, he'd be going out with her, just the two of them. It might have been Mikey's imagination, but Sabrina seemed a little bubblier too.

Mikey had been practicing opening and closing the 'doors' of his meridians when he was around other people, and it was becoming easier. The discomfort was still there, but Mikey was getting used to that too. Eating regular food seemed to help, and a quick one-minute drain when it got too much was all he needed to quell the itch in his hand and the full-body hunger pangs.

Lunch with his friends was fun but uneventful. That was until they were leaving for class, and Marcus mentioned their 'date' tonight, which got Sabrina flustered. Mikey laughed at their antics and came to Sabrina's aid by saying they were just going to hang out at a coffee shop before training.

Marcus continued in art class by occasionally humming the 'sitting in a tree, k-i-s-s-i-n-g song. It ended when Sabrina threatened to only call him Marky for the rest of his life.

When art class was over, Marcus said his goodbyes and that he looked forward to meeting Arthur. Mikey and Sabrina waved him off before heading across the field to their bus area. They found a seat near the front, and Mikey asked her about her art piece and what brought her joy.

"I'll show you when we get to the café," Sabrina replied with a smile. Then she looked out the window.

I guess I'll find out what that means?

They got to her bus stop around four p.m. and walked past the residential area to a busy street filled with shops and restaurants. There was snow piled up in different corners—some almost ten-feet high—to create pathways to get to the stores.

As they walked, Mikey saw a girl in an alleyway across the street staring at him. Although gorgeous, Mikey only noticed her because she wore clothing that didn't match the weather.

She had strange eyes that seemed to glow, but Mikey couldn't tell from this distance. Mikey could see her arms' warm olive skin because they were exposed. It was twenty-two degrees, and everyone around had on multiple layers. Her legs were covered with black leggings and brown boots with white fur around the rim. She wore a black T-shirt with a poofy red winter vest. Her straight, dark-brown hair showed underneath a red beanie the same color as her vest. The girl smiled and stared at him as they walked past.

Weird.

Shaking his head, Mikey turned back to Sabrina, who hadn't noticed the odd exchange. She led him past a few more shops before stopping in front of a black brick building with a matching black sign above that read in cursive, 'Chill Pill Café.' There was a little yellow and blue pill capsule logo next to it that made the bottom portion of the pill look like a cup filled with a hot drink. And the top part was cracked open like the lid to a thermos.

"Awesome name," Mikey pointed. He really liked the logo and thought the name was clever.

"Yeah, it's a great name," Sabrina smiled. She motioned for him to go in. As they entered, Mikey heard an acoustic version of a famous rock song that had been playing on the radio. The shop was divided into two sections. The right side had a large countertop with various pastries and treats, immediately catching Mikey's eye. Behind that was another counter against a chalkboard wall with multiple coffee bean types and syrups. Menu items and prices were written in chalk by hand on the board. There were three college-aged workers behind the counter.

The left side, closest to the door, had tables and chairs where several people were sitting and chatting. Some were using laptops that were conveniently charging from stations placed throughout the seating area. Further back were several couches and coffee tables. One guy was sitting on a sofa with headphones on, reading what looked like a textbook.

Sabrina went to stand in line to order. It hit Mikey that he'd never been in a coffee shop and needed help figuring out what to get. There were always jokes on TV where a young person would order a 'nonfat soy latte with half caramel foam, half hazelnut foam, and a dash of cinnamon.' And Mikey didn't know what most of that meant.

"What do you recommend?" Mikey asked. He figured it would kill two birds with one stone. He'd get an idea of what to order and learn more about what she liked.

"Oh, I always get one of two things. Either the vanilla bean Frappuccino or Chai Tea latte to have something warm. I saw you eyeing the pastries. Their kitchen sink cookies are amazing," she grinned, leaning slightly against him.

Mikey liked seeing this bubbly side of her. The fact Sabrina seemed happy he was there with her made it even better. "I've never had chai," Mikey admitted. "Let's try it, and you sold me at the word cookie."

"Chai is different. I hope you like it," she seemed less certain of her recommendation.

They both ordered, and Mikey had a new conundrum.

Do I pay for her?

Arthur cosigned a credit card for him that had $200 on it to build up credit and use in emergencies. Mikey figured this fit the bill. But before he could decide what to do, Sabrina paid for both of them.

"Wait, I—" Mikey started to say.

"Relax, I invited you here. You can get us the next time," Sabrina reassured.

He still felt awkward not thinking to pay first, but Mikey was more focused on the fact she said, 'next time.'

Hopefully.

After they got their orders, Sabrina led them to one of the lone couches towards the back. When they sat down, Mikey noticed she was looking at him expectantly. He must have had a puzzled look because Sabrina bumped him, laughing, and pointed to the drink.

"Try it, dummy."

"Oh, duh," Mikey laughed at himself. He took a sip of the latte and was surprised by how different but delicious it was. "Wow, this is really good." Mikey smacked his lips, "It's like a spicy sweet if that makes any sense."

"No, that's a good description. Glad you like it!"

After taking a bite of the kitchen sink cookie, Mikey was in heaven. "Oh my gosh. So soft. Mmhmm," he mumbled. The cookie had peanut butter cups, chocolate chips, caramel, and sea salt.

A quatro made in heaven.

But before Mikey knew it, the cookie was gone.

"What are you part pelican? You practically swallowed that cookie whole," Sabrina teased.

"Sorry, 'sweet tooth' is a real medical condition. The doctors are searching for a cure, but for now, I have to suffer," Mikey managed to say with a straight face.

"Dork," Sabrina snorted.

They sat together, enjoying the music and drinks until Sabrina's earlier comment on the bus popped into his head. "I recall you saying I'd have to wait until we got here for you to tell me about your art piece," Mikey said.

"Oh, right," she nodded, reaching for her backpack. She pulled out a laptop, opened it, and Mikey saw she had been writing something. Sabrina saved that file, and the cursor went to her desktop and opened a folder called 'chronicles.' There were at least a dozen documents, including one labeled 'relics.' She clicked it and handed Mikey the laptop. After reading for a minute, Mikey realized it was a collection of all the information she had gathered about the leg armor relic she wanted and others. It was all very detailed and organized, like an encyclopedia.

"This is amazing; you wrote all this yourself?" Mikey asked.

"Yeah. I'm obsessed with history and writing. While searching for the relic, I realized there were no real reference books for them. All the information is scattered in various diaries and scrolls. The same goes for other stuff. I secretly want to be a chronicler for Haven and our history for the next century," Sabrina admitted.

"Why does that have to be a secret? That's a great goal. You found something lacking and are trying to make it better and easier for future generations."

"If only my mother felt the same way," she sighed. "'You are not a historian. You are the future leader of this Sect,'" she imitated Elder Cassandra perfectly.

"I can see her saying that," Mikey admitted. "But that doesn't mean you still can't do it. If you become Sect leader, you don't have to do the same things your mother did. In fact, I think learning Haven's history and contributing to lacking knowledge would make you an even better leader."

"Thanks," she brightened up. "I hadn't really thought of it that way. I spend so much time training to be the best and learning about how the Sect runs, going to the meetings she wants me to attend. Sometimes, I feel like I never have any time for myself. Other than hanging with you and Marcus, coming here is the only time I get to do what I want to do."

"Well, I'm glad you let me be a part of it," Mikey said. "And for suggesting I try Chai," he grinned, taking another sip of the spicy sweet concoction. "I think what you are doing is great, and you shouldn't let anyone stop you."

Sabrina smiled and leaned into him.

This is nice.

He leaned back. They spent the next couple of hours talking about the different subjects Sabrina wanted to write about. She told him how she wanted to visit other libraries from other Sects to search for more information about relics. Sabrina asked about Mikey's life and audibly gasped at all he had been through.

"You should be way more messed up than you are." Sabrina shook her head. "I can't believe you spent your life so alone and with no idea what was going on." She looked heartbroken.

"It wasn't easy. But if all you do is focus on the negative, then that's all your life will be," he said. "Thank goodness Arthur found me and took me in."

When it was almost time to go, Sabrina excused herself to the bathroom, and Mikey said he would wait outside for her.

I need to open my meridians for a little bit.

Outside, Mikey saw the sun had already gone down. Looking around, he froze when his eyes glanced across the street. There, in the same alleyway, the girl from before was staring and smiling as if she hadn't moved. Mikey had the urge to go over and ask what was going on, but four guys walked up and started talking to her.

He couldn't see much but clearly heard her say, "STOP" before she disappeared further down the alleyway. Worried, Mikey covered the distance in an instant.

Was I always that fast?

"Come on. Relax. You must be freezing out here with those clothes. Let me keep you warm," one of the guys said.

"I'm quite warm, thank you. Though I could use a little snack," she grinned devilishly.

"That's fine, honey. You come with us, and we'll give you all the snacks you need," another snickered.

"Yay. Here is my handsome hero to the rescue!" the girl suddenly shouted.

Mikey was confused because even though she was in real possible danger, the girl said it like an overdramatic actress in a play. They all realized she was talking about him as the guys turned around.

"Uh. Hi," Mikey shrugged.

"Get lost," the first neanderthal barked. He was short and stocky. Even though the guy was wearing several layers, Mikey could tell he was well-muscled.

There's the leader.

Mikey had never been in a fight before, at least one where he fought back. And other than learning to control his Source a little, he hadn't done any of the Jaecar training yet. That didn't mean he was going to leave her here alone with these guys. It was clear they didn't have the best intentions. Ignoring them, Mikey looked at her and offered his hand, "Do you want to come with me and get out of here?"

"That sounds fantastic," she grinned, walking to Mikey until the leader stuck out his arm, stopping her from going further. The girl made an 'O' shape with her lips before shrugging. The big grin on her face confused Mikey even more.

Why isn't she worried?

It was then he got a good look into her eyes. The irises were yellow, with an inner core of deep green. Her pupils weren't round but marquis-shaped, like a pointed oval.

Those are the most incredible cat eyes I've ever seen.

"We weren't done with our conversation," short and stocky interrupted. "Last warning." He pushed Mikey in the chest.

"I'm pretty sure the lady made it clear she'd rather come with me," Mikey said coldly. Getting pushed in the chest brought Thomas to mind, and Mikey's blood boiled. His meridians instinctively opened, but Mikey realized it would hurt the girl, and they snapped shut. He was really getting fed up with people starting fights for no reason.

"Just let her through and go on with your night," Mikey growled. It was very uncomfortable closing them off so suddenly, and his patience was wearing thin.

The other three men walked towards him, spreading out. Mikey's eyes followed the guys who went behind before he felt a sudden change in the air. He turned in time to see the ring leader's fist coming at his face, comically slow. Mikey was so surprised that he didn't even think to dodge. When it connected with the side of his head, Mikey heard bones shatter and briefly thought his skull had been fractured. That was until he saw the ring leader's mangled hand and realized his head was fine.

Arthur's voice replayed in his mind. *'Your dad is a vampire.'*

Thinking back to his past, Mikey couldn't recall when he'd felt pain or was even sick. The first time was when Thomas attacked him in the field at school. That thought started to make Mikey even angrier because it meant Thomas had actually tried to hurt him.

"Bastard. You broke my friggin' hand," the lead neanderthal squealed. "What are you doing?" he yelled to the others. "Beat the shit out of him!"

The air shifted behind Mikey, but this time he had the sense to dodge the fist coming at his throat.

Okay. These guys want to play dirty.

Mikey's lips curled in a wicked grin. He grabbed the outstretched arm at his throat and heaved the guy over his shoulder with surprising ease. The man flew down the alley twenty feet before landing in a large pile of snow. The girl had to jump out of the way to avoid being hit.

Mikey panicked.

Oh my god I killed him!

Mikey audibly sighed in relief at the moaning and movement coming from somewhere inside the snow pile. When his eyes went to the other two guys they lifted their hands and backed off. Seeing their friend thrown impossibly far, right after their group leader broke his hand on Mikey's face, made them come to their senses.

"I knew you had it in you. My hero," the girl booped Mikey on the nose. "They should thank their lucky stars. They got off easy dealing with you." The mysterious girl eyed them hungrily as they ran away. "Thanks, though. It was hilarious seeing the looks on their faces."

"Uh, you're welcome?"

I have no idea what's going on...

The girl began walking in a circle around him, her eyes roaming up and down his body. "I have never seen anything like you." She took Mikey's left hand into her own, flipping it over and tracing the lines along his palm. "Beautiful," she inhaled deeply through her nose like she was breathing him in.

"What do you see?" Alarm bells started ringing in Mikey's head that maybe those weren't contacts. He was in uncharted territory. Despite that, he became astutely aware of how warm she was and how it didn't fit with the freezing temperature outside. She smelled like nature, wild berries, and flowers.

Their eyes met, and she took a step closer, her lips just a few inches from Mikey's. "That's a secret; maybe you'll find out one day." She dropped his hand, then locked her arm underneath his before leading him out of the alley to the sidewalk.

"Mikey?" Sabrina's voice called from across the street. He turned to see her standing next to the Black SUV he'd come to associate with as the Sect car. The driver's window was rolled down with Chase's head sticking out. He looked from Mikey to Sabrina and the girl, then smirked before rolling the window back up. Mikey got the hint.

Crap. This doesn't look good, does it?

The girl narrowed her eyes at Sabrina and then turned to Mikey. Impossibly warm hands grabbed the side of his head and pulled him close. Mikey froze as the girl's soft lips met his, and they kissed. His heart started pounding until it felt like it was going to explode out of his chest.

"Later, Hercules," she whispered in his ear, shooting goosebumps down his spine. Letting go of his arm, the mystery woman began walking down another alleyway before turning back. "I'm Viki, by the way." A moment later, she seemed to fade into the darkness.

A hand on his shoulder brought him back into reality. Sabrina was staring into his eyes, a concerned look on her face.

"Are you...okay?"

"That wasn't—" Mikey motioned down the alley, "I don't know what that was," he started to say. "She—"

"Do you know that vampire?" Sabrina interrupted.

"Vampire? That—she was a vampire?" Mikey's jaw dropped.

"Yeah. Didn't you see her eyes?" Sabrina asked. "Also, you can kinda tell from the way they move. It's like they glide."

"I just thought they were cool contacts," Mikey said. "And no. I've never met her in my life. Some guys were harassing her in the alley, and I went to help, but she didn't seem worried. I was super confused..." he recalled.

Mikey went on to explain what happened, about his super strength, and the guy breaking his hand from punching him. He didn't know how to explain the grabbing of his arm or the kiss, but Mikey tried to make it clear she did that on her own out of the blue.

Are all vampires like that?

"Yeah, the utter surprise on your face gave me a clue," she teased. "I'm not sure I like the part about her watching you, but I'm hoping she's someone who knows of you from your father's side. Or maybe she thought you smelled the same or something. I haven't really interacted much with vampires. Be careful, though. From what I've been told they want you too."

"I heard. At least I didn't get the feeling she wanted to hurt me," Mikey offered.

Sabrina snorted, "It seemed like she wanted to do quite the opposite."

Mikey thought he detected a hint of jealousy in her voice and hoped he didn't imagine it.

"Yo Romeo. As much as I like watching all this teen drama, I'd like to get this show on the road," Chase yelled out the window. He grinned and pointed to the back of the car.

"Sorry, Chase," Mikey apologized.

They hopped in, and Chase headed for the factory portal zone.

"I thought your mom was going to pick us up?" Mikey asked Sabrina.

"Oh, she's already at the Sect. There's some big meeting about the increased number of monster attacks she's getting ready for. Happens all the time. Perks of being Sect leader," Sabrina sighed.

"She cares about you a lot," Mikey reassured her. "In her own way."

"I know," Sabrina nodded. "I don't even want to imagine having all those lives under my responsibility and running a Sect. She's always under a ton of stress. Anyways, you need to get back into the mindset of forming your core. I hope that other than your run-in with the Vampire Princess, you had a good time," she teased.

"I had a great time. Thanks for inviting me. I can see why you really like that place. Everything was delicious, and the atmosphere really was like a chill pill."

"We...will have to do it again sometime," Sabrina leaned into him.

"I'd like that," Mikey nudged her back.

"Ah, young love. Reminds me of when I first met Shelly and had two hands," Chase chimed in.

"You need to focus on driving before you lose your other hand," Sabrina quipped.

"Ouch, yes ma'am," He pretended to salute and made a show of how focused he was on driving. But Mikey could see him smiling in the rearview mirror.

When they arrived at the Sect, Sabrina apologized, saying she needed to see her mother about the meeting, but they would drop him off at home in a couple of hours. The pair walked together until Sabrina paused at the master hallway leading to the Sect's different areas. Mikey headed straight toward the isolation room after Sabrina wished him luck. She turned left, confirming Mikey's previous suspicion that it was a command area for the elders.

Reaching the training room, Mikey sat in the middle and focused on blocking all distractions. He closed his eyes and tried to imagine forming his core. Unfortunately, it was complicated because every fiber of Mikey's being protested against it. He hadn't made any progress in almost a week, and trying always left him utterly exhausted. And he couldn't get his day with Sabrina, or the fact a vampire was his first kiss, off his mind.

No. Focus Mikey!

He felt ashamed this was the amount of effort he could muster to master his abilities. Shaking his head and closing his eyes once more, Mikey called upon his Source and started moving it towards his left hand.

Over the last few days, Mikey had, in fact, made some progress. He could bring energy toward his hand much quicker, but the result was always the same; it disappeared as soon as he stopped actively gathering it. The task was like using your hands to form a snowball, but as soon as you moved your hands away, it instantly melted into a puddle. Soon enough, Mikey was covered in sweat, too exhausted to continue.

Whatever I'm supposed to do, this isn't it.

"How goes it?" Mikey heard a familiar deep raspy voice behind him. Elder Ryan stood in the doorway with Sabrina in tow. "The meeting was over, and Sabrina here said you were training."

"Not going well," Mikey sighed in frustration. "Whatever I'm doing...I don't think it is ever going to work. No matter how much Source I bring to my left hand, it takes all my energy to keep it there. And when I let go, it dissipates. It feels like I'm using all my energy just to gather it." Mikey wasn't sure what else he could do.

"We should have Elder Neema examine you again. Perhaps she could advise you on what is wrong," Elder Ryan suggested. "I can help you use your Source once you have formed your core, but I cannot enter the body and observe like she can."

"Actually, that would be great." Mikey perked up. If anyone could see what was going wrong inside him, it would be her. Mikey liked the old Healer and figured he could also say hi to Luke.

"Alright. I will try to set it up for Saturday morning before I have the other acolytes come for shield training. Is that acceptable?" he asked.

"Yeah, that works. Thanks!"

Elder Ryan nodded with a grunt and left the room.

"Neema will be able to help you. I'm sure of it," Sabrina put a hand on his shoulder.

"I'm sure she will, too," Mikey hoped.

Sabrina held out a hand to help him up, "Let's go. My mom has to stay late, but Chase will give us a ride. We'll drop you off first."

"Thanks. Could I stop at the cafeteria first for a snack? I'm starving," Mikey asked.

He got a cookie for himself and left one for his friend.

Feeling better after some chocolatey goodness, Mikey walked with Sabrina back to the porter room where Chase was waiting for them. Sabrina rolled her eyes as Chase grumbled out a few comments about him' slaying monsters' and 'saving countless lives' only to become a teenage taxi driver. Mikey cracked a joke about painting the SUV yellow and giving Chase IOUs for all the rides. The back-and-forth didn't end for the rest of the drive.

When they pulled into his driveway, Mikey thanked Chase for the ride and Sabrina for inviting him to her café. He headed in after confirming she was still able to come over tomorrow.

Arthur always went to bed at around nine because of his early schedule. So, when Mikey came in, he was already in the sweatpants and baggy white T-shirt that were his pajamas. Arthur asked about his 'not date' with Sabrina and how training went. Mikey told him everything about the cafe and Sabrina's secret hobby.

"That girl has a good head on her shoulders. The next generation of Jaecar will be in good hands," Arthur approved.

The conversation turned when Mikey mentioned his encounter with Viki, the 'Vampire Princess.'

"Did she have yellow and green eyes? Olive skin? Red beanie?" Arthur questioned.

"Yeeaah..." Mikey said slowly, his brows furrowing.

"I went to get some things at the store...paper plates and cups for your friends tomorrow. A young vampire accidentally bumped into me, matching that description," Arthur replied, scratching the white stubble on his chin. "She apologized and helped me pick up the stuff I dropped. Seemed nice enough; I thought nothing of it."

"You saw a vampire and thought nothing of it?"

How does everyone seem so calm about this?

"Like I told you before. After signing The Accords all those years ago, they don't kill humans. At least they don't do it in a way they'll get caught. There aren't many, but I see one at least every month or so," Arthur explained. "Though the fact she ran into me first and then specifically went searching for you raises my hair a little bit. I didn't sense any hostility from her, and it sounds like she didn't want to hurt you, either. But I agree with Sabrina. You need to be careful."

"I know."

There wasn't much Mikey could do except be cautious. A small part of him was curious, though—*what if she knew my dad? Maybe she could tell me about the Verdaat?*

Arthur didn't seem surprised when Mikey got to the part about fighting the guys in the alley.

"I guess I didn't get to tell you any details before Cassandra came. The Verdaat have senses like you can't believe. It's said their eyes can see the Source. They are stronger than any Jaecar, excluding elders. And I've heard that some ancient ones can move faster than the eye can see. They don't go in the sun much. To be honest, I'm not sure why," Arthur shrugged. "Maybe it does burn them like the movies say, but I doubt it. Surely you could have some of those abilities too. We were so focused on your Source drain that we didn't pay attention to any of your other possible gifts. At least your eyes are normal, or you'd stick out like a sore thumb."

Makes sense," Mikey nodded. "I realize now, though, I have to be more careful with my strength. I could seriously hurt someone."

"That you do. Good thing nothing awful happened to those hooligans today," Arthur added. "But I know you, Mikey Black. You'll always try to do the right thing."

"I hope so."

"I know so," Arthur stood up. "Alright. I need my beauty sleep. Otherwise, I won't have the energy for you youngins tomorrow. Have a goodnight."

Mikey went to bed, but sleep didn't come easy. His mind was a whirlwind.

CHAPTER 14

Mikey noticed during their bus ride to school the next day—much to his delight—that Sabrina was more comfortable with him after their evening at the café. She sat much closer than before and would gently push him or lean into him with her shoulders when he made her laugh. Her smile made him feel like everything was just a little bit brighter.

Marcus must have also noticed it because his taunts from the other day resumed at lunchtime. Mikey added more fuel to the fire by sitting next to Sabrina instead of Marcus. But he didn't care. Mikey was enjoying it all the same.

"Boo, it's no fun teasing you if you aren't going to get all flustered Sabrina," Marcus sighed after she repeatedly failed to take the bait. He overdramatically winked at Mikey when she wasn't looking. The fact Sabrina didn't seem to get worked up by the teasing was a good sign, Mikey thought.

Girls and relationships of any kind were not his strong suit.

Without Arthur, Mikey might've spent his whole life not really talking to anyone. But whatever was happening between Sabrina and him, he liked where it was going.

When Marcus realized his teasing was getting nowhere, he decided to switch gears and talk about Arthur and all the questions he had for him. They agreed on what pizzas to order, and Mikey emphasized the chocolate cookie pizza for dessert.

"Do vampire hybrids get cavities?" Sabrina chuckled.

"With all the sweets I eat, I probably should. I brush my fangs twice a day like my vampire dentist tells me to, though," Mikey said as straight-faced as he could muster. Sabrina laughed out loud, bringing warm fuzzies to his chest. A bell dinged, like the annoying buzzer in a gameshow, signaling the end of their fun.

"See you in art," Sabrina waved as they headed for their following classes.

Is it me, or is high school just dragging on now?

Those thoughts were the theme for the rest of the day until the final bell rang. The acolyte trio rushed out of art class heading for Marcus's car. Arthur came out to greet them as they pulled into Mikey's driveway. Marcus bolted towards Mikey's foster father like a fanboy seeing his favorite celebrity.

Mikey looked at Sabrina as she rolled her eyes.

"Oh my god. Arthur...sir, it is an honor to meet you," Marcus reached out his hand, "I'm Marcus, Mikey's best friend. I'm sure he's told you all about me." Marcus talked so fast Mikey thought he was turning into a gnome.

"Hi, Marcus. I'm Arthur. Of course. Mikey has told me about the both of you," Arthur smiled warmly, looking up at Sabrina. "Thanks for being there for him. I'm glad you've all found each other. Having those you trust to watch your back is one of the most important things for a Jaecar."

"Speaking of Jaecar, is it true that you can make your shield so strong that it wouldn't even break from a bugbear club?" Marcus asked. Mikey could have sworn his eyes were twinkling.

"Haha, are they still telling that story?" Arthur turned slightly red. "Maybe not anymore, but back in the day, my team investigated reports of mangled bodies of animals and people in Yosemite. We found a bugbear in a cave using a boulder to cover the entrance. At that time, I could manage two shields strong enough to withstand a few bugbear clubbings before I was spent. Saved my friend's butt and my own a few times," the old Elder reminisced.

"Well, how do—" Marcus started before Sabrina stepped in front of him and stuck out her hand.

"Ignore my friend over here. I'm Sabrina. It's an honor to finally meet you," she smiled. "I'm sure he will answer some of your questions later," Sabrina snapped to Marcus, who had a pouty look.

"Of course, I will, Marcus. And it's wonderful to meet you, Sabrina. I've heard a lot about you from Mikey," Arthur grinned.

"Hmm, is that so?" Sabrina looked to Mikey, raising an eyebrow.
Why does my face feel suddenly hot?

She smiled at his reaction, and Mikey let out a breath he didn't realize he was holding.
Phew. Leave it to Arthur to throw me under the bus...

Though it seemed she wasn't upset about it. Arthur had a wife and daughter; he probably knew way more about the nuances of relationships than he did.

"Whelp, have you kids decided what kind of pizzas you want?" Arthur rubbed his hands together. "I know Mikey wants the chocolate chip cookie one for dessert. But if you need pineapple or anchovies, please just put it on one." Arthur faked throwing up.

"As much as tormenting you with an anchovy and pineapple pizza would make my night, we decided to keep it simple. One large pepperoni and cheese, and one large everything. And, of course, the cookie pizza," Mikey added.

"Thanks for being gentle on me," Arthur joked. "I'll call the order in. There is soda and plastic cups on the table. Icemaker in the fridge." Arthur walked to the living room phone, and Marcus whispered to Mikey that he'd never seen a landline phone before.

"He's old school," Mikey whispered back. "He has an old flip phone but doesn't like using it much."

"Good thing the Source hasn't been technologically upgraded then," Marcus teased.

Arthur returned shortly, confirming that the pizza should arrive in half an hour. They spent the night telling stories and eating good food with even better company. Mikey found out about some of Arthur's crazy monster hunts. The most dangerous and exciting of those was when his omada was sent to investigate reports of people suddenly dropping dead near a swamp in Mississippi.

It turned out to be a Gwyllion, which according to Arthur, was a rare gnome-type creature that looked like—in his words—'a swamp hag.' Humans were moving into her territory, so she felt threatened. They were generally peaceful and would sometimes offer wisdom to those they deemed worthy, but they would just as quickly curse you to death. Arthur and his team very carefully spoke to her, promising the Jaecar would purchase the land and keep others from encroaching on her territory.

"She wasn't too thrilled to see us at first," Arthur recounted the tale, "one wrong move, and that could've been the end of us."

Mikey was fascinated.

"That's amazing and terrifying all at the same time!" Mikey exclaimed. "I wonder if there are creatures we've never even heard of before that are out there somewhere."

"I know there are!" Sabrina chimed in. "On top of chronicling relics, I'm also going to compile all the information we have on OS and try to find even more." Sabrina looked out in the distance like she was envisioning the crazy adventure.

"That is a lofty goal, young lady. But I'm sure if anyone was going to achieve it, it'd be you," Arthur encouraged.

"Yeah, yeah. Sabrina is going to be the best chronicler in Jaecar history and a super badass Mover, but let's get to shielding, the most awesome and best archetype," Marcus interrupted. "I want to pick Arthur's brain for a little bit. How often do you get the chance to learn from one of the best Shielders ever?" Marcus made a shooing motion with his hand. "Go have some more pizza or something."

"Well... I'd like to see some more of your artwork. If you have any?" Sabrina suggested.

"Uh, yeah, it's up in my room...." Mikey trailed off. He didn't know the protocol for inviting a girl to his bedroom. Was it better for him to just grab some of his sketchbooks and bring them down?

"That's perfect," Marcus saved the day. "Go give her the tour of the house and your room. But keep the door open, you two!" He shook his finger at them like a concerned parent. Mikey and Sabrina managed to roll their eyes in unison.

"I'm going to have to test his shielding strength right now with a punch to the chest," Sabrina voiced to Mikey.

"I'll hold him down while you do it," Mikey joined in.

"Uh-huh. Test me when I've learned from the master. Now shoo," Marcus reiterated.

Mikey led Sabrina upstairs. He thought about giving the 'tour' like Marcus had suggested, but the only rooms upstairs were his own, the bathroom, and a storage area that was also supposed to function as an exercise room. And like all exercise rooms with a treadmill, Mikey couldn't remember the last time he or Arthur had used it.

"There's not much to show you, tour-wise," Mikey confessed, rounding the top of the stairs. "Storage room, bathroom, and my room," he pointed. This was one of the few times in his life that

Mikey was happy he always kept things neat and clean. When he was younger, Mikey hadn't wanted to give any foster families more reason to get rid of him, so he made sure to be clean and tidy.

"Cleaner than my room." Sabrina whistled. She walked up to the wall of art above his desk. It was filled with drawings of Wendies and some of his other favorite creations.

She pointed to one of his drawings that depicted the night his parents were taken. He had drawn their car flipped over, with all the Wendigos surrounding them.

"Was that how many were there that night?" Sabrina gasped.

"That I could remember." Mikey nodded.

"I can't believe you survived that. Only some of our strongest elders or top omadas could have taken on that many. Why would there be so many there out of the blue?"

"I've thought about that almost every day of my life. I had no idea before finding out about all this. But now I think they were after me. Haven wanted me. The Verdaat wanted me. It makes sense that other things might want me, too," he guessed.

"I can tell you for certain, no one in Haven had anything to do with Wendigos. It's odd, though. They are very rarely seen in groups this big," Sabrina puzzled. "But their numbers and activity have been increasing lately; all monster activity is up in general."

"That gives me even more motivation to get my abilities under control," Mikey growled. "The more of those things that are dead, the better." Those memories brought out a wave of anger that Mikey usually kept buried. He'd had that same rage when his parents were killed.

"I'm sorry," Mikey felt Sabrina's arms wrap around him.

Mikey froze in surprise but relaxed and gave in after a couple of seconds. Sabrina seemed to take all that pain away. Mikey had never met anyone so kind yet fierce. They stayed like that for a few more moments before Sabrina grabbed his hand.

"Come on. Show me some of your sketchbooks," she asked, trying to lighten the mood.

Mikey appreciated it and really did want to show his work off. He squeezed her hand before heading to his desk to pull out a few of his best sketchbooks from the right-hand drawer. They sat on the bed together, flipping through the books and talking, and that's when Mikey realized how much he cared for Sabrina.

"Ugh, that one is equal parts creepy and awesome. I hope there are no monsters like that in OS," Sabrina grimaced at one of his drawings.

The creature had white, hollow eyes and a large mouth filled with razor-sharp teeth that spiraled inward like a portal to hell. Its black and orange body was long, round, and segmented like a caterpillar with hundreds of spines jutting out, the tips dripping with vile liquid. Each segment had four legs that ended in razor-sharp pointed blades.

"Yeah, we'd all be done for," he grinned.

"I should get you to do the drawings for my future creatures of Otherside compilation textbook," Sabrina mused.

"That would be the coolest thing ever," Mikey nodded.

What better way to use my talent for drawing monsters than actually drawing monsters?

"We should probably go rescue Arthur from Marcus," Sabrina suggested.

Mikey looked at the clock. Thirty minutes had flown by.

"Definitely. By now, Arthur's ears have probably fallen off," Mikey chuckled.

They headed back downstairs to the sound of Arthur, deep in explanation.

"Your instructors will try to take their Source and thicken a single shield layer to make it stronger. Now, don't get me wrong, that method is effective. But it's a waste of your Source and won't be as strong as it could be. You need to practice creating a sizeable, thin shield, then folding it in on itself several times," Arthur explained.

"Uh, can you elaborate?" Marcus looked confused. He saw the duo walking downstairs and ignored them, focusing on Arthur's explanation.

"Wow, he didn't even joke about us being upstairs for half an hour," Sabrina whispered to Mikey as they sat at the kitchen table. He had decided to go for another slice of pepperoni.

"I know. Marcus being serious about learning doesn't feel right," Mikey smirked, taking a bite. He did want to finish hearing what Arthur was saying.

Arthur paused for a moment, watching them go into the kitchen. "Mikey, hand me a piece of paper from the drawer," Arthur asked, pointing to the dining room cabinet where they kept pens and scratch paper.

Mikey put the remaining slice in his mouth while he nabbed the paper and handed it to Arthur.

"Now, how many layers would you have if you folded this one time?" Arthur demonstrated by folding it.

"Two, obviously," Marcus answered.

"Exactly. Now, how many if I folded it four times?" Arthur questioned.

"Uh—" Marcus paused.

"Sixteen," Sabrina chimed in.

"Correct," Arthur winked at her.

Marcus stuck his tongue out, and Sabrina blew him a kiss.

"How many layers if I folded the paper twelve times?" Arthur challenged. That question made every one pause. "Hmm?"

"It's Friday, and I'm too full for math," Mikey called out.

"Over four thousand," Sabrina answered.

"Correct again," Arthur nodded. "If you can take your single layer of Source and fold it as many times as possible, you can strengthen your shield exponentially. Of course, you can't fold a regular piece of paper more than seven times, but you can fold Source as often as man times as your precision and control will allow.

"Wow. I mean... that's unbelievable. Why don't they teach us that at the Sect?" Marcus looked stunned.

"Honestly, it is a technique I developed myself. It's challenging to master. You must have full control of your shield—it needs to feel like an extension of yourself. But I have a feeling you'll be the ones looking out for Mikey. Which is why I want you to have all the tools on your belt. It won't be easy, but if you can fold your shield seven times, come see me again, and I'll have another present for you," Arthur offered.

"I don't care how long it takes. I'll get it done," Marcus vowed.

"Good." Arthur nodded.

The gang hung out for another hour before Marcus and Sabrina said their goodbyes. They all agreed to do it again sometime. Arthur said he would take Mikey to the Sect tomorrow morning, and Marcus offered to drop him off.

"I need to get a friggin' car," Mikey said aloud.

"No worries, man. I don't mind driving you at all. Thomas is... well, Thomas now, and my parents aren't the same either. Trust me, I'd rather spend my time hanging with you," Marcus assured.

He must be going through a lot.

"All right. I just don't wanna be a burden."

"You aren't. I'll see you tomorrow. Hopefully, Elder Neema can help," Marcus replied.

Sabrina seemed to hesitate when Mikey turned to say goodnight. She looked to Marcus and Arthur, then back to Mikey. As if making up her mind, Sabrina walked up to Mikey and kissed him. "Thanks for tonight. And last night."

Mikey's hand instinctively went to his lips. "I uh...um... you're welcome," he stuttered. "Thank you..." Mikey was trying to find words, but he was drawing a blank, "...for that," he finished.

So smooth, Mikey. So smooth.

Sabrina chuckled, then leaned in, whispering 'anytime' just loud enough for him to hear. She turned to go with Marcus, who looked more surprised than Mikey about her bold move. He started humming the 'sitting in a tree' rhyme again before Sabrina pushed him into the snow.

"Violence is never the answer," Marcus yelled, brushing off the snow and heading to his car.

"You have some good friends there, bud," Arthur said quietly next to him in the doorway. "And from what I can tell, maybe Sabrina might become more than a friend," he teased.

"Maybe," Mikey touched his lips again and smiled. "And yeah, I have great friends. Thanks, Arthur, for this, for tonight, for everything."

"You're welcome," he said, putting his hand on Mikey's shoulder. "Now, let's get some shuteye. You have a big day tomorrow."

CHAPTER 15

As Mikey walked through the portal in the Wonder Bread factory the following day, he saw The TC was as active as ever. Acolytes were already training their Source and combat skills in the many rooms as full-fledged Jaecar prepared for their secret missions to save Saps from the monsters of OS. Walking through the Sect was slowly becoming second nature as Mikey shrugged off the familiar stares.

When he walked through the clinic doors, Mikey was glad to see Luke there to greet him.

"Hey, man. Congrats on controlling your Source absorption," he smiled warmly. "I'm sure the elder will get you fixed up so you can start training and give me some work to do." Luke eyed Mikey like he was Dr. Frankenstein and Mikey, his monster.

"I'd gladly trade some cuts and bruises to get my core formed," Mikey laughed. "How are things here?"

"It's been quiet the last couple of days. There's a lot of talk in Haven about the increase in monster activity. A couple of omadas around the country were hit hard. Some are saying the creatures seem afraid. We haven't been hit that bad here yet," Luke explained. "Head on back. Elder Neema's in the same room as before."

"Awesome, thanks."

"Oh," Luke called out as Mikey walked through the doorway. "Elder Ryan told all the acolytes that needed help with their basic shield to come to the TC in a few hours. I'll see you then."

"See you then," Mikey headed in. When he entered room 204, Elder Neema was sitting down. The calming scent of lavender and honey filled his nostrils.

"Ah, Mikey. I hear you are having some trouble forming your core? But it seems you were able to control your Source vampirism a bit, eh?" She grinned. "Why don't you sit on the bed and tell me what you feel."

"Hello, elder," Mikey bowed before moving to the examination bed. The parchment paper crinkled as he sat down. "It's nice to see you."

"And you. I wanted to examine you again once you formed your core, but doing it while you try and form your core sounds just as intriguing. Now tell me, what happens when you attempt it?"

"Well...we figured out my left hand was where I absorb the surrounding Source, so everyone thought that was where my core should be formed. But after trying for days...it's like I'm using my own Source to gather it there, and when I do, it just disappears. I can't get it to condense no matter what I do," Mikey explained.

"Hmm...interesting. I would have thought the same," the Elder mused.

"All right, I want you to repeat exactly what you do when you try to form your core, except this time, I will examine you. Is that all right with you?" Elder Neema asked.

"Yes. Please."

"Close your eyes and start when I tell you," Neema instructed. The Healer's small, shriveled hands grasped the side of his head. Mikey felt the Source tendrils enter his body, breaking again into smaller and smaller branches. Knowing what to expect made it much easier this time.

"Begin," Neema said.

Mikey started gathering his inner energy, bringing it to his left hand. Beads of sweat began to trickle down his forehead. When Mikey felt like he had enough, he tried to condense it, to no avail. It disappeared just like all the other times.

"Hmm, perhaps we were wrong about where best to form your core. We did not know last time to examine your left hand. The meridians in your left hand feel odd. Let me look at it more closely," Neema stated.

Mikey felt the tendrils of energy shift their focus solely on his left hand. As they concentrated there, he felt the doors of his meridians open, and Neema's Source began to get sucked in. Mikey fought to keep them closed until the tendrils suddenly withdrew from his body.

"Oh my," the Elder gasped. "Your left hand...I don't know how to explain it. There is already some sort of core there...except it is nothing like I've ever seen. It's like a black hole—a void that steals all life. No wonder you couldn't condense your Source there. It would be like trying to force all the water in a river back upstream. The fact you were able to gather your Source and keep it there at all is unbelievable!" Neema exclaimed.

She let go of his head, and Mikey opened his eyes to see the old Healer pacing around the small operatory, deep in thought.

"I wonder..." the Elder stopped pacing and turned to Mikey as if a light bulb had just flashed in her mind. "Okay. I have a hypothesis. You have two meridians, yes?" Neema worked through her idea aloud.

"Yes..." Mikey nodded.

"Then it is feasible to think that perhaps your body might have two separate cores, as well," she guessed. "I'd like to give you some of my Source and follow where it flows through your body. It might give us a clue," Neema suggested.

"Sounds like as good an idea as any," Mikey nodded. Something about her suggestion seemed instinctively right. It had felt—wrong moving the Source into his left hand.

Mikey still flinched as the tendrils entered his body again. Some focused on his left hand, but the branches spread everywhere.

"All right, open your meridians a little. I'm going to send you some unfocused Source," the Elder informed him.

Mikey opened the doors to his void core slightly as he felt the Source seep into him. The uncomfortable itch and hunger from keeping them closed washed away. He could feel the Healer's tendrils flow with the energy he took in. The Source moved from the void core to his right hand and then back throughout his body.

That's odd.

The Source went back to his right hand a second time. Anytime Source approached his left arm, it bounced away, flowing back to his right before circulating again.

Of course! Mikey realized what was going on. If his left hand was the vampiric aspect of taking in Source, he should've figured his right hand might be where he formed his core from his own Source.

"My right hand," Mikey voiced to Neema, with his eyes still closed.

"Ah, seems you can feel it too. I agree. Your left hand absorbs the Source around you, and your right hand is used to condense and harness it," Elder Neema guessed. "Let's see if our hypothesis is correct. Try and pull the Source into your right hand and condense it," she instructed.

As soon as the Source began to gather, Mikey knew they were right. The Source rushed to Mikey's hand as he condensed it. He pictured the core in his mind building up more and more energy until something clicked inside him. It felt like finally popping a crick you had in your neck...for sixteen years. The relief was immediate and just as quickly, interrupted by a yelp from Elder Neema.

The Source tendrils vanished from his body. Mikey's eyes flew open when he felt the smack on his arm. Standing before him was a glaring Elder Neema, rubbing at her hands.

"I... I'm sorry. Are you okay?" Mikey felt terrible. "I think I formed my core. My Source was condensing, and it all just clicked together, then—"

"It's all right," Neema cut in. "I'm sorry to smack you. It was just a reflex. You did form your core, and it was so intense it was like the damn sun! I don't know if it's possible to burn Source, but that's what it felt like when I touched it," she scolded.

"I didn't mean to, I'm sorr—wait, I formed my core? I really did?" Mikey asked excitedly. He focused on his right hand and knew it was true. He could feel its energy, condensed and ready to be set free.

"You did indeed," Neema said somberly. The change in tone brought Mikey out of his body and back to the present. "You both fascinate and terrify me," the Elder confessed. "To form your core in one go..." Elder Neema started pacing across the room again, her tiny feet shuffling. She walked over to the counter and took a few deep breaths of the incense. Then, grim-faced, she leveled her eyes at Mikey

"You have the power to destroy anything in your path. And, like two sides of a coin, to save those you wish to save. It's as if you've got a black hole in one hand and the sun in another. If you were to master both..." she trailed off.

Mikey didn't know what to say. He didn't want anyone to be terrified of him.

Am I really that strong?

Last week, he was a nobody, a freak with no friends that everyone steered clear of. Now he was someone who could 'destroy anything in his path'?

I don't want to destroy anyone or anything.

However, Mikey knew that wasn't true after thinking about it momentarily.

His eyes narrowed as he responded to the Elder. "The only things I want to destroy are the things that hurt the innocent. Vampires, gnomes, Jaecar, it doesn't matter to me. If they are innocent, I want to make sure they get home to their families like I never got to," he declared.

The Healer's eyes softened. "Don't ever forget that. You may live for thousands of years and see your loved ones, friends, and family come and go. Even living as long as I have, I've seen the rise and fall of many nations. It can change you. Do not let it alter who you are and what you wish to protect. Cherish the time you have with those you love," Elder Neema urged.

Mikey swallowed. *Thousands of years?*

He was going to ask what the Elder meant but realized precisely what she was saying. He was half vampire. They live for thousands of years, maybe even forever.

What if I do too?

It was all too crazy to even fathom. Sabrina and Marcus would be gone in 100 years at best, and Mikey would just...*live on?* How did his dad stay with his mom, knowing she would grow old and die right before his eyes?

That's just too much to process right now.

There were other, more pressing issues and Mikey wanted to celebrate the fact he had formed his core and could start real training.

The Elder seemed to be waiting for him to respond.

"I won't," Mikey replied.

"I hope you don't," Elder Neema snorted. "For now, you are ready to start your training. We will be monitoring you closely. The sooner you realize your strength, the sooner you will learn to temper it when needed. I would like Elder Ryan to train you separately so you can get a gauge for yourself. There is a real possibility of seriously injuring one of the other acolytes or another Jaecar."

"Actually... I'd prefer that," Mikey recalled the scuffle with the guys in the alley.

"Wonderful. Ryan informed me about your training in a little while. His idea of using your void to help train the acolytes in shielding is a great one. Report to the TC at 10:00 a.m. Which gives you"— she checked the clock on the wall— "an hour."

"Congratulations, acolyte," Elder Neema met his eyes, smiling warmly. Her face disappeared in the wrinkles, but it was infectious.

"Thank you for everything." Mikey was overwhelmed with joy. Despite their brief time together, he grew fond of the old woman. And Mikey knew none of this would have been possible without her.

"It is my pleasure. Now go enjoy your hour before training. Don't attempt to use your Source on your own. It is forbidden to use it against another Jaecar unless during official training or a life is in danger," Neema instructed.

Mikey recalled Thomas saying he had violated the rules of their order and felt a twinge of guilt. That was until he remembered Marcus and Sabrina were feeling the same and didn't just start violently attacking him.

Hopefully, Thomas won't be here for training today.

It would be just the thing to sour his good mood.

A loud grumble from his belly helped Mikey decide how to spend his time before training. With his stomach guiding him, Mikey headed for the cafeteria to grab a bite.

And maybe a little morning dessert for me and my faerie friend.

He wanted to avoid overeating, knowing he'd probably take in a decent amount of Source at Elder Ryan's training. But that was later, and his stomach wanted sustenance now.

Mikey grabbed a sausage corndog, a syrup dipping cup, and two chocolate chip cookies. He scarfed it all down before heading to get training clothes and drop off his gift.

Every time Mikey left his sweet treat, he'd hoped his little friend would pop out again. Unfortunately, the Brownie had only shown herself the one time. But that didn't dissuade Mikey in the slightest. It looked like today would be no different, but as Mikey kneeled to drop off the cookie in the usual spot, a flash of auburn hair caught his eye.

Mikey pushed down his excitement. He pretended not to watch as his little friend struggled to push what looked like a small, old-fashioned treasure chest—no bigger than a fifty-cent piece but a third of her size—out from behind the bin. When she managed to push it far enough that Mikey could clearly see it, the Brownie started jumping up and down, waving her hands.

Does she really want my attention?

Not knowing if he was doing the right thing, Mikey turned to look at her. The faerie's big grin let him know that was, in fact, what she wanted. He was able to get a good look at her for the first time. The folklore depicted Brownies as small, ugly creatures that were usually male. Maybe that was true for the male Brownies, but Mikey wouldn't describe her that way.

Besides being eight inches tall, the fairy had a pretty face covered in freckles and long, slender ears. She wore the same outfit as the first time Mikey had seen her. He noticed her feet were bare, and she only had four toes.

"Hello. Nice to see you again. I'm Mikey," he greeted.

The tiny woman waved, then pointed to her mouth and shook her head as if to say she couldn't speak.

"You can't talk?" Mikey asked to clarify.

The Brownie shook her head.

"But you can understand me?"

She nodded, then pointed to the chest. The Brownie opened the lid, exposing a small, white piece of paper resting on top. She hoisted the article over her head, revealing a gold coin underneath. After struggling to unfold the tiny parchment, her arms reached to hand it to him. Even though it was about half the size of a gum wrapper, it might as well have been a large poster in her hands.

Looking at the paper, Mikey saw it had two drawings on it. The left-most drawing was some sort of pond or lake, and the right was...*a chicken*? With no clue what this meant, Mikey looked to her for some explanation.

Grinning, the fairy pointed to the paper and then pointed to herself.

"Is this where you live?" Mikey probed. He didn't want to upset his little friend but had no idea where this was going.

She shook her head, then her expression changed to one of concentration. Like she was trying to find a way to explain it to him. An idea must have come because the Brownie pointed to Mikey and rolled her hand forward as if to say, 'and you are....'

"Mikey," he stated, pointing to himself.

She nodded excitedly, pointing back at the paper and then to herself.

"Oh. This is your name," Mikey figured it out. He couldn't help but smile when she started nodding vigorously and jumping up and down. "Okay, I can figure this out," he said determinedly.

"It's not...pond chicken?"

She crinkled her nose and shook her head.

"Thought so," he smirked. "Okay. I assume it's two words put together to make your name?"

She nodded.

"So, let's get the first word down, then go from there," Mikey suggested. He proceeded to name bodies of water until she clapped when he said 'lake.'

"First part is lake. Okay..." Mikey tried to think about what the chicken meant.

Lake chicken makes no sense. Hmm.

He thought it might be another word for chicken. Lake...hen?—*Laken!*

"Is it Laken?" Mikey hoped.

She squealed in excitement and pointed to herself, smiling from ear to ear.

"We did it! Nice to meet you, Laken." Mikey beamed.

Laken pointed to the cookie bag and her mouth before putting her hands together as if to say thanks.

"No problem. I love them too."

Laken walked back over to the chest and made a little show of pushing it toward him.

"You don't have to thank me. I'm just happy to have made another friend here," he offered.

But Laken wasn't having it. She shook her head and puffed out her cheeks in a pout. She pointed back to the chest and to Mikey before stomping her foot.

"Okay, okay. I'll take it. Thank you." Mikey conceded, reaching for the tiny box with the gold coin and putting it in his pocket. As much as he wanted to take a closer look at his present and talk to his new friend, the training was going to start soon.

Nodding with a pleased look, Laken pointed to him and then to the cookie bag before putting her hands together again.

"Don't worry. I'll bring you more every chance I get," Mikey promised. "I have to do some training now, but I'll visit you again."

She gave him a thumbs-up, dragged the cookie behind the bin, and disappeared. Mikey lingered there for a moment, processing the whole interaction before shaking his head in wonder at this crazy new world. He finished grabbing the large-size training clothes and headed to his old room to change.

CHAPTER 16

The Training Center was less lively than it had been earlier that morning. Mikey searched for Elder Ryan but spotted Marcus instead. He was standing near the entrance of one of the many practice rooms.

"Over here," Marcus called out, seeing him simultaneously. "This'll be our room. Just waiting for Elder Ryan," he pointed when Mikey got closer. A few others were standing nearby watching them. Mikey waved and did his best to be friendly.

Not again. Mikey sighed.

He noticed Thomas walking towards them, a small entourage behind him.

"I guess this is where the pathetic acolytes go who need to depend on a vampire to get stronger," Thomas sneered.

"I'm pretty sure you can't keep a basic shield going either," Marcus retorted.

"Not yet. But I certainly don't need help from this freak. We kill his kind, not make friends with them. They would do the same to you." Thomas glared at Mikey with such hatred that he almost took a step backward. "This is all part of those bloodsuckers' plans to destroy our order." The posse behind Thomas nodded in agreement.

"But don't worry, everyone," Thomas continued. "I'll make sure this monster never becomes one of us."

"Look, I didn't know about any of this stuff until a week ago. I didn't even know who I was. All I want to do is make sure no one loses their family like I did." Mikey replied.

"LIAR!" Thomas snarled. "How many monsters like him used deceit to kill our people?" he turned to the gathering crowd. "It's in their very nature!"

"Tom." Marcus stepped beside Mikey. "Mikey's not like—"

"And the vampire has its claws in my little brother, too. Or is that what you're really into, Marcus?" Thomas mocked.

"Dude...what is wrong with you? You know I'm all about Ryan Reynolds," Marcus joked. But Mikey could tell the comment had hurt his friend. "Besides, Mikey only has eyes for Sabrina." As soon as the words left his lips, Marcus turned to Mikey, wide-eyed, realizing that was probably not the best thing to let slip. 'Sorry,' he mouthed.

Thomas roared as Mikey was hurled through the open training room door, smashing into the back wall with a crunch.

Aaargh! Mikey was getting sick of this. Thomas lumbered towards him, practically frothing at the mouth. But Mikey's eyes went wide as strange colors swirled around him.

What—what am I seeing?

It was all so much brighter and crisper. As if Mikey was wearing blurry and dull glasses all along but finally put on the right pair. A few feet from him, Thomas froze. And then Mikey saw it. Glowing, dark-red swirls of energy flowed within Thomas, gathering to his fists.

"You see. Look at his eyes!" Thomas screeched, pointing at Mikey. "The monster shows itself."

Others audibly gasped.

Confused, Mikey turned to Marcus. His friend had the same swirling energy. Except Marcus's was a dense, rich green that reached out from his chest to cover his entire body.

It's...so beautiful.

Marcus gasped, his eyes going wide as they met Mikey's. His friend, as if unsure what to do, hesitated for a moment before ultimately rushing to Mikey's side.

"Uh, your eyes went full vamp. Like—they are super blue and practically glowing," Marcus whispered.

"Huh?" Mikey's eyebrows shot up.

Marcus took out his phone and after a few seconds, handed it to Mikey in camera mode.

Okay. That's freaky.

Mikey's eyes had indeed changed. They were the same shape as Viki's, but instead of yellow, his were a deep blue. The Source continuously shifted behind them, almost like smoke rising. It gave them an eerie glow.

"We have to stop this monster now!" Thomas snarled. The red energy around his fists flared as he lunged at Mikey.

I think I broke a rib.

Mikey winced as he dodged the Source-filled punch aimed at his head. The void core in Mikey's hand fought to be opened. His body demanded more Source. An aggressive instinct tried to take over as Mikey struggled for control.

Thomas screeched in rage, punching out a blast of fiery red Source.

It was much easier to dodge now that Mikey could see the ball of energy barreling toward his chest.

Marcus was yelling for them both to stop, but Mikey wasn't the one who started it. He was done apologizing for doing nothing wrong. His parents were amazing people, and Mikey wasn't going to feel guilty for either of them or himself.

Clamping down on his doors to keep the void closed, Mikey reached for his own Source, pulling it towards the core in his right hand.

He gasped as dark blue claws erupted from the tips of his fingers.

Thomas hesitated, sensing something had changed.

Mikey took the opportunity to analyze the blue curving blades projecting from his fingertips. Something inside of him knew they were incredibly sharp. A sudden desire to test out just how sharp they were, began to gnaw at him. The itch to open the void in his left hand grew exponentially. Mikey had to suppress the urge to scratch it with his claw.

"ENOUGH!" Elder Ryan bellowed behind them.

Mikey blinked in surprise, and the world returned to normal. The rivers of color disappeared, and dullness returned. He let the Source in his hand dissipate as Elder Ryan stomped over to Thomas.

"You disrespect our rules and attack a fellow acolyte unprovoked!" The elder fumed.

"I don't recognize this freak as one of us," Thomas spat.

"It is not your place to decide. ACOLYTE!" The elder's voice boomed.

Surprisingly, Thomas came to his senses enough to bow his head. "I am sorry, Elder. I will accept my punishment."

"You will. And Mikey will decide what it is." Elder Ryan turned towards him.

"Um...what? I don't think that's appropriate. Thomas hates me enough as it is, shouldn't—" Mikey stammered.

"I don't think he will hate you anymore or less, no matter what you decide," Elder Ryan interrupted. "Keep in mind that if you were a different acolyte, that blow might have killed you."

Thomas's eyes were seething with hatred as he stared at Mikey.

The elder has a point about him hating me no matter what.

And to his surprise, Mikey wanted to make him pay.

But how? Physical pain isn't enough. He wanted to hit Thomas where it really hurt.

A sudden pang of guilt overcame Mikey at the thought of Thomas acting out because he had lost his brother. But he quickly realized that wasn't an excuse for Thomas's actions. Mikey had witnessed the deaths of his parents. He'd seen their bodies lying there lifeless. He spent the next decade locked away with no one to talk to and only his memories of their love to keep him going. If Arthur hadn't come into his life…Mikey could very well have become the monster Thomas thought he was.

And like Marcus said, his brother was out of control. Thinking about Thomas's words, an idea started to form in his mind.

It'll kill two birds with one stone.

"If it is acceptable elder Ryan," Mikey began. "The only punishment I want from Thomas is for him to participate in the upcoming Tribunal. Because I will be," he declared.

Several gasps rang throughout the large crowd Mikey realized had formed around the training room door.

"Hmm. That is an unusual request. The Tribunal is a serious matter," the elder mused. "Though not common, death is a possibility. The main issue is that the Tribunal cannot be done alone, and it wouldn't be acceptable to force others to enter," Elder Ryan answered.

"I accept the punishment!" Thomas announced. "I will form an omada and enter the upcoming Tribunal. If only to save our order and prevent him," Thomas practically spat at Mikey, "from ever becoming a Jaecar."

"Then I'll allow it," the elder answered. "But if you cannot meet these terms," he grinned wickedly, "then I will be the one to determine your punishment, acolyte Thomas."

"Understood," Thomas bowed. He glared daggers at Mikey, then left, his entourage following behind.

"Well, this was unexpected," Elder Ryan turned to Mikey. "I apologize for putting you in this situation by asking for your help today. I understand if you want to try another time."

"It's not your fault. And I'm still good to go if anyone wants to work with me. After that whole thing—" Mikey gestured towards the cracked wall where his body hit, "I'm definitely craving some Source to heal."

"Excellent," the elder clapped his hands together. He turned to the remaining acolytes. "Anyone having trouble forming their basic shield, I urge you to participate in this training. Marcus here can attest to its efficacy."

Marcus nodded. "It's true. My shielding control has almost doubled by just being around Mikey for a week." Marcus paused as several murmurs buzzed throughout the small crowd. "And as I was saying before my delusional brother had an episode, Mikey just wants to help."

Only four from a group of at least thirty decided to enter the training room. Mikey recognized Luke, who looked at the splintered wall behind them and then back to Mikey, a questioning look on his face.

Is he asking if I need healing?

Mikey shook his head, and Luke's shoulders sagged.

I'm sure you'll get your chance.

The other three were two guys that Mikey had seen in passing and a short, dark-haired girl five-foot tall at best. She walked up to Mikey with an appraising look before sticking out her hand. "I'm Janet. I hope Thomas isn't right about you, and you can help me with my shielding."

"I'm Mikey. I hope so too. Er—not about the Thomas part, but about the shielding. My mom was a Jaecar. I'd never want to hurt an innocent person."

Janet's eyes narrowed briefly before she shrugged, seemingly satisfied with his answer.

The other two introduced themselves as Isaac and Anthony. They seemed warier but determined to improve as Jaecar.

The next few hours went by with Marcus and Elder Ryan instructing the acolytes on keeping their shield up against Mikey's void core. Mikey used the opportunity to strengthen the mental doors he'd formed, letting them open slightly more each time. At this point, he could let them open about a quarter of the way with the ability to close them, never wanting to go past the point where he wasn't sure he'd be able to stop.

The extra Source did wonders. By the end of the training, Mikey's rib felt just about healed. Those who chose to stay had vastly improved their shielding abilities, Janet especially. Luke spent more time pestering Mikey with questions like, "If you lost a hand—do you think it would grow back like a lizard...or would we have to sew it back on?"

The others thanked Mikey for his help and seemed a little more comfortable by the end. Elder Ryan said he felt they could do training on their own and that Mikey had a lot of work to do if he was going to enter the Tribunal.

"I want to do one-on-one training tomorrow in the isolation room. Be there tomorrow morning at nine. Remember to continue your reading. A written test is part of it as well," Elder Ryan added.

Luke and Marcus stayed after everyone left. Marcus blurted as soon as they were alone, "And just how were you planning on entering the Tribunal by yourself? Hmm?"

Mikey stood there like a deer in headlights.

Crap.

"You're right...I didn't really think that part out. If I'm being honest, it was a spur-of-the-moment thing. I guess I hoped that you and Sabrina would join me?"

"I thought so," Marcus tsked and shook his head.

"I'm sorry. I know I shouldn't have even considered roping you guys into anything without—"

"I'll join," Luke interrupted.

"What?" Mikey asked, dumbfounded.

"I said I'll join your omada," Luke shrugged. "My only goal is to surpass Elder Neema as a Healer someday. What better way to get there than to join you? I have a feeling I'm going to get a lot of practice joining your team." Luke's eyes seemed to sparkle.

He's probably imagining me getting decapitated so he could try and put me back together again.

But Mikey wasn't going to say no to the help. And despite Luke's...quirkiness, Mikey liked him.

"Whoa. No fair!" Marcus brought his hand to his chest, feigning offense. "I was gonna mess with him a little longer, but I was going to join. I'm sure Sabrina will too. Besides," Marcus clapped Mikey's shoulder, "with our future super slayer here, we can become some of the youngest Jaecar ever. And I can't pass up the chance to one-up Thomas."

Mikey fought the knot forming in his throat as he looked at his two friends. "I—don't know what to say...other than thanks." He blinked away the mist forming in his eyes.

I hope I can live up to their expectations.

"Don't mention it. Just like Luke said, I get the feeling I'll be able to get much stronger being a part of your team. Plus, we're friends," Marcus replied. "Let's talk to Sabrina about it tomorrow. We need to up our training big time if we want to have a shot at being ready in five months."

"Agreed," Luke nodded. "I gotta do some work at the clinic, but I'll catch you guys tomorrow."

"All right. And thanks again," Mikey waved goodbye.

They decided to call it a day, and Marcus dropped Mikey off. He'd wanted to see Sabrina before they left, but she must've been busy with Sect business. He sent a text telling her he hoped she was doing all right and had something big to tell her the next day. Realizing that was probably too vague and could be misinterpreted differently, he clarified "Jaecar business."

Arthur was on the couch watching TV when he walked in. They started talking about their days when a knock at the door surprised them; Arthur got up to answer it.

"What are you doing here? How did you know where we live?" Arthur's eyes narrowed.

"Look, I'm here to see Mikey. I promise I don't mean either of you any harm. I just want to talk to him."

I know that voice.

Mikey went to the door, and his suspicions were confirmed. It was Viki.

"Hey you," she smiled warmly when he came into view, "Can we talk? In private, please? It can be right here on the steps if it makes you feel safer."

Like before, Mikey didn't get the sense she had meant him any harm. If anything, he was more curious about what she wanted to talk about.

"Mikey, I don't know...." Arthur hesitated, his expression concerned.

"It's all right," Mikey assured him. "We'll just be out here on the steps."

"Holler if you need me." Arthur eyed Viki warily but went inside.

When they were alone, she motioned for Mikey to sit on the front step before joining him.

"You're probably wondering who I am and why I'm here?" Viki started.

"Among other things," Mikey nodded.

"Honestly, I was sent here to watch over you. Our people heard you were alive and might be held hostage. So they sent me to make sure. And if needed, rescue you."

"Wait, the vamp—I mean, Verdaat thought I was in trouble?"

That's partially true, Mikey realized. Elder Cassandra had threatened to keep him at the Sect indefinitely if he couldn't control his abilities.

"Yes. Is it really so hard to believe? You are one of us—possibly even more. And the Source users' whole reason to live is to kill us."

"Okay. I can maybe see how you'd think that. But why are you here now? I'm obviously not being held, hostage. And what about the theatrics yesterday in the alley?"

"I was told to watch over you regardless. And the alleyway thing was just me seeing what you could do...and having a little fun," Viki blushed.

Mikey's face felt suddenly hot as he recalled her 'little fun' on his lips. "Well, as you can clearly see, I don't need watching. So you can tell your peop—"

"OUR people," Viki corrected. "You are more one of us than one of them."

"I... don't view things like that. Us and them. I don't care what someone is as long as they don't hurt the innocent," Mikey voiced. "And you can tell whoever you report to that I'm fine."

Viki cocked her head. "You're an odd one. And I don't mean that just because you're the first hybrid ever. But orders are orders, so I'm going to keep an eye on you."

"I prefer you didn't," Mikey sighed.

"I thought I'd feel the same way. I figured this would be a crap job. Until you dashed across the street to rescue little ol' me." Viki pretended to fan herself. "It was actually sweet. Besides, if you were actually in any trouble from those goons, I would've stopped it. No worries."

He didn't like the idea of someone 'keeping an eye' on him. Especially a beautiful vampire. A random thought suddenly crept its way into Mikey's head.

What if she's like a thousand years old?

"I know you aren't supposed to ask this, so please don't get mad. But how old are you?"

"Ha. Would it freak you out if I was like a thousand or something? Or would that be something you're into?" She leaned against him, then laughed again when Mikey became visibly flustered.

"Relax, I'm seventeen."

"Oh, I'm sorry," Mikey said somberly.

To be turned into a vampire at seventeen. And now they have her taking orders and doing missions.

Viki tilted her head quizzically. "Sorry?"

"Er...you know. For being turned into a vampire so young."

Mikey jumped as Viki suddenly started laughing hysterically.

"What?" his brow furrowed.

"Oh, my," Viki wiped away a tear. "You don't know anything about us, do you?"

Mikey's face turned red. "No, actually. I lost my parents before I got to learn about any of this."

Her face softened. "You're right. That was stupid of me to say. How about I tell you about our people and answer some of the questions you have as an apology?"

"You don't have to apologize, but that sounds great," Mikey perked up.

"Okay, first, I was born. Verdaat babies are rare, but they exist. We age until our bodies fully mature. After that, they pretty much stay that way forever."

"So, you are immortal?"

"No Mikey. WE are immortal. That's why you belong with us. All your little friends will grow old and die while you stay like this forever."

That topic is still on pause...

"Does the sun really burn you guys?" Mikey tried to change the subject.

"Nope. That is made up. Direct sunlight is uncomfortable, though, because we run hot. It feels like a burn, in a way. Next question."

Mikey felt like he had hundreds more churning in his head, but his encounter with Thomas was at the forefront.

"About your eyes. Today when"— Mikey thought secrecy was best for now— "when I was training. My eyes changed, and I could see all these colors...."

"They what?" she grabbed his hands excitedly. "Your eyes look human right now. Are you telling me you can switch between the two?"

"I'm not positive. I think so. It happened once. But is it true? That you can see the Source?"

"Yeah. Why do you think I was so enamored with you yesterday? You look like nothing I've ever seen before."

"What do I look like?"

"As I said before, that mystery should be for you. The next time your eyes shift, take a look for yourself. But I'll leave you with this. If you are like us, as you reach maturity, your abilities will come easier. But, your hunger for Source will grow with it."

Pretty sure I've already had a little taste of that.

When she mentioned the word hunger, Mikey had to know. "Have you ever—killed anyone?"

"Yes," her eyes narrowed. "But they deserved it. I was fourteen, and two men tried to—kidnap me. When I saw what they had planned to do to me and had already done to others...I ended it." Viki raised her head defiantly as if daring Mikey to judge her.

"That's terrible. I'm sorry that happened."

"What? It doesn't repulse you that I killed them?" Viki looked surprised.

"I said innocent people before, remember? Just imagining what the poor girls went through...." Mikey shuddered.

"I've never harmed a human that didn't deserve it, though. If that puts your mind at ease," she answered. "Anyways," Viki leaned in and kissed his cheek before standing up, "I'll see you around."

Mikey called out that he had more questions, but she was already gone.

Holy hell. How does she do that?

He sat there for a few minutes, processing it all before heading inside. He gave the gist of what had happened to Arthur, who ultimately told him to 'be careful.'

When Mikey finally collapsed on his bed, he thought about his life and its drastic changes in the last couple of weeks. He briefly tried to process being immortal and how it would impact his relationship with Sabrina if it ever blossomed that far, but it hurt his head. Instead, Mikey thought about the upcoming Tribunal and if he should have brought his friends into it.

No. Luke and Marcus know more about what they're getting into than I do. I'm not forcing them and should respect their decision.

He hoped Marcus was right and that Sabrina would want to join too. His last thought before sleep came was about his shimmering blue Source claw.

I gotta try that out.

CHAPTER 17

Mikey got to the isolation room a bit before nine. He stopped at the cafeteria to get breakfast and dropped off a cookie for Laken. He'd hoped to see the little Brownie, but she didn't show. It reminded Mikey to mention the coin to Marcus and Sabrina. With the chaos yesterday, it had slipped his mind.

Elder Ryan or someone must've repaired the concrete while he was away because it was brand new. Mikey could barely contain his excitement to test out his newfound ability.

I mean...this is the room to practice things, right?

Unable to argue with his flawless logic, Mikey reached for the Source within, pulling it to the core in his right hand. When he looked down, Mikey frowned.

I can't see it.

His eyes were normal. It wasn't the same.

Thinking back to the day before, Mikey tried to replay what had happened. Thomas slammed him into the wall, then Mikey got up and wanted—he wanted to hurt Thomas. To feed on his Source until there was nothing left. Mikey shuddered at what could've happened if Elder Ryan hadn't shown up.

I can't let those urges take over. Ever.

Mikey closed his eyes and concentrated on how he had felt yesterday, bringing the rage, hunger, and even embarrassment to the forefront of his mind. When he opened them, the world was crisp and bright again. He would've done a little dance if it weren't for the delicate balance of controlling his powers and resisting the aggressive urges they brought.

He hadn't realized it yesterday. But when Mikey looked closely, a rainbow-like mist of Source was floating around him. It wasn't like the hyper-concentrated Source running through Thomas or Marcus. It seemed...*diluted.*

Mikey opened his void core, sticking out his hand. The mist began to swirl in the air, tunneling into Mikey's void like water down a drain. There wasn't a lot of Source in the ambient air, but it was something.

As the energy flowed, Mikey channeled it, along with his own Source, to the core in his right hand. Dark blue blades erupted from his fingertips.

So badass. I've got lightsaber claws!

Elated, Mikey practically skipped over to the concrete shelf and swiped at it.

No way.

Within the concrete, five long gashes went entirely through. Each slice was several inches deep and about the width of a nickel.

"Impressive!" Elder Ryan clapped at the doorway. Mikey jumped back away from the counter, letting go of his Source as his eyes returned to normal.

"Sorry—I...this happened yesterday, and I wanted to test it out, and I figured this was the isolation—"

"What did I say about apologizing?" the Elder raised an eyebrow. "There is no need to be sorry. You were correct. This is the place to practice, and I am late. Thankfully, I got here in time to see that." He pointed to the concrete.

"When Thomas attacked me, my eyes changed, and I was so angry... I pulled the Source into my core and this claw formed," Mikey activated it again, lifting up his hand.

"Ah. So it's a claw. I can only feel the Source from your hand. It is powerful," Elder Ryan said. "Tell me. What does it look like with those eyes?"

"It's like...long, deep-blue knives sticking out of my fingertips," he answered.

"Hmm," Elder Ryan looked puzzled. "I've never heard of someone being able to make a blade from nothing. That would take an incredible reservoir of Source. But with your vampiric core, I guess that isn't much of a concern."

Mikey liked the fact that his own hand was a weapon. Instinctively it felt like fighting with a sword, or something similar wasn't right.

"I have arranged for this to be your permanent practice room as you prepare for the Tribunal."

"Thank you, Elder," Mikey bowed. He was truly grateful. Practicing in private seemed the safest way to go about it for everyone, especially after the very public incident with Thomas.

"I'd like to begin sparring." Elder Ryan motioned to Mikey's hand. "I needn't remind you how dangerous that claw is. So let's just practice as if it was active. Then you'll practice the same movements to build your endurance."

"Okay." Mikey understood the sense of that. He shuddered as the thought of accidentally scratching his nose with the claw popped into his head.

I've got mental problems.

They spent the next few hours going through hand-to-hand maneuvers before starting short weapons training. Elder Ryan figured that would be closest to his Source claw. It became quickly apparent that Mikey had a knack for physical combat.

With his memory, he recalled the movements easily. Mikey had barely felt a thing when Elder Ryan's attacks landed with no Source behind them. When the Elder—obviously frustrated—noticed that was the case, he started using Source to enhance his blows. Then Mikey felt it.

I should've pretended it hurt more.

His vampire sight activated at the moment a lightning-fast Source punch landed in the center of Mikey's face. He growled, sticking out his left hand. The urge to drain the Elder dry of his Source clawed at the edge of his mind. But Mikey bit the inside of his cheek for focus, taking a few deep breaths until he felt like himself again.

"Staying in control while using my abilities is not easy."

"I didn't think it would be. That is why we are here. I am not supposed to tell you this. But I feel I should. The High Council of Haven view you as too dangerous an asset if you don't prove yourself...controllable," the Elder shared.

"What does that mean?"

"It means, Mikey, that if you are deemed a threat to Haven, you will be eliminated."

"But I was able to control my Source drain. I'm not a threat anymore."

"Think. In a single day, you were able to conjure up blades of pure Source from your hand. You have an unlimited supply of energy at your disposal and all the powers of a vampire. And those are just the things we know about. In terms of threats, you are at the top of the list as far as Haven, and the rest of Otherside are concerned," the Elder explained.

"If our leaders view you as a wild card. They will take steps to get rid of you. It is important to portray yourself as in control at all times. I'm sure there are spies for other Sect leaders within our own. It was not looked upon favorably when other leaders found out we had invited you into the order without their knowledge."

Damn.

It was a good thing Mikey hadn't acted against Thomas the other day. A hit order might've been placed on his head even though Thomas had started it. Mikey was even more grateful that Elder Ryan had gotten there in time.

"I have some other students to train. But I want you to practice using your vampiric abilities and staying in control," Elder Ryan instructed. "I will train you in combatives on Sundays at 7:00 p.m., starting next week. Don't forget your reading."

"Thank you for all your help, Elder Ryan." Mikey meant it. The gruff teacher hadn't taken it easy on him. But he'd made Mikey feel like one of their own. And that meant a lot.

"Think nothing of it. You are an acolyte, and I am your teacher. I believe with your personality and abilities, you have what it takes to become a Jaecar. Maybe even in five months. Elder Cassandra and I have vouched for you to the other Sect leaders. Don't let it be in vain."

"Why are you doing all of this for me?" Besides Arthur, Mikey wasn't used to people going out of their way to help him.

"Because I knew your mother and father and respected them both. They were good people forced into terrible circumstances. And I see a lot of them in you. Now I must go."

"Yes, Elder," Mikey nodded and found himself alone in the training room. His bloody nose was already starting to heal.

I'm lucky Elder Ryan was my instructor. Mikey shuddered to think what it could have been like if someone like Thomas had been given the task instead.

He decided to get back to training, and after a few more tries, Mikey brought forth his vampiric eyes again.

"Holy shit!" Mikey cried out when he saw his left hand.

Inside the center of Mikey's palm and the tips of his fingers were—*actual black holes?* The world inside of his hand was devoid of all life and light. It was like looking into a gateway to nothing. Nothing but the abyss.

And from those pits of darkness, black veins stretched across his arm to intertwine up his shoulder before anastomosing with his human meridians. Their swirls were the same rich blue as his claw and eyes, and he knew what Viki was talking about.

A half hour into practicing, Mikey began to feel like he was getting the hang of it.

"Whoa—" a familiar voice called from behind.

"See! I told you. Vampy eyes," Marcus pointed.

His friends were standing in the doorway. Sabrina's face was a mask of surprise.

"Hey guys," Mikey let go of the Source sight, and within the next blink, they'd returned to normal.

"Guess you were able to get them back," Marcus grinned.

"What do you see? How does it work?" Sabrina blurted.

"I see Source. All around me and inside everyone," Mikey explained. "The Source inside everyone—it's all different colors. Like Marcus is a rich green color."

"Can you bring them back again? I have to know what my color is!" Sabrina urged.

"Yeah. Give me a second. I've gotten a little bit better at it." Soon, Mikey's eyes were deep blue and marquis shaped.

"How does it feel?" Sabrina asked.

"Honestly, it makes me a little...vampy," Mikey shrugged. "Not like an 'I want to suck your blood kind of way.' More like, 'I want to open the doors in my left hand and take in all that ruby-red Source you have, Sabrina."

"Sorry. I didn't realize it did that to you." She stepped closer and caressed his face with the back of her hand. "Better or worse?"

"Both," Mikey laughed.

"They're beautiful. It's like looking into the ocean."

"Okay—third wheel here," Marcus scoffed. "Let's take a second away from Mikey's 'beautiful ocean-blue eyes' and focus on what made that?" Marcus pointed to the gashes and sections of concrete that had crumbled away.

"Oh. That's my other thing."

"Other thing?" Marcus faked annoyance. "You've got vampire eyes and now have an 'other thing' that can tear away chunks of concrete? This isn't even fair." Marcus threw his hands in the air. "But seriously, what is it?"

"I'm sure Marcus already spilled the beans to you about my plan yesterday, Sabrina. But even if he didn't, I guess I should show you what I've got so far." Mikey began to focus but realized how much Source he had used practicing.

"Um...this is a little embarrassing. But is it okay if I take a little bit of your Source?" Mikey asked them. "I used up too much," he pointed to the concrete rubble, "doing that."

"Sure. Just a little off the top," Marcus quipped.

"Yeah. No problem," Sabrina nodded.

"Thanks," Mikey was grateful. When the doors in his left hand opened, Mikey stared in awe as the ruby red and rich green Sources spiraled towards the black vortex in his hand. Their energies passed through his black-veined arm, changing into the same deep blue as his own Source.

Using the two energies, Mikey condensed them, and razor-sharp claws shot out of his fingertips.

"I can...I can definitely feel it," Marcus said. "What the hell is that?"

"It's a claw, really. Blue Source blades are coming out of my fingertips. They are slightly curved, and concrete doesn't seem to put up too much of a fight against them."

"Incredible," Sabrina exclaimed. "I've never heard of someone conjuring their own weapons. At least one that isn't a projectile."

"That's some serious firepower, man!" Marcus slapped him on the shoulder. "How can we not pass the next tribunal?"

"That reminds me. Sabrina," Mikey swallowed, "I'd like to officially ask you to be in an omada with me to take the upcoming Tribunal. Oh, and Marcus. And Luke," he finished.

Mikey's palms were sweaty. This seemed bigger than a date. It was asking someone to trust you to watch their back when lives were on the line. An omada was usually forever.

"Actually. When you got your powers in check, I was going to do the same thing. Which, by the looks of it, you did and then some," Sabrina answered.

She laughed at the dumbfounded look on both of their faces. "I've been training my butt off for years to pass the Tribunal. I was planning on asking Marcus and...Thomas. But after everything that happened, I kind of put it off until you came along," Sabrina winked at him. "So yeah. Let's do this."

"Is using the term' dream team' too corny?" Marcus asked.

"Yeah."

"Definitely," Mikey nodded. "But I'll allow it."

"Really? Pfft. You're a softie Mikey Black," Sabrina leaned into him. Mikey's idiot brain immediately thought of Viki the other night and their conversation.

"That reminds me...I forgot to tell you guys that Viki the vampire stopped by my house last night. To talk."

"About?" Sabrina prompted.

"Um. She said she was sent here because the Verdaat found out I was alive. And maybe the Jaecar were holding me hostage, and she needed to make sure I was okay and was sent to protect me," Mikey stammered.

"Protect you from what?" Marcus scoffed.

"I guess from you guys." He grinned. "But I set her straight and said I didn't need protecting and that I wasn't being held hostage."

"And?" Marcus rolled his hand forward to continue.

"And she said too bad, she's going to keep an eye on me to keep me safe. I don't know. Then she said, 'see you around,' and literally disappeared," Mikey finished.

"Great. Now you have a bazillion-year-old vampire security guard stalker!" Marcus exclaimed.

"She's actually only seventeen and was born, not turned. It's rare, I guess," Mikey shrugged.

"I don't like her," Sabrina announced. "Seems fishy."

"Never met her, but I'm on Sabrina's side," Marcus declared.

"I got a sense she was holding some things back but not lying exactly. She didn't seem like a threat, though," Mikey said.

"I'm sure she was very non-threatening, like the other day, right?" Sabrina pursed her lips.

"Would it help if I said not as bad?" Mikey held his arms up in defeat.

"What's this? Seems like I'm missing something here?" Marcus chimed in.

"I forgot to mention that Viki, the vampire princess threw herself all over Mikey. She even kissed him." Sabrina shook her head. But Mikey could see the smirk at the corner of her lips.

Phew. Not mad. "I swear I didn't do anything."

"It's fine. I know you didn't. You aren't a liar, Mikey Black." She flicked him on the forehead.

"Now I kind of want to meet this mysterious vampire protector," Marcus changed his tune.

Mikey sighed. "I get the feeling we will all be seeing her again. Anyways, I'm about done. What about you guys?"

"Yeah, we were done too. That's why we came to check on you," Sabrina answered. "Want to grab a bite somewhere and start making our Tribunal plans? I know a little bit more about what it entails."

"Let's see if Luke is free too," Mikey suggested.

"Sounds good. Me and Brina have a bet on whether Luke is gonna dissect you in your sleep."

"Okay—first, good try on the Brina. But nope. Second," Sabrina struggled to hold in a laugh, "don't you dare tell him which side of the bet I'm on Marcus!"

"Wait—does that mean you bet Luke WOULD dissect me?" Mikey laughed.

When they got to the clinic, Luke apologized but said he was too busy.

"I have Next Sunday off from clinic, so you all can fill me in on your plans then. Don't worry, though. In the next five months, I'll have my basic shield in top-notch shape. I'm also working on something special in the damage department. We can practice and catch up."

"Sounds like a plan. We'll keep you updated," Mikey promised.

"Try not to have too much fun," Marcus smirked.

"Practice makes perfect," Luke replied.

After they left the clinic, Mikey suggested the Chill Pill Café. "I could go for a Chai."

Sabrina agreed, making it two against one. A grumble from Marcus and a 'fine' let them know their destination was set.

"Oh. I forgot to mention to you guys—" Mikey pulled the small chest holding the coin out of his pocket. "Laken, the Brownie friend that I made, gave me this. Do either of you know what it is?"

"What the frick—is that what I think it is?" Marcus's eyes went wide.

"That's...a faerie coin," Sabrina's expression was the same. "I've—I've only heard about them. In fact, I don't think anyone alive has ever seen one." Sabrina shook her head. "Wow."

"Don't let anyone see you with it! Make sure you put it in a safe place!" Marcus motioned for Mikey to put it back in his pocket. "They are literally legendary."

"What does it do?" Mikey wondered.

"They say if you flip a faerie coin and catch it with the same hand, it'll reveal a great treasure," Marcus shared.

"There is never a dull moment with you," Sabrina stared at Mikey in amazement. "What did you do for...Laken, was it? For her to give you this?"

"...I just gave her chocolate chip cookies."

"What?" Sabrina burst out laughing. "All this time, any of us here could've gotten a legendary item by just leaving cookies around."

Mikey shrugged. He didn't realize how big of a gift Laken had given him and felt awkward about its extravagance.

"Should we see what kind of treasure it is?" Mikey pulled the gold coin out of its case.

"No!" Sabrina and Marcus yelled in unison.

"It's not like—official. But the legends about faerie coins make it seem like you should only use it if you are in need," Marcus tried to explain.

"He's right. You should keep it safe and only use it when you're in a pinch," Sabrina nodded.

But I really want to know what it'll turn into...

Mikey harumphed internally but knew his friends were right. He looked at the rune-inscribed coin one last time before placing it back in its chest and his pocket.

Marcus and Sabrina grumbled words like 'lucky bastard' and 'over a freaking cookie' all the way to the car.

The Café was slightly less busy on a Sunday night. The trio made their orders and took the two couches in the back.

"So, what exactly is the Tribunal?" Mikey asked.

"Well—you know it's the test to become a Jaecar. It has a written portion first, then a Source-control portion, and a team battle. The whole thing ends with a final hunt. Everyone in the omada has to pass each part before continuing."

"Anything else?" Mikey probed.

"The Jaecar are forbidden from discussing it with acolytes. Only those eighteen and older are allowed to watch the last fight. My mom has told me a little bit more than she should've probably. But justified it as 'priming a future leader.'"

"Like what? I've heard all of that," Marcus said.

"Just that it's brutal. Its main purpose is to wake the acolytes up to the reality that this stuff is life or death. The monsters of OS won't hesitate."

"That sounds reassuring," Marcus blurted. "But hey. On the bright side. I've been working on folding my shield and have gotten up to three folds. I can only do it in a small section, but it's way stronger already. So, making progress," Marcus gave an exaggerated bow.

"That's great," Mikey congratulated.

"That will definitely come in handy," Sabrina rolled her eyes before her face turned serious. "As far as the written portion goes. I think Mikey will have an advantage there with his memory. We just have to make sure we've memorized all two hundred-ish books of the traditional Jaecar education."

"I'll uh...do my best," Marcus turned pale.

"Don't worry, Marky. I'll cram all that knowledge into your little, teensy, tiny, itty-bitty wittle brain." Sabrina mimicked in an astonishingly accurate baby voice.

"I want out already," Marcus sighed. "Honestly, I think Mikey is going to have an advantage in every category of the Tribunal. Look at what he's done in just a week. Imagine what he'll be capable of in five months!"

"I don't think we should underestimate it," Sabrina urged. She bit her lip and then turned away. Mikey thought she looked frustrated.

"What is it?" Mikey nudged her.

"I'm not supposed to talk about it. Like, really not supposed to. It could ruin me ever becoming a Sect leader," Sabrina looked torn. "But screw it. Who are you going to tell?" She leaned in to whisper. "The High Council of Haven knows about Mikey and what he can already do. My mom pissed them off by bringing him into Haven without telling them. So...they might "alter the tribunal accordingly," Sabrina air quoted.

"What does that mean?" Marcus looked puzzled.

"I don't know. That's all I can tell you about it. And that was more than I should've. Haven takes that stuff seriously," Sabrina whispered.

"Thanks. To both of you. That's a lot more info than I had before." Mikey jumped in. "I hope I don't let everyone down. Half of me just wants to make Thomas blow a fuse. But the other half really does want to protect the innocent. The faster I can learn to do that, the better."

"Hear, hear," Marcus raised a glass of peppermint white-chocolate mocha.

"Well said," Sabrina beamed. "In five months, we'll be Jaecar."

Mikey followed Sabrina's gaze as she looked past him, her smile turning into a frown. Viki had just walked in. The vampire's lips turned up in a wicked smile as soon as her yellow-green cat eyes locked onto them.

CHAPTER 18

"Hey, you," Viki winked at Mikey. She sat down on his other side, acting like Sabrina and Marcus weren't there.

"This is a private conversation," Sabrina scowled.

"Not really. I can hear everything you guys are saying from outside. But it was getting boring out there," Viki shrugged.

"This is so exciting," Marcus clapped. "I'm Marcus. Mikey's best friend." He stuck out his hand.

She seemed thrown off by the gesture but recovered and returned Marcus's handshake. "At least one of your friends has some sense, Mikey."

"What is she even doing here?" Sabrina's scowl deepened. "No one invited you. And as you can see. Mikey is fine."

"As I'm sure Mikey has told you, I am here to keep him safe. My people figured it was best for our Wonderboy here to learn to control his sorcerer powers before an invitation to be with his own kind."

"You didn't tell me that," Mikey snapped.

"Huh. I guess that part didn't come up in our conversation," Viki shrugged.

"The Verdaat...want to invite me?"

"It's probably a trap," Sabrina cautioned.

Viki rolled her eyes. "If it was a trap. I would've kidnapped him in the alley or something."

"Well, I still don't trust you," Sabrina snorted.

"My-my, are female humans always this—snappy? Or," Viki narrowed her eyes and smiled, "is it that Sabrina here has a thing for Wonderboy?"

"Oh, they totally have a thing," Marcus chimed in.

"It's okay," Viki grabbed Mikey's wide-eyed head and turned it towards her. Their noses touched. "I can wait. She'll be old news in like fifty years, max."

"Wow. That's cold on so many levels," Marcus grinned.

Sabrina glared daggers. The awkward silence that ensued was thankfully interrupted by Viki clapping her hands. "So, a Tribunal to become a sorcerer. Sounds dangerous!"

"Again—None. Of. Your. Business." Sabrina enunciated each word.

"Wonderboy, here is my business," Viki replied. "That's fine, though. I'll leave you to your little planning session. I was just in the neighborhood and wanted to say hi," Viki stood up. "And that I'll see you tomorrow."

"Wait, when tomorr—" Mikey started.

But she had already glided out the door.

"I like her," Marcus declared, drawing the stares of both Mikey and Sabrina. "What?"

"Very funny," Sabrina rolled her eyes.

"Wait, I thought you were like really mad?" Mikey was confused.

"That was nothing. I was just trying to rile Viki up to see if she would let anything slip. I'm serious about not trusting her," Sabrina explained.

"Oh. Well, I'm sorry about...that."

"Yeah, well...I didn't like the fact that you sat there and lapped it right up," Sabrina added.

She's got a point. Why did I just stand there?

Truthfully, Viki was beautiful...if not a little scary. Then the answer came to him.

"Vampire hormones," Mikey blurted.

Shit. That sounds terrible out loud.

"Huh?" Marcus and Sabrina replied in unison.

"I think the reason Viki, um--gets me all frazzled...is that, according to her, once a birthed Verdaat gets close to maturing, their urges and stuff will get stronger. So, it's probably my vampire hormones raging."

Yeah, Mikey. Keep digging that hole deeper.

Sabrina suddenly burst out in a fit of giggles. "Seriously?" she wiped at her eye. "Your response to why you let that succubus all over you is, 'my vampire hormones are raging.'" She was overcome with laughter again.

At least she's not upset anymore...

"Seriously, dude," Marcus clapped him on the shoulder, shaking his head. "You don't just come out and say it like that."

"Yeah...I realized—once I said it."

"No." Sabrina got a hold of herself. "At least you're honest. It's something that's been lacking in my other relationships. Anyway, let's head home. I'd say this meeting was productive."

"Agreed. I'm beat. Especially after watching all this drama. Who needs TV?" Marcus joked.

They all agreed to call it a night, and Marcus dropped them off. Arthur was barely awake but wanted to make sure Mikey got home safe. As he walked to his room, Mikey heard him grumble something about 'teenagers' and 'up all night' even though their oven clock said it was a little past nine-thirty.

"Night, Arthur."

"Uh-huh. Night."

The following day was overcast as Mikey's bus pulled up to the high school.

When they got off, he let go of Sabrina's hand with a wave, promising to see her at lunch.

It's going to be a good day.

During the bus ride, he and Sabrina had reached for his bag at the same time and ended up holding each other's hand for the rest of it.

"You're so warm," she had commented but didn't let go. Mikey smiled as he recalled the moment before heading towards History, his day's first class.

Oh no. Please no.

Mikey froze when he entered the classroom.

"Your eyes are so cool!"

"Are those contacts? Where can I get them?"

In the back of the room, sitting on a desk, was Viki, with a crowd of students around her.

"I had them laser altered in Germany. Then I got them tattooed. See?" Viki proceeded to poke at her eye, showing them there weren't any contacts to move around.

"Whoa. Can you see, okay?" One student asked.

"Yep. Perfect vision. Speaking of perfect," Viki saw Mikey and then made a beeline for him.

"Miss me?" she wrapped her arm around his.

Okay. She's strong.

Mikey could see several of the male students scowling through the corner of his eye.

"What are you doing here?" he whispered.

"I'm going to high school. What does it look like?" Viki smirked.

"You know what I mean," Mikey rolled his eyes.

"How else am I supposed to keep an eye on you? The Verdaat have influence throughout the entire world. Getting into high school is a breeze."

"I don't need you to keep an eye on me," Mikey hissed, grinding his teeth.

Viki just shrugged and winked.

The class began to take their seats, and the vampire menace took hers right behind Mikey. The teacher arrived shortly after and did the whole 'introduce yourself, new student' spiel. Viki obliged, garnering oohs and ahhs from the rest of the class. Mikey felt his eyes would get permanently stuck after the number of times he rolled them. Then a horrible thought came to mind.

His worries were confirmed true when the end-of-class bell rang, and Viki appeared next to him.

"Ready to go to our next one?" she grinned.

"Why do the gods hate me?" Mikey looked to the ceiling and shook his head.

"Come on, don't be like that. This is exciting. It's the first time I've gotten to go to high school. I don't even care that it's a bit boring since I already know all of this."

"Wait, you've never gone to school before? And what do you mean you know all of this?"

Viki's demeanor changed, a pained expression behind her eyes and she looked down at the ground.

"I never got to hang around people my age before...As I said, Verdaat children are rare. My father hired the best tutors; I've technically graduated from college. Several times over. You know how our memory is." She looked up at him.

"Yeah. I thought mine was just photographic," Mikey's tone softened.

I guess she kind of grew up lonely too.

"I'll say," Viki laughed. Her expression returned to normal, but now Mikey felt some of it was a facade.

What was her life really like?

"Come on," she grabbed his arm again, pulling them to their next class.

It was the same every time. All the students surrounded Viki, bombarding her with questions about her eyes, where she was from, and if she was single. Mikey suspected she was secretly enjoying all the attention and talking with people her own age.

The ire of all the male students befell Mikey in every class as Viki made it apparent she was there with him.

"Dude, please tell me she's your sister?" The guy next to him elbowed.

"Uh, nope," Mikey shrugged.

"Lucky bastard," the student in front of him mumbled, obviously listening in.

Mikey turned to look at Viki behind him. She was grinning from ear to ear.

Dread filled Mikey as he thought about lunch after their next class.

I think a full-on riot is going to happen. Please don't let Thomas be there.

He was still determining what Thomas would do if Mikey was at school with another vampire. Or even Sabrina.

As they walked to their next class, Mikey thought it was best to just reason with Viki about the situation.

"Look—" Mikey pulled his arm away from her. "I get that you are ordered to watch over me or whatever. But I'm with Sabrina. And as beautiful as you are...."

"You really think I'm beautiful?" Viki interrupted. She seemed taken aback by his comment, but Mikey wasn't sure if it was a ruse.

"Obviously. But that isn't the point," Mikey tried to get back on track. "I can't have you hanging on to me like that. But on a bigger note, there is an acolyte here who hates vampires, me especially. And if he sees us together, I don't know what he'll do. He's already attacked me a few times. Promise me you won't start anything, and please tone it down with Sabrina."

Viki raised an eyebrow.

"And," Mikey continued, "If you do, I won't make a fuss about you being around. I do want to know more about you and about my dad's side of the family."

She seemed to consider his words and then nodded. "Okay. I already told miss stick-up-her-butt what's what when it comes to you. Though I don't think you realize the implications of being immortal yet. But I promise I will keep myself under control."

"Okay. It's a deal," Mikey stuck out his hand.

Viki grabbed his right hand. "Deal." But she didn't let go. She stared at his hand before turning it over. "I don't know if I'll ever get used to your body. It's like a miniature blue sun."

"Can you not say stuff like 'I'll never get used to your body' out loud?" Mikey looked around to make sure no one heard.

"Ha. I guess that does sound...forward," Viki chuckled.

A knot had been forming in Mikey's gut that only seemed to get worse the closer they got to lunchtime. It was relieved a little when Viki promised to behave, but not by much.

The knot had turned into a full-blown boulder by the time the next bell rang. Thankfully, Viki didn't grab Mikey but walked beside him to the cafeteria instead.

Phew. Maybe it won't be so bad?

"What the hell Mikey. Why is she here?" Sabrina barked behind him in the cafeteria line.

Or not.

"She, uh, enrolled at our school...." Mikey trailed off, realizing he should have prepared exactly what he would say. "But don't worry, she promised to behave herself."

Sabrina scoffed, rolling her eyes. "I feel so much better now."

"Hey. It's Viki," Marcus walked up behind Sabrina. "'See you tomorrow,' I get why that's so funny now."

"Listen," Viki sighed. "I'm here to protect him," she motioned to Mikey, "I swear. Maybe I was having a little too much fun messing with you all. Even though he said I was beautiful, he obviously wants you, Sabrina."

Of course, she had to include the beautiful part.

But it seemed to be enough for Sabrina. She harumphed, and they both waited for Mikey to get his lunch before heading for their usual spot.

"Ow. Watch it," someone yelped behind them.

"Move!"

The group turned at the commotion to see Thomas barreling towards them. A few people followed behind him, and Mikey recognized some of the faces from the Sect.

Thomas froze mid-step as his eyes locked on Viki. "Get out of this school. Now," he growled. "Your kind isn't welcome here."

"Hmm, I don't think that I will." Viki acted bored and sat down at their table. "Run along now. No one here will be harmed, I assure you."

"Your words mean nothing, bloodsucker," Thomas snarled.

Sabrina and Marcus just stood there, seeming unsure of what to do.

Mikey was getting tired of this. "Just take your posse and go, Thomas. This is getting old. For the life of me, I have no idea how they can't see how unhinged you are. But put your fists where your mouth is at the Tribunal and leave us alone."

"Don't worry, I'm going to kill you then," Thomas spat.

The slight screech of a chair was the only warning they had before Viki was in front of Thomas. She had both of his wrists pinned down at his sides. The other acolytes jumped back at the sudden explosion of speed. Mikey was thankful they had fanned out and blocked the view from the rest of the cafeteria.

Hatred and panic filled Thomas's eyes as Viki whispered in his ear. She let him go and casually strolled back to her chair and sat down with her back turned to them.

Thomas stood there, his fists turning white. Veins bulged from the side of his head as he shook with fury. Mikey braced himself for the attack he thought was imminent. But to everyone's surprise, Thomas turned and walked away.

The trio stood there with their jaws open.

"What did you say to him?" Marcus asked.

"I just told him if he didn't leave now, I was going to shove the chair leg where the sun doesn't shine," Viki smirked.

"I've never seen anyone move that fast," Mikey commented.

"With some practice, you should be able to," Viki stated.

Sabrina stayed unusually quiet.

"You okay?" Mikey nudged her.

"Yeah," she smiled, but it didn't reach her eyes. "I'll tell you later."

"So, you're telling me we can probably add super speed to Mikey's ability list?" Marcus tried to break the ice. "The Tribunal doesn't stand a chance. And I'm sure Thomas was just kidding about the killing you part...."

"I don't think he was," Sabrina said somberly. "It's like...he blames vampires for the death of Simon or something." Her brows furrowed.

"I agree. I don't think that Source user was joking around," Viki nodded. "But with your gifts, you should be fine. It would take an elder to take down a Verdaat. One that wasn't an ancient, of course."

The rest of lunch was spent talking about the Tribunal, and Marcus pestered Viki with questions. Mikey didn't mind because he was curious too. Sabrina chimed in here and there, but Mikey could tell something was still bothering her.

Soon, the end-of-lunch bell rang, and they all went to their following classes. Viki had wiggled her way into every one of Mikey's classes, so they walked together to the next. By the end of the day, Viki had become one of the most popular girls in school. Her 'tattooed laser eyes' were a big hit.

Mikey wished he had been more interested in art class, but Sabrina's solemn mood had continued. He hoped she'd open up at the Sect when Viki wasn't around.

"That was fun! High school is fun," Viki cheered as the last bell rang. "I know you're gonna go do your sorcerer stuff, so I'll see you tomorrow. Don't get killed before then."

She vanished again as they walked through the woods to the parking lot and buses. The three of them decided to go straight to the Sect to start practicing and studying. During the car ride, as Mikey had hoped, Sabrina opened up.

"You okay, Brina?" Marcus asked. Mikey was glad he had also noticed.

"Did you see how fast she moved? Thomas was rendered useless in the blink of an eye!" Sabrina cursed. "And he is one of our strongest acolytes."

"I'm not following...." Marcus looked puzzled.

"If that—" she pointed towards the school, "is what we are dealing with in the real world. We have a lot of work to do," she tsked. "At our current level, we wouldn't stand a chance against a monster like that."

"Hey—" Mikey started.

"No offense, stud," Sabina leaned over and pecked him on the cheek. "But we will just hold you back if we don't step up our game."

"I'm glad I'm not the only one who felt that way," Marcus agreed. "When she said Mikey would be able to move like that too...I thought I was in a little over my head."

"I'm sorry I dragged you guys into this mess," Mikey lamented. "We don't have to do this."

"You didn't drag us into anything. I was going to do this anyways, remember?" Sabrina assured. "If anything, today has woken me up. I know we probably won't get to your level. But we need to get to a point where we won't hold you back."

"I think with Arthur's method, I'll get there in time," Marcus declared.

"Good. We also need to keep in mind the elders are probably going to pull something unexpected." Sabrina reminded.

They pulled into the parking lot at the Wonder Bread Factory.

"Well, let's get this show started," Marcus stuck his hand out.

"Don't do it," Mikey grinned, placing his hand on Marcus's.

"So lame," Sabrina sighed and did the same.

"DREAM TEAM!" Marcus cheered.

CHAPTER 19

"Dammit. It needs to be stronger and faster!" Sabrina cursed.

The following Sunday came quickly, and the trio agreed to spar in their training room before meeting up with Luke.

"Ugh. It felt plenty strong and fast to me," Mikey grumbled. He pulled himself out of the rubble where Sabrina's Source-infused kick sent him flying.

"You're still standing," she smirked. "So definitely stronger and faster."

"I don't know if I'll ever get tired of seeing you get thrown into walls, Mikey," Marcus teased.

"Yeah, well...if I used my speed to dodge, I might've thrown myself into the wall."

After what Viki told him, Mikey had tried to move as she had at school. Instead, he ended up slamming face-first into a wall.

"I wasn't being specific. You throwing yourself into a wall counts too."

"Come on. Let's try the precision control of your void core, like we talked about. Is there any Source in the room?" Sabrina suggested.

After several discussions on what they all needed to practice, Mikey's void core had come up several times. He needed to be able to pinpoint which Source to absorb; otherwise, his team would be at risk.

In the week of training, Mikey had gotten to where he could acti-vate his vampiric eyes at will. The desires that came with it didn't lessen. But his control of it had.

"Yeah. There's some in the air. Let me see if I can only take that in," Mikey said. The doors in his void opened, and he tried to focus only on the ambient Source around him.

Rainbows of Source swirled into his hand as his friends' green and ruby red began to combine.

Come on! Mikey tried to tell his hand which energy to take, but it was no use.

"Nope. Shut it off," Marcus called out.

Mikey closed off the void, and his shoulders slumped. "I'm not sure it's possible to control that part of it."

"Don't lose heart," Sabrina squeezed his hand. "You didn't think this was possible before, right?"

"True," Mikey smiled a little.

"And if it isn't, we need to know how far of a reach it has so we can still use it as a trump card as long as we get out of range," Sabrina added.

"You're the best," Mikey kissed her.

"I really need a boyfriend," Marcus grumbled. He started making barfing sounds as Luke walked in.

"You need me to take a look at that?" Luke looked at Marcus with concern.

"He's just being a dork," Sabrina laughed.

"Yeah, young love just makes me ill. How've you been?" Marcus asked.

"Good. Looks like you've all been busy." Luke gestured to the destroyed concrete counter and wall. "I've got some stuff to show you that I've been working on. But I need a volunteer...Mikey?" he grinned. The sparkle of crazy in his eyes made Mikey want to run.

"Um, how about Marcus?" Mikey suggested.

"Nope. He called you man!"

"Don't worry. You'll be fine," Luke waved off their concerns. "You are a hearty vampire, and I've gotten this to work like three times now." Luke motioned for Mikey to come over, holding out his hand.

Mikey gulped and stuck his arm out.

"Now... I call this restore and decay. It might hurt a little bit." Luke threw in. "Just be still."

"I don't know about this," Sabrina interjected.

"Shh. Just watch. It'll be worth it," Luke insisted and closed his eyes. "Hold still."

Mikey jumped as white-blue tendrils came out of Luke's hands and entered his body.

"Stay still," Luke snapped.

Thirty seconds passed, and Mikey was about to say something until the skin on his arm began to itch. A black dot the size of a mole appeared on his forearm. Then Mikey stared in horror as the hole widened and grew deeper. His flesh rotted away, and the tissues underneath became visible. Amazingly, it hadn't hurt at all.

But then, it started to tingle...

Ouch. I'm starting to feel something now...

Pain shot through Mikey's arm like someone had stabbed him with a hot poker.

"Argh," Mikey yelped. "Make it stop. It burns!"

"Okay. Okay. That was decay. Time for restore." Luke's forehead crinkled as beads of sweat poured down his face. The pain started to ebb, and Mikey's skin and tissues began filling in and stitching together.

A minute later, Luke collapsed, panting but grinning from ear to ear. Mikey's arm looked untouched.

"That was some freaky stuff," Marcus said, wide-eyed.

"Incredible," Sabrina praised.

"What did you do to me?" Mikey examined his arm in awe.

"Essentially..." Luke held up a hand to catch his breath. "I turned my Source into flesh-eating bacteria. Of course, it's not bacteria, but I made it do the same thing they do...plus, I ramped up the speed. The rest was just normal healing."

"What would've happened if you hadn't healed me?" Mikey wondered.

"Well, the process would've continued, and your whole body would've necrosed until the Source wore out. It was a little touch and go there, but I was right about your vampiric healing helping the process along."

Sabrina's eyes narrowed. "What do you mean touch and go? How did you practice this?"

"On dead bodies, of course," Luke replied like it was obvious.

"Dude, that's messed up," Marcus grimaced.

"What?" Luke looked confused. "What else was I supposed to practice on? The issue was, once you're dead, you can't heal anymore. But I was pretty sure I could reverse it on Mikey."

"Pretty sure? You were pretty sure?" Sabrina scolded. "You could have killed him!"

"I needed to practice the technique!" Luke threw his hands up in exasperation. "I thought you guys would be excited. He's fine!"

They all looked at each other before Mikey shrugged and placed a hand on Luke's shoulder. "We are excited. It's an amazing ability. But next time, let's not practice on us?"

"Fine. But I could improve it much faster if you let me practice it on you," Luke grumbled.

The rest of the time, they discussed how they could use Luke's 'restore and decay' in combat. When it was time for Mikey's combatives with Elder Ryan, Sabrina suggested the rest of the team study until he was finished. Mikey tried not to laugh as they all acted like he was going to his funeral.

They were partially right.

"Again!" Elder Ryan bellowed as Mikey tried to dodge a barrage of orange-red Source bullets.

I think I dodged a few more than before?

In the hour they'd been training, Mikey's body had been bruised from head to toe. He felt like a practice dummy at the paintball range.

I shouldn't have told him about Viki.

When he'd mentioned her, the elder decided to change tactics and focus on improving Mikey's speed and reflexes using his vampiric eyes. Mikey thought it had been a good idea until, without warning, the elder had launched twenty bullets at him within a few seconds.

He'd dodged two of them.

"You did well. We'll continue same time next weekend. I would've liked to have gone a little longer. Unfortunately, I have other matters to attend to tonight." The Elder inclined his head, leaving Mikey panting in the corner.

Unfortunate for who?

Mikey decided to go to the cafeteria and get food for himself and Laken. After finding out how valuable her gift was, Mikey felt like a cookie wasn't enough.

He asked the worker at the cafeteria for a piece of paper and a pen. Mikey ripped a tiny square off and drew a heart with the chest next to it. He put it on the cookie, hoping she'd understand his gratitude. Mikey was disappointed the fairy wasn't there when he dropped it off.

Undeterred, he headed toward the TC and was glad to find the rest of his omada hard at work.

Marcus whistled as soon as he saw Mikey. "Boy, Elder Ryan sure did a number on you."

Sabrina turned and winced as soon as she saw him. "Ouch. Are you okay?"

"Yeah, it's more painful than it looks," Mikey chuckled. "Remind me to never get on the elder's bad side."

"If you'd like, I can use my repair and—"

"No thanks Luke," Mikey interjected. "I'll be fine. Would you mind if I took a little of you guys' Source?"

When they all agreed, Mikey couldn't believe how lucky he was to have such great friends. Relief flooded him as his void core took in the offered energy. The pain ebbed, and Mikey knew his body was already beginning to heal.

"Thanks, guys."

"You're welcome," Sabrina smiled. "Now sit your butt down and open up a book. Just because you have a perfect memory doesn't mean you don't actually have to read this stuff. Let's get in another hour."

"Yes, ma'am," Marcus saluted.

Luke and Mikey joined in on the salute. Sabrina rolled her eyes, shaking her head.

Omada Taktiki wasn't being used by anyone, and Mikey remembered Marcus mentioning it. He opened the first page and dug in.

A bajillion more books to go.

CHAPTER 20

The months flew by as the dream team trained and studied.

Viki had become a part of their group at school and after. She'd trained him—rather violently, in his opinion—to use his Verdaat abilities. With her help, he could soon dodge almost all of Elder Ryan's bullet barrage. Sabrina still wasn't Viki's biggest fan but accepted her support for his sake. Mikey had come to call the pesky vampire a friend.

Thomas had steered clear, surprisingly. Marcus had told them his brother wouldn't even talk to him anymore. He'd put on a front for them, but Mikey knew all this wasn't easy for his friend. But they agreed to focus on nothing else but the Tribunal.

In what little free time he had, Mikey worked on something in secret. It still wasn't stable, but Mikey felt he'd have it ready in time. Unfortunately, there was no progress when it came to his void core. It drained everything within a hundred feet of Mikey, starting from the center.

"We'll just have to use it as a trump card if we can get clear of you," Sabrina had said.

Sabrina's Source control improved by leaps and bounds. Shortly after their first two weeks of sparring, she'd had an epiphany. She could propel herself at incredible speeds if she blasted her Source behind her legs. After several broken bones, which she begrudgingly let Luke help heal, Sabrina could almost keep up with Mikey. Coupled with her natural ability to project Source from her legs, she was a force to be reckoned with.

Marcus had gotten to the point of folding a shield five times—almost six—he liked to remind everyone. Though he could only hold it for a couple of minutes, it was close to impenetrable. If Marcus projected it to someone else, it dropped to thirty seconds. He'd also become proficient with a short staff which Mikey hadn't known his friend was practicing with.

Luke's 'restore and decay' had become something truly terrifying. Mikey had agreed to one last demonstration the week prior after Luke promised he had it completely under control.

Within a few seconds, the skin on Mikey's entire arm had rotted away. Mikey waited for the burn, but Luke smiled, saying the nerve synapses couldn't fire and he wouldn't feel a thing. The Healer's repair had grown the skin back almost as fast as it had eaten it away.

"Just give me a few moments to touch an enemy, and they'll be done," he'd told them. That wasn't all. Luke had taken the ability a step further and had become somewhat of an Adept. He could toss out globs of decay Source about six feet in front of him.

Snapping himself out of his thoughts, Mikey walked through the Sect, which had transformed into organized chaos as the Tribunal grew closer. Elders and Jaecar from all over the globe had come to watch.

"Where is it held?" Mikey asked Sabrina as their group headed for their isolation room for some last-minute training.

"The written and individual tests are held here. But I have no idea where the omada portion is held. You have to porter to it, though," Sabrina answered.

A group of Jaecar Mikey had never seen strolled towards them down the hallway. A tall blonde man in the middle was wearing the gold Orion pin on his shirt. Mikey thought he looked like a TV weatherman. He would have just said the customary 'elder' and continued, but the man looked at him like he was the plague.

"Ah. If it isn't the half-monster orphan boy," the man snickered. A few of the Jaecar behind him did the same.

Why does every asshole get an entourage?

"Elder Tem," Sabrina inclined her head.

"Oh, your poor mother, Sabrina. To have a daughter join an omada with this," the man eyed Mikey up and down with disgust— "being."

Mikey didn't care if people made fun of him or looked at him the way Thomas did. He was used to that. But when someone put down his omada, that crossed the line. Mikey's jaw clenched as he wrangled with his desire to strangle the man. But Elder Ryan's warning rang in his head.

Cool it, Mikey. Now you're acting like Thomas.

"My mother is doing quite well. Thank you," Sabrina retorted.

"I'm sure she is," Elder Tem sneered.

"I'm Marcus, and this is Luke," Marcus chimed in.

"I don't care," he turned up his nose. The elder turned to Mikey with a sinister grin plastered on his face. "I am looking forward to your tribunal."

"Elder," Mikey inclined his head.

They won't get a rise out of me.

"Who was Elder Bond Villain?" Marcus chuckled after they'd left.

"Elder Tem is one of the ten elders of the high council. They're the head honchos of Haven. He's the Sect leader in California and a total snake. Every chance my mom has had to join the council, he's done everything in his power to sabotage," Sabrina snapped.

"I thought Jaecar were all noble warriors," Mikey teased.

"There are crappy people in everything," she replied.

"I'm not sure I liked how he talked about the Tribunal," Luke added.

"No use in worrying about it now," Marcus said. "Let's just focus on kicking Mikey's butt for a couple of hours."

"Deal," the other two said a little too quickly for Mikey's comfort.

His omada had agreed—excluding Mikey, of course—that since he was technically a creature of OS, it would be best to train against him. He didn't mind, though, as the three vs. one had forced him to get stronger much faster...or be mincemeat.

As they arrived in the training room, his opponents wasted no time. Sabrina used her Source-powered legs to maneuver behind Mikey and go for a leg sweep. Grinning, Mikey dove out of the way and activated his vampiric eyes.

Always with the surprise attacks.

Mikey brought the Source into his right hand, and the claw flared to life. His three companions backed him into a corner. Mikey lunged for Luke, slashing at his chest. Sparks of blue and green Source bounced off the contact, but it hadn't connected. Marcus's shield had appeared just in time. Mikey didn't slow as a ruby-red ball of Source hit the wall where his head had been. His eyes went wide at the softball-sized indent.

"Hold him down so I can use my decay," Luke smirked.

"Not happening." Mikey blurred behind Sabrina, wrapping his arms around her from behind. "Save me from the monster," he whispered in her ear. His strength was no joke. There was no way Sabrina would be able to wriggle out.

"Nope," she grinned as the Source blasted from her legs, hurling them backward. Mikey's back slammed into the concrete counter. He still held on to Sabrina as the air was knocked from his lungs.

"Careful. I have a beautiful hostage, and I'm not afraid to—" Mikey teased until Marcus's staff, which felt more like a crowbar, smashed into the side of his leg. Simultaneously, Luke landed a punch on the opposite side of his face.

Mikey leaped over Sabrina with his one good leg as pain radiated from all over. He landed in a roll and turned to his attackers in the same motion. Blood poured from his right eye obscuring his vision. His left leg was throbbing, and Mikey could hardly put any weight on it.

"I think you broke my back Bri," Mikey wheezed.

"It's the price you pay for taking a hostage," she grinned. "Let's take a ten-minute break, then get back to it. But no playing around this time." Sabrina gave Mikey the 'I'm serious' look.

He put his arms up in defeat.

I thought it was funny.

"Way to take advantage of the situation, guys," Mikey grimaced as he slumped to the floor.

"Like Sabrina said... shouldn't have taken a hostage," Marcus sat next to him.

"I'm just glad I get all this practice," Luke grinned as he began to heal the team. Soon, they were back at it again.

By the session's end, all four were bloodied, bruised, and exhausted; Mikey was a little more so. He'd forced them to give up three times to his five. Two of those were because of Luke's decay. It was more painful than having his meridians shut off.

"Is it just me, or is your death touch even more painful?"

"No. It's not just you," Luke puffed out his chest. "I tweaked it again so it activates pain receptors as it travels. Nice, right?"

"No. Not nice," Mikey shook his head.

"Exactly," Luke smirked.

"I think we should just rest up until the Tribunal," Sabrina suggested. "It would do us some good, and two days more won't make much of a difference."

"I agree," Marcus chimed in. "We've been going nonstop for months. Time for some R&R."

"Sounds good," Mikey agreed.

"That's fine," Luke added.

"Hangout at Mikey's place?" Marcus suggested. "I want to talk to Arthur about a couple of things."

"I'm sure he won't mind if that's cool with everyone else," Mikey answered.

Luke apologized, saying he had some things to work on at the clinic before heading out.

Probably wants to tweak decay, so a whole limb falls off in half a second.

"You know Viki is going to show up," Sabrina crossed her arms as they headed for the porter room. "She's a stalker."

"Be nice. Without her, I'd be slamming into walls still. And she's stopped with the whole handsy thing."

"I still don't trust her," she shook her head.

"Still? After all this time..." Mikey trailed off. They'd had this conversation many times before.

Viki had opened up to him one night when they were alone. She'd told him about her father forcing her to fight and train at the age of four. How she was always alone except for her mother and a woman named Brittania. Mikey couldn't explain to Sabrina what growing up with the kind of loneliness they had was like. It was more painful than anything. More than Luke's decay.

"I don't care," Marcus blurted, bringing Mikey out of his somber thoughts. "I've hit a roadblock and need some advice from the top dog. To the Marcmobile!"

"Such a dork," Sabrina snorted.

Mikey laughed, grateful for the distraction.

When they got to Marcus's car, and Mikey got a signal again, he texted Arthur to let him know their plans.

"*Sure. Pizza?*" he texted back.

"Hell yeah!" Marcus cheered when Mikey showed him the text. "We're going to Mikey's and getting pizza."

Mikey texted back the pie requests, and soon they'd arrived at his house.

"Hey, gang." Arthur greeted them at the door. "Pizza should be here in about five minutes."

They each gave him a hug before heading in.

"Okay. Arthur. I need some more of your ancient wisdom. You two can run along upstairs or whatever," Marcus waved them off.

Whoa, déjà vu.

Mikey didn't mind, though. He hadn't had alone time with Sabrina in a few days.

"Sure. Holler if you need rescuing Arthur," Sabrina teased before grabbing Mikey's hand and heading for his room.

They lay on his bed, cuddling while Mikey stroked her arm. So much had changed in the last five months. He'd changed. And so much of it was because of her.

"What's wrong?" Sabrina wiped the tear from his eye.

"Nothing. Just happy right now. I never imagined I'd be able to do this with someone, let alone someone as wonderful as you."

"Oh—" She snuggled into him. "Me too."

"Any room for me?" Viki's voice came from the doorway.

"I knew you'd show up," Sabrina sighed.

"You know you guys missed me," she rolled her eyes. "How did training go? Did Mikey show your little squad what's what this time? Did he show you his special sorcerer move?"

"What special sorcerer move?" Sabrina's brows furrowed as she turned to Mikey.

"Oop—" Viki covered her mouth, feigning surprise. "Was I supposed to keep that a secret? I mean, your big tournament is only a couple days away, right? I thought he'd use it."

"I could strangle you," Mikey glared at Viki, then turned to Sabrina. "I've just been practicing something, but it's not ready yet. I wanted to save it for the Tribunal. And after today, maybe see the surprised look on Elder Tem's stupid face."

"Why does she know about it, then?" Sabrina's eyebrow rose.

"Only because of what you said before. Viki's a stalker."

"I am not a stalker. I am a diligent security detail," the yellow-eyed vampire harumphed.

"Except no one hired you. And you...what? Hide in the bushes outside Mikey's house? How else do you know when he's home?"

"Pfft, I have cameras up..." Viki trailed off.

"Stalker," Mikey and Sabrina smirked.

"I—" Viki struggled for a comeback when Marcus yelled from below.

"Pizza's here. You can stop the hanky panky and come downstairs."

They hurried downstairs to grab a slice. Marcus was notorious for hogging.

"Did Arthur help you with your questions?" Mikey asked between bites of his pepperoni lovers.

"Yeah. Like always. But...any chance you could let me skip the seventh fold and give me the present you talked about now, Arthur?" Marcus inquired.

"If you can't fold your shield at least that many times the compactor would be useless," Arthur told him.

"It's called the compactor? Now you gotta tell me what it is!" Marcus pleaded.

"Nope. You need the incentive. You'll get there," Arthur patted his shoulder. "Keep your head up. It took me almost ten years to develop the shield fold and several more to get to six."

That seemed to brighten up Marcus's sour face.

"How are your nerves, son?" Arthur turned to Mikey.

"Not bad. I have complete faith in my team. I'm just worried about the basic shield part. I have a nagging feeling about what 'altering the Tribunal accordingly' means."

After months of trying, Mikey had yet to form a primary shield. He had talked to Elder Ryan about it, but he told Mikey not to worry, that his natural defenses more than made up for it.

"I think Ryan was right about the shield part. You're tough as nails." Arthur reassured him. "It's the part about changing the Tribunal that concerns me. It would take a lot of powerful people to agree to that."

"I'm not worried. I'm sure Wonderboy here and his little team can handle a few human sorcerers," Viki stated. "Besides, Sabrina can just attitude them into submission."

Sabrina stuck out her tongue, and they all laughed.

"In all seriousness," Arthur continued. "If what you've told me is true and they consider you a real threat to Haven, they might do something drastic, and Cass might not have any say in it. Keep your wits about you. I wouldn't put anything past the high council."

"Elder Tem made a snide comment about it earlier today," Marcus added.

"Ugh. That scoundrel," Arthur frowned. "He was always trying to weasel his way to the top. I shouldn't have left Haven just to stop him from taking my seat.

Mikey's eyes went wide. "I didn't know you were on the high council."

"I did," Marcus nodded.

"Yep. Me too," Sabrina joined in.

"Actually. Me also," Viki admitted.

"Man! Just when I thought I was up to speed with everything," Mikey tsked.

"Sorry. I guess it never really came up. But it doesn't change much. Just be ready for anything," Arthur warned.

"Right," Mikey nodded.

"I just wish I could be there to see you. But I gave up that right," Arthur's shoulders slumped.

"It's all right, gramps," Viki winked. "I can't go either. But I have faith in our Mikey--and his team, I guess."

"If you call me gramps again, you can stay outside from now on," Arthur smirked.

Viki raised her hands in submission, laughing.

The night passed too quickly for Mikey's tastes, and soon the party was over. Marcus and Sabrina went home, and Viki went—wherever Viki went. Mikey decided to spend the next few days improving his new technique and keeping his anxiety at bay.

Despite what he'd told Arthur, he was nervous about the Tribunal. Thomas was working himself to death with the goal of ending Mikey's life. Elder Ryan's and Sabrina's warnings about the council also didn't sit well.

Mikey walked up to his room after saying goodnight to Arthur, hoping that drawing would ease some of his fears. It had been almost two months since he'd picked up a pencil. There hadn't been time. After several hours and one perfect abomination put to paper, Mikey crawled into bed. He was right. The drawing had helped, and sleep came quickly.

CHAPTER 21

Nerves were high, and the sect was abuzz. The training center had been transformed into a testing center with various rooms set up for individual written and practical exams. *Well, the TC is still the TC.* Mikey chuckled to himself. His omada stood in line with the rest of the acolytes determined to become Jaecar. Thomas was there with some of the goons Mikey had seen following him around. When he noticed Mikey, he brought a finge and slid it across his throat.

The dude's got problems.

"We'll take him out quick like we planned, then the rest of his team should fall easily," Sabrina whispered next to him.

"Yeah..." Mikey sighed.

"Take your test booklet and answer sheet and proceed to the room written at the top right corner of your form." A woman Mikey had seen before handed him a thick, white paper packet. He noticed her blue Orion pin.

Damn. How many test questions are there?

Mikey looked at Marcus, who went white as the Jaecar handed him a packet.

"You got this!" he encouraged.

"Easy for you to say with your genetic cheat sheet." Marcus tapped Mikey on the head for emphasis.

"Relax," Sabrina said calmly. "This is what we've been busting our butts for. After we all pass the written portion, there are our basic shielding and individual archetype tests. Then, it's just the omada portion tomorrow...somewhere."

At the mention of the shielding test, Mikey's anxiety grew.

What if I overestimated how easy the written test was going to be? What if I fail the shielding part and let everyone down?

Taking several deep breaths, Mikey pushed his fears down and followed the others through a white door into a hallway he'd never seen. It was empty except for light-grey walls and numbered doors every six feet. It was even plainer than the rest of the sect.

Mikey found the door with his number and walked into a red-walled room slightly bigger than a walk-in closet. In the center was a brown school desk with two pencils and a small plastic sharpener resting on top.

"Hello," a voice boomed from a speaker in the corner of the room, making Mikey flinch. "This is Sect leader Cassandra. You all have chosen to become Jaecar and take the Tribunal. You have three hours to take the exam. There will be no breaks. You will stay in this room until you are finished. Everyone in your omada must pass, or you all fail. I wish you the best of luck. Begin."

Here we go.

Marcus had been right. This part of the Tribunal was practically cheating for Mikey. The first part of the test was on fighting formations, which depended on which archetypes and number of people were in the omada. For example, a tight square formation was best if a group consisted of four Movers. Each Mover would scan their angle for threats and notify the others.

There were questions about different types of supernatural creatures, their abilities, and the best ways to kill them.

Three hundred and eighty questions encompassing the basics every Jaecar should know by heart. Mikey had finished with over an hour to spare. He briefly thought about getting up and seeing if he could leave but thought better of it. It could cause too many issues.

What if that was disqualifying?

Elder Cassandra didn't say anything about leaving when you were done. And he didn't need to give anyone else more reason to dislike him. They'd resent him even more if he walked out way ahead of the others.

So, Mikey sat there patiently. Knowing his team was doing their best and hoping it would be enough. Until now, it hadn't really occurred to Mikey how much an omada meant to becoming a Jaecar. Throughout the entire Tribunal, if anyone failed, they all did. He realized now how big of a decision it was for his friends to join him. He chuckled at the memory of Luke volunteering out of the blue. The crazy Healer he'd come to call a friend.

I'm a lucky guy.

"Your time is up," Elder Cassandra's voice boomed through the speaker sometime later. "Put the pencils down. Leave the room with your test and answer sheet and hand them to the person who gave them to you. You'll be notified in one hour if you pass. Be at the TC before then. The basic shielding portion will begin shortly after."

As Mikey searched for his team, other acolytes poured out of their testing rooms. Marcus came out of the room two doors down from him, looking like he'd seen a ghost. Sabrina and Luke were further down the hallway.

"We'll see," was all Marcus would say. It looked like the test could have gone better.

"Regardless, I'm proud to be in an omada with you," Mikey stated.

"Until we get the test results," Marcus snorted. But his comment had seemed to put Marcus more at ease. "We'll see," he mumbled.

Sabrina and Luke seemed to be in better spirits as they joined them.

"We did our best," Sabrina shrugged, seeing that the test had gotten to Marcus. "Let's go get some grub."

The group headed for the cafeteria, and Mikey reminded himself to leave a present for Laken. He'd left a Rice-Crispy treat a few weeks ago, which seemed to have been a hit. The last time she showed herself, Mikey tried to introduce Sabrina, but Laken disappeared and wouldn't return.

"Maybe it's because you aren't fully human?" Sabrina suggested.

Whatever the reason, it was clear that she didn't want to be seen by anyone else but Mikey.

The next thirty minutes were spent with Marcus, asking them the answer to every question he could think of on his test. Mikey was grateful when Sabrina told them it was time to head back. He dropped off a marshmallow treat for his little friend.

Back at the TC, the acolytes waited to find out their results. The loudspeaker crackled before Elder Cassandra's voice came through. "I will now call out the results. Remember that even if your team cannot continue today, there is another Tribunal in six months. Use this as a lesson to train and study harder."

Mikey gave his team a thumbs up.

"Acolyte Sabrina Adelmund—"

Everyone seemed to hold their breath.

"—Your omada passed."

"Woo!" Marcus cheered.

"Quiet," someone from another group hissed.

"Acolyte John Rise," Elder Cassandra continued. "Two of your members failed."

One of the members, clearly from John Rise's omada, punched a wall before storming off. Four acolytes went after him.

Relief flooded Mikey. He didn't even pay attention to the other groups being called until he heard Thomas's name.

"Acolyte Thomas Sante...one of your members failed."

"No!" Thomas roared. He turned to the three members of his group. "Which one of you idiots failed!"

The rest of his omada cowered at his rage when Elder Ryan stepped up behind him. "Enough! That is no way to treat the members of your team. Maybe if you focused on helping them instead of just yourself, you would have succeeded," the Elder scoffed.

"That's...I—I'll take them on myself!" Thomas blurted. "You can make an exception. I don't need the others."

The rest of the acolytes snickered, but Mikey looked concerned. Thomas seemed desperate and afraid.

What is going on with him?

"That is not allowed. Your group is no longer a part of the Tribunal. I will find you sometime later to discuss your punishment for this outburst. You may go," Elder Ryan replied.

Thomas looked hopeless. Like a lost puppy that didn't know where to go or what to do. It was so pathetic that Mikey wanted to comfort him.

Or not.

The look Thomas now gave him wasn't the loud 'spit in your face' kind of hate he was used to. It was calm and cold, sending shivers down Mikey's spine. Without another word, Thomas left the TC.

"I liked it better when he was screaming," Luke said.

"Me too," Mikey replied.

At the end of the written exam, only four of the seven omada that had come to take the Tribunal were left.

"I wasn't expecting that," Marcus looked worried. "He's hardly home and spends all his time studying and training. I tried to get him to open up about this obsession of his..., but he just gets angry. I miss my brother."

Mikey wanted to comfort his friend, but Elder Ryan's voice rang throughout the TC. "Congratulations to all who have passed the written exam. Next, you will be tested on your basic shield control and individual archetype abilities. There will be three elders to judge your performance. Lucian Blodwell, will you please go into training room 103."

Elder Ryan called out the acolytes one by one, assigning them a room. He squeezed Sabrina's hand when her name was called and wished her luck.

By the end, Mikey found himself alone. He didn't think anything of it until Elder Ryan stood in front of him, his expression serious. "I'm not supposed to say anything. But they've gone too far. Maintain your control and do not give in. No. Matter. What."

"What does—"

"Remember what I said. Room 107," Elder Ryan motioned toward the door of his room.

Okay. That's not vague and ominous at all. You've got this, Mikey.

He took a few deep breaths to steady his nerves before opening the door to Room 107. It looked like the same training rooms Mikey was used to, except near the entrance was a large table with three metal folding chairs. One of those chairs was occupied by Elder Tem, the other by Elder Cassandra. The door was shut behind them as Elder Ryan took the third and final seat.

"Acolyte Mikey," Elder Cassandra greeted. "We have been informed that you cannot form your basic shield. But Elder Ryan has assured us that due to your—heritage, your natural defenses should prove sufficient. I motion that we skip this portion and move straight to the archetype test."

"I concur," Elder Ryan declared. But the look on his face gave Mikey the impression it wouldn't be that easy.

"As much as I respect and trust the word of my fellow elders here. As a high council member, I must see for myself," Elder Tem interjected.

"Is this really necess—" Elder Ryan started, but a look from the Sect leader ended the discussion.

"Stand at the opposite end of the wall, acolyte," Elder Tem ordered, cracking his fingers. Something about the look in his eyes unnerved Mikey. Still, he did what he was told.

"Now, the purpose of a basic shield is to offer a modicum of protection from monster attacks. If your natural toughness is akin to our shields, this shouldn't do too much damage."

Before he could figure out what Elder Tem meant, the Elder's hand punched outward in a blur. Mikey activated his vampiric eyes just in time to see a soft-ball-sized, crimson orb of Source slam into his shoulder. The impact spun his body, lifting him into the air. Mikey landed with a crack, skidding across the floor until the wall at the back of the room stopped him with a crunch.

Bastard!

Mikey realized how much Elder Ryan had been pulling back his shots in their training. He struggled to stand. His right arm refused to obey. Undeterred, Mikey managed to get to his feet despite the room spinning and his right arm hanging loosely at his side.

"I think that was a little extreme," Elder Cassandra scowled.

"What? The boy is obviously fine. Just a little dislocated shoulder," Elder Tem waved it off.

"Even with a basic shield, the strength of that blast would have taken a normal acolyte's arm off," Elder Ryan glared daggers at him.

"I had faith in your reports that the boy could handle it," Elder Tem shrugged. "Besides, you have Neema here."

Elder Ryan slid his chair back and walked over to Mikey. "Here, let me pop it back into place."

"Thanks," Mikey was grateful.

"Alright, on the count of three."

Mikey nodded, bracing himself.

"One..."

"Wait, you're not gonna do the thing where you say it's on three, but you do it on tw—aagh," Mikey yelped as his shoulder popped back into place. The pain gave way to relief as feeling rushed back to his arm.

"Wonderful. I agree that the boy's natural toughness is sufficient. On to the next test," Elder Tem clapped his hands together excitedly.

"Remember what I said. Stay in control," Elder Ryan whispered so only Mikey could hear.

Instead of returning to his chair, Elder Ryan went outside the room, and Jaecar Michelle followed behind him, holding another chair. When she looked at Mikey, her expression changed for a moment.

Was that guilt? And what is she doing here?

Michelle placed the chair in the center of the room, and Mikey saw it wasn't like the foldable chairs the elders were sitting on. It was wooden and had straps on the armrests and feet. She sat in it, and Elder Ryan secured her arms and legs.

"How is this supposed to test my Source control?" Mikey puzzled.

"Well, it does test your Source control, in a way," Elder Tem snickered. "I've been told all about your abilities, and the thing we on the high council are most concerned about isn't you controlling your Source. It's controlling yourself."

"What do you mean?" Mikey's brow furrowed.

"I mean," Elder Tem scoffed like Mikey was an idiot. "We've been told you enjoy taking Source from others, and the longer you use your abilities, the less you are in control. How dangerous would it be for your companions if, after a tough battle, your darker urges took over?"

"That would never happen," Mikey shook his head. But he realized quickly the road this conversation was going down. He HAD lost control. Several times.

"Oh? Is that right? Then how come we've received several reports of that exact occurrence. Hmm? And it happened once at your high school no less. Thank goodness Arthur was there to stop you," Elder Tem feigned concern.

Mikey realized that denying it would get him nowhere. Even though all he wanted to do was leap over the table and drain the Elder's Source within an inch of his life.

"What does Michelle have to do with this?" Mikey growled. "And why is she strapped down?"

"I thought that would be more enticing for you. There aren't many vampires who could resist a bleeding helpless human in front of them. And since you aren't attracted to blood like your other kind, I have decided to try something else to entice you. Let's see if the monster within you can be stopped."

"I don't—What do you want me to do?" Mikey sighed.

"I want you to activate that claw I heard about and keep those eyes going until I say stop. And if I feel you steal even a hint of Source during any of it, I will disqualify you."

"You don't have the authority to disqualify him," Elder Cassandra barked. "I didn't have a say in this mockery of our Tribunal, but there are three here for a reason. It takes two votes to fail an acolyte."

"If the boy keeps his claw activated and his meridians closed for, say... thirty minutes. Then he passes. Is that acceptable?" Elder Ryan suggested.

"Ha. The boy will be foaming at the mouth for Source. I don't even know of a Jaecar who can use an ability like that constantly for more than fifteen. You have a deal," Elder Tem grinned smugly.

Thirty minutes?

Mikey had never kept his abilities going that long. He'd be starving for Source even if he could.

This isn't fair.

After all the work he'd put into controlling his Source, they throw it in his face.

No. Not them. It was Elder Tem, it was Thomas, and others like him. Mikey realized it was essential he made the distinction.

The anxiety Mikey thought he'd finally gotten rid of these last few months began to rear its ugly head. It told him to quit. To go back home with Arthur and back to drawing. He'd learned to shut the void core in his hand. A normal life was possible now. Marcus and Sabrina would forgive him, and they could still go to school together. His omada would fail the Tribunal, but someone else would come along.

Maybe after I'm gone, Thomas will join back with them.

"Don't let them break you...." a whisper dragged him out of his thoughts.

It was Michelle's voice, Mikey realized. She was strapped down in the chair two feet in front of him. "Don't let it be all for nothing." Her mouth barely moved, but Mikey heard it.

She's right.

What was the point of the last six months? Of all the broken bones, the pain, the joy, and the friends he'd made. Was he going to throw it all away because of a few assholes? Like Sabrina had said, they were everywhere. And if he gave up, they'd get what they wanted, him out of the picture one way or another.

And who was Mikey kidding? The high council wouldn't let him just live in peace. They'd probably think it was too risky, and maybe he'd join the Verdaat, and it was best to take care of him. It might even put Arthur at risk.

No.

His best bet was to succeed here and now. To join the Jaecar and grow stronger. It was the only way he'd be able to protect those he cared about and, at the same time, give a big 'screw you' to the assholes that stood in his way.

"Mikey," Elder Ryan cleared his throat. "Do you accept these terms?"

"Thank you," Mikey mouthed to Michelle before turning to the elders. "Yes. I do." He raised his head defiantly.

"Good," Elder Ryan nodded. "Then the time begins when your Source weapon is summoned."

Mikey turned his back to the elders and took a few deep breaths before bringing the Source to his right hand; his claw flared to life.

After a few minutes, Mikey began to think the test might be easier than he thought.

But as the ten-minute mark approached, the slight itch in his hand had turned into a gnawing ache. The doors of his void core fought to be opened. Sweat dripped from every pore of his body, and the hunger grew. Still, Mikey held on.

The minutes ticked away, and Mikey began to doubt he had enough Source to keep his claw going.

A voice grumbled somewhere in the distance. Mikey briefly registered Elder Tem, who was no doubt trying to make him lose focus. But Mikey could barely note which voices were real and which weren't. He suspected his mind was playing tricks.

"Remember how good it feels? It'll make all this pain go away..." it whispered to him.

Mikey had needed to look away at some point. Staring at the vibrant green of Michelle's Source would've pushed him over the edge. Mikey's body began to tremble.

*Don't let them break you...*Mikey replayed Michelle's words. He held onto the thoughts of Sabrina and his friends. How they put their faith in him. How they were a team.

But as Mikey's hunger grew, an inhuman, bestial part of himself began to emerge. It wanted out. Demanded it! All while promising all the power in the world.

"Hungry. Hungry. Hungry. Open your eyes. Look! Look at the Source in front of you. It's yours for the taking. It could all be yours. Let me out! LET ME OUT!"

Mikey was overcome with profound terror. The Wendigos, his childhood, and even the thought of losing another person he loved didn't come close to the horror of what would happen if this creature inside him was freed. It showed him visions of what would come. Blackened, grotesque tendrils erupted from the darkness in his left hand as it stabbed into the people around him, draining them of their life. Nothing could stand in his way as Mikey drained them all, whether it was vampire, human, or beast.

"Never!" Mikey yelled as the darkness inside warred for control. It couldn't be set free.

His eyes flew open at the familiar icy jolt of his meridians being forcefully shut off. Everything was blurry, but soon, the concerned face of Michelle began forming as his vision cleared.

"Mikey. Mikey, it's over. You did it." She shook him.

"Wha—what?" Mikey mumbled.

"Open your meridians. Take some of my Source," Michelle offered, grabbing his left hand.

Mikey was disoriented, but his body greedily took the offered energy and cried out in relief. The creature inside of him had disappeared back into wherever dark part of him it dwelled. As Mikey became more aware of his surroundings, the realization of where he was flooded back. He closed his meridians again and turned to the three elders behind him.

Elder Ryan and Cassandra were both smiling, while Elder Tem managed to look both surprised and angry at the same time. Usually, Mikey would've been happy at the look on his face, but none of them knew how close they'd been to losing their lives. He didn't realize how truly powerful the elders were, but Mikey believed the beast inside of him had shown the truth.

He shuddered at the memory.

"Well. I believe that concludes this test," Elder Cassandra stood up. "Pass."

"Pass." Elder Ryan nodded.

Elder Tem's upper lip curled with disdain as his eyes narrowed at Mikey. "Pass."

"Thank you, Michelle, for your assistance." Elder Cassandra inclined her head.

A thought occurred to Mikey. How could Michelle have been beside him when she was tied down? Mikey got his answer when he saw the chair. The straps, along with the armrests, had been ripped clear off. Michelle must've torn herself free as soon as his time had been up.

Their eyes met as she saw that he'd come to the realization of what had happened. Michelle smiled warmly at Mikey as he mouthed 'thank you' once again before she left.

"Mikey," Elder Cassandra addressed him once the door closed behind Michelle. "The omada battle will be tomorrow morning. Be at the TC at nine a.m. sharp. You should rest until then."

"Does that mean everyone else passed?" Mikey wondered. He almost laughed at the prospect of one of his friends not making it after what he'd just been through.

That would be the icing on the messed-up cake that is my life. He suddenly hoped the cafeteria had some cake.

"Yes. I received confirmation while you were...indisposed. Congratulations. We will see you tomorrow." The elders left. Elder Tem gave him one last look of disdain, and Mikey thought he saw a hint of fear.

Yeah. I scare myself too.

He laid on his back, staring at the ceiling for a few minutes before heading out to meet his friends. They recounted their tales of harrowing triumph, and Mikey hoped he appeared as excited as possible. But the memory of the monster inside him and a nagging worry about tomorrow's battle left him uneasy.

After they'd celebrated at Marcus's favorite restaurant, an arcade down on Main Street, the gang split early to get a much-needed break. Mikey had hoped Viki would show up earlier so he could ask her about what had happened during his test. But for some reason, she was in the wind.

It was only when Mikey was just about to fall asleep that a tap on his window made him jump up. He pulled back the curtain to reveal Viki standing on the roof waving. She'd do it every so often, and Mikey felt she just wanted someone to talk to.

"I got your text. What's up?" Viki said, climbing through.

"Surprised you weren't 'guarding me' today," Mikey chuckled.

"Uh, yeah. I had some other stuff to do," Viki crossed her arms. "But it went well, it seems?"

"If you call changing the rules and forcing me to starve myself of Source so they can see if I turn into a Source-sucking monster...then yeah, it went well."

"Ouch. So, did you...turn into a "source-sucking" monster?" She asked, doing air quotes.

"No. But I almost did."

"What was it like?" Viki probed.

"Honestly, it was terrifying. It felt like—like there was some sort of demon inside of me. And it was talking to me. Telling me to let it out so it can take the Source from everyone. I saw visions of me scouring the earth for Source; nothing could stop me...."

"Holy crap. I mean—it kinda sounds like Edax but more extreme. I've never heard of it making anyone have visions or it talking or anything," Viki said.

"What's Edax?"

"It's what the Verdaat call their hunger. It means devouring or devourer. There aren't many reasons one of my kind wouldn't go without blood for long, but it's happened before. It's like this hunger takes over, and that's all you can think about."

"That kinda sounds like it for the most part. Mine seemed more separate from me," Mikey puzzled.

"Maybe because you're half human...yours is different?"

"It's as good an explanation as any," Mikey shrugged. "Still, it scared me."

"Like you said, though, it tried to take over, and you beat it. You'll just have to do it again if it ever comes to that."

"It's all I can do," Mikey nodded somberly. He knew Viki was trying to cheer him up, but the thought of that thing taking control of him...

Am I too dangerous to be alive?

"Hey. Cheer up, you passed your baby competition." Viki punched his arm playfully.

"Sorry. I'll be fine. You're right. After tomorrow it's just the ceremonial hunt."

And then it's official.

He'd be a Jaecar and get to see the world. Sure, some of the time would be spent hunting dangerous monsters. But there was a lot of time off too. Maybe he'd go with Viki to visit the Verdaat. Though seeing her father didn't sound appealing. But Mikey did start to feel a bit better thinking about what his life would be like. He'd be doing something noble with Sabrina and his friends.

It was late, but they talked for a bit longer. Viki told him more tales of her travels. About the different creatures she'd encountered and the places she wanted to go next.

Mikey liked it when Viki talked like this. She seemed more herself.

She said some things that gave Mikey the impression that she wanted to get something off her chest, but that moment never came.

"Hey, Mikey..." Viki started, but she wouldn't meet his eyes.

"What is it?" Mikey invited.

Her eyebrows crinkled in frustration, but then her face hardened. "Nothing. Just good luck with your thing tomorrow. Don't die."

"Thanks?"

Like always, Viki disappeared off to god-knows-where, and Mikey was left with the stillness of the crisp winter night. After crawling back to bed, he laid there for a while, concerned sleep wouldn't come. But exhaustion won out; after making sure his alarm was still set for 7:30 a.m., he was asleep.

CHAPTER 22

"Baby got back!" Mikey's phone alarm rang. He groaned, turning it off just as Sir Mix a Lot got to "big butts, and I cannot lie."

He laughed and tried to remember when Marcus could have gotten him again. It was the third time he'd changed his ringtone. Mikey stretched and was pleased to realize the ache in his shoulder was gone.

Thank goodness I was able to get some sleep. And for vampire healing.

Today, he would face whatever the high council would throw at him. There was no reason to believe this would be their only attempt to kill him or ensure he got the message that he worked for Haven.

The organization ultimately had good intentions, but Mikey realized it wasn't the beacon of justice and valor he'd initially thought. It had its problems. That didn't matter, though. Today he would start the next chapter in his life. A life he never would've thought possible before.

Mikey smelled those blueberry pancakes again as he came downstairs. "You're the best!"

"It's a big day." Arthur smiled, handing him a stacked plate and their special syrup.

Mikey hadn't told him the truth. He hadn't told anyone but Viki what really happened at the test. As far as they knew, he just used his abilities and showed the elders he had complete control over them. It didn't seem right to ruin their joy or make them worry. Besides, he'd passed. Mikey hoped that because the Tribunal portion happened in front of many Jaecar eighteen and older, Elder Tem and the rest of the high council couldn't do anything too horrible.

"With your and your team's abilities, you should have no problem taking on any of the other omadas. And Thomas isn't even a factor, so it's a win-win."

"Yeah, I hope it goes that smoothly."

"But still, don't let your guard down." Arthur tried to finish sternly, but his smile was still there. His enthusiasm made Mikey feel a little lighter. Plus...pancakes.

Arthur let Mikey borrow their car for the day, and as Mikey appeared on the porter platform, the Sect seemed to be even busier than before. He made his way to the TC and found Sabrina and Luke together.

"Hey." Sabrina kissed him. "How are you feeling? You seemed a bit off last night,"

"Feeling much better now. I was just tired yesterday. And I'm a little nervous about what might be in store for us," Mikey said.

"Whatever it is, we'll get through it together." Sabrina squeezed his hand.

"Exactly," Luke added. "And hopefully, I get to practice my...skills."

"I hope not. For the enemy's sake," Mikey smirked.

Marcus came shortly after, and the three remaining teams waited for instructions. At 9:15, Elder Cassandra walked in, and the chatter in the room cut off like someone had flipped a switch.

"Good morning," the elder's voice boomed. "And congratulations to all who have made it this far. The final test will be held in a special place. You can only get there with one of these." Elder Cassandra held up her hand to show a blue porter watch.

"Each of you will be given one. To use it, go to the leftmost platform once you enter the portal room. You will receive further instructions there. As a reminder, anyone caught discussing the Tribunal will be thrown out of our order permanently. No exceptions," Elder Cassandra warned. "Now, form a line for your watch."

When his group received theirs, they waded back through the crowd and reached the leftmost platform in the portal room.

"Ladies first," Marcus motioned to Sabrina, who rolled her eyes before pressing the green button on the blue watch. Mikey followed close behind.

The new portal watch seemed to behave the same as his own. One second, Mikey was at the Sect; the next, he was standing next to a large stone pillar. He glanced around, realizing they were in some kind of Roman colosseum. Except it was much smaller. Mikey estimated it was about half the size of a football field.

Pillars of rock outlined the dirt clearing, which Mikey figured was their battlefield. Stone benches rose upwards like stadium seats away from the center. On either side of the field were short towers with winding steps that led to the top.

That must be where the judges watch.

"Whoa, this is so cool!" Marcus looked around wide-eyed.

"Not what I expected," Luke nodded.

His team looked at each other, the excitement on their faces.

"Ahem," someone cleared their throat to their side. They all turned to see Jaecar Chase leaning against the tower.

"It's my favorite band of misfits," he grinned. "Welcome to the Colosseum of Atlantis."

"Chase!" Mikey beamed. He hadn't seen him in months. "Wait... Atlantis," he paused, "Like THE Atlantis?"

"The one and only. It used to be a Jaecar city until a big battle happened between the humans and...other things. This colosseum was the only thing they saved. Or so they say," Chase explained.

"Wow, so they hold Tribunals here?" Mikey stared in awe. "I'm fighting in a piece of Atlantis."

"Oh, speaking of fights," Chase started. "Good luck today. Head down this path between the seats until you get to a stone building. Wait in there, and we'll grab you when your time is up. You guys are the last fight."

"Who are we—" Sabrina started to ask.

"No idea," Chase interrupted. "I was only told to give you those instructions and nothing else. They specifically ordered me to say nothing else. So go, chop chop."

"Alright, we're going," Sabrina snorted. They followed his instructions and found the small stone building. Inside were plain wooden benches and not much else. His team sat down as their nerves began to hit them all. A short time later, cheers rang out from the colosseum.

A voice that sounded like Elder Tem seemed to reverberate throughout the stadium. Unfortunately, none of them could make out what was being said. Cheers rang out for what seemed like forever until a knock on the door brought them all to attention.

"Follow me, ladies and gents," Chase motioned forward.

His team paused as they all stared at each other.

"We got this," Marcus stuck his hand out.

"This isn't a thing," Mikey grunted but placed his hand on top.

"Not even close to a thing," Sabrina sighed, doing the same.

"DREAM TEAM!" Luke cried out as soon as he placed his hand atop theirs.

"Noooo. Dammit. That was my part," Marcus whined. Sabrina and Mikey walked away laughing.

Feeling much lighter, they followed Chase until they reached the edge of the open field. They looked back, and Chase motioned them to step out. Murmurs broke out on all sides as his team walked into the center.

"And the battle you've all been waiting for," Elder Tem's voice rang out. They followed it, gazing up to the top of the right tower. The elder was sitting there with Cassandra and Ryan next to him.

What is this, a game show?

"I'm sure you are all aware that Elder Cassandra's Sect has taken in the son of Angela Black and the ancient vampire Jacob Black, both deceased. I have witnessed with my own eyes his extraordinary gifts, all of our abilities and that of a vampire; none of the weaknesses...." Elder Tem paused for dramatic effect.

Mikey could see where this was going but not where it ended.

What was the point of getting the crowd to distrust him? Was it to make his time as a Jaecar more difficult?

"But where does his allegiance really lie?" Elder Tem continued. "What if it was a choice between one of us? Or one of his own?"

More murmurs rang throughout the audience.

"This is bogus," Marcus whispered. "You didn't tell me you had to deal with this dickwad Mikey."

"I thought I'd save the joy and surprise for all of you," Mikey smirked.

"So—the high council has decided to change the rules a little bit," Elder Tem grinned wickedly.

"Uh oh," Marcus blurted.

"We have recently caught a vampire confirmed to have captured and killed at least a dozen humans, including a small family. And per The Accords, the vampire will be executed. But I thought it would be an excellent opportunity to test where our new acolyte and his omada's loyalty.

"He's not saying what I think he's saying?" Sabrina looked horrified as the arena broke out in deafening chatter.

"They are making us fight a vampire?" Luke said a little too excitedly.

This is pointless. These idiots don't freaking get it. Wanting to see if I'd choose a vampire over a human?

Mikey didn't care about what someone was. It only mattered what was in their heart. This creature had killed people, and children. He'd torn families apart just like his own. Stopping monsters like that is what he'd been training for.

"This is preposterous. My daughter is down there. You would release a vampire on children?" Elder Cassandra shouted.

"These are not children," Elder Tem barked. "These are acolytes who wish to become Jaecar. Is that not what this test is all about? To see if they have what it takes to root out evil and exterminate it?"

Nods could be seen throughout the stadium.

"Besides," the high elder continued. "Your daughter knew the risks when she decided to form an omada with—him."

"The council is going too far—" Elder Ryan started.

"Silence!" Elder Tem thundered. "This was sanctioned by the high council. We must know for certain! There are a dozen elders on standby in case of an emergency."

That last bit of information seemed to calm the crowd's concerns. *How powerful is an elder really?*

Gasps began to ring out of the crowd on the opposite end of the colosseum. Mikey activated his vampiric eyes and had to squint from the sudden brightness. Walking towards them between the stands was the vampire. Instead of humans that had meridians throughout their body, a Verdaat's body WAS Source. It looked like Viki's, except...*dimmer?*

Four Jaecar elders followed behind the vampire, their Source at the ready. They ordered the prisoner to halt about ten feet away.

"Oooooo," the vampire stared at Mikey, licking its lips. "What are you? I don't care. I'm so hungry! I'm Ivan. I'll be drinking you dry," it cackled.

Other than the black-red eyes—the same as its Source—the vampire looked like a malnourished, ordinary man.

"Also, he might be weak and a little out of his mind from hunger," Elder Tem added. "Begin!"

One elder came and unlocked the shackles with the other three close behind, ready for any sudden movements. Once the vampire was free, the elders retreated back into the shadows of the stands.

The vampire's frenzied eyes locked onto Sabrina. *Shit, we aren't in formation.* Mikey cursed. They were so caught up in the craziness of it all it hadn't even come to mind. He began inching closer to Sabrina, hoping Ivan wouldn't notice.

"One of them told me for every one of you I eat, I'll get a two-second head start before they try to kill me. But I'm so hungry I would've done it anyway," the starving vampire squealed with laughter.

The next instant, Ivan blurred as he charged for Sabrina. Thankfully she was ready for it, dashing backward with a flash of speed. The vampire pivoted to intercept, but Mikey was there. He slashed at the vampire's head with his Source claw but hit empty air. Mikey ducked backward as sharp fingernails darted for his throat.

He's not faster than me. And I think I'm stronger. But why does it seem like he is? Mikey didn't have time to think it through as Ivan pivoted again, this time heading for Luke. As Ivan closed on the Healer, the vampire quickly changed course, diving to the side.

"Dammit, I forgot you vamps could see Source," Luke groaned. "I was hoping it'd touch you a little."

"Whatever that is... it's bad news," the vampire's eyes widened. "I should—" Ivan jerked sideways as a ruby-red ball of Source flew over his back.

"No. Definitely the girl first," the vampire grinned wickedly, glaring at Sabrina. "Hungry. Hungry. I need it. Hehe. Your blood, that is. It smells soooo good. You should be helping me, though," the vampire paused before twisting its head toward Mikey. "You smell...like me. Have some—" he gestured to his friends, "I'll share. But the girl's mine. So yummy."

This must be Edax.

Mikey shivered at how eerily similar the vampire's rantings sounded to the monster inside him.

"You hear that, Sabrina. Mikey's not really that into you... you just smell yummy," Marcus chuckled, attempting to draw the vampire's attention. With Arthur's training, Marcus's barriers were no joke. They'd have at least a few seconds to take it down if it attacked the Shielder.

"You... you have nothing," the vampire eyed Marcus. "Except a stick." It chortled.

"A big stick," Marcus smirked.

Mikey and the rest of his group tried to get into formation to take down the crazed vampire once it dove for Marcus.

"Nope, I said the girl first," the vampire croaked as it somehow came to a dead stop and dashed straight behind them for Sabrina.

At that moment, Mikey realized what the vampire had that he didn't; control and experience.

"No!" Mikey called out too late.

Sabrina dove out of the way as soon as she realized, but the vampire already had momentum. While she was still in the air, a lightning-fast chop slammed into her side with a crunch. She gasped as the impact pushed the air from her lungs.

Mikey got there just in time to force the vampire back.

"One down. Heehee," it squealed.

Marcus and Luke tried to maneuver closer to them. It was dangerous with them divided.

"This is madness!" Elder Cassandra roared from the tower.

"This is reality! Will you defy the high council?" Elder Tem replied coolly.

Mikey didn't get a chance to hear her response. The vampire blurred, once again charging for Luke before diving away. Despite being completely bonkers, the vampire was doing a good job keeping them apart. Mikey couldn't leave Sabrina undefended.

It's now or never.

"Marcus, Luke," Mikey called out. "I want you to start walking towards me. Marcus, you need to shield whoever he attacks. Especially Luke, okay?"

"All right...what are you gonna do?" Marcus replied.

"I'm going to make him slow down. Luke, get your decay ready."

"Yes!" Luke beamed.

"Ah, the boy says his plans out loud. Tricky. Who to kill? Who to kill...." Ivan debated with himself.

Mikey used the distraction to condense the Source in his right palm, molding its purpose. A fiery blue orb the size of a pebble flashed to life in his hand. He fed the sphere more of his Source, and it grew. The fog of Mikey's breath became visible as the temperature around the orb fell quickly. Mikey formed a small barrier around the skin of his hand—the best he could do for protection—but it already began to feel numb.

After several terrible cases of frostbite, Mikey discovered he could mold his Source to behave like a heatsink; an object that absorbs the surrounding heat and releases cold instead. He'd gotten the idea months ago when Marcus had commented that it always felt colder near Mikey's claw. After he had dug deeper into the Source that powered the blades in his right hand, Mikey felt the energy absorbing nearby heat and lining it along the claw's edges.

"Whaaaa—" Marcus's jaw dropped.

"An Elemental—" Luke was equally stunned.

The stadium fell silent.

"Now," Mikey signaled.

Even Ivan could tell the power behind Mikey's ball of ice. When Marcus and Luke stepped forward, he hesitated. They continued making ground. The vampire's eyes shot back and forth between them as Mikey waited for his opportunity.

The vampire snarled and then lunged at Marcus. Sparks flew as Ivan's claws raked at the Shielder's formidable barrier. Mikey's elemental attack impacted the ground at their feet, sucking in the heat around the blast radius. Ice formed in the blink of an eye as Ivan dove away, screeching. His left hand had shattered after being flash-frozen solid. Marcus had dashed backward, his shield protecting him. But the effort had visibly exhausted him.

Ivan hissed, turning to Luke. He had been creeping ever closer to the group, but now Marcus's retreat had created space. The desperate vampire charged for Luke as a ruby-red orb flew past Marcus to slam into Ivan's calf, snapping his shin like a twig.

Luke rushed forward with two globs of decay in hand— a maniacal grin plastered on his face. Ivan screamed as the decay landed on his forehead and chest. Most of the crowd turned as the vampire began to necrose. Huge, gaping wounds started forming. The screams ended when the decay had reached Ivan's neck.

Mikey's claw quickly removed the vampire's head.

The team rushed to Sabrina, who struggled to get up.

"Sorry I was out for a bit," she blushed. "I think he broke a few ribs."

"Yeah, well, that slapshot at the end redeemed you," Marcus winked. "And uh—that was equal parts disturbing and amazing, Luke."

"Thanks. Worked as intended," the Healer puffed out his chest.

Mikey looked up at the murmuring crowd and then at Elder Tem, who wasn't doing a good job hiding his disappointment.

"Congratulations," Elder Ryan clapped. "Not only have you slain a monster that had taken the lives of many innocents, but one of your team has shown us a skill that only one person alive can use today. I would be proud to call any of you Jaecar."

Elder Cassandra stood up and joined him. "Well said."

A single clap rang somewhere in the crowd until another joined, then another. Soon the colosseum was roaring with applause and cheers for the new hunters.

"Yes. Yes." Elder Tem jumped up, raising a hand to silence the crowd. "We can add Elemental to the boy's growing list of abilities. Let's truly hope he is on our side."

Many in the crowd booed, but there were enough whispers among them that Mikey knew his comment had reached a few.

The elder sneered at Mikey before looking back out to the crowd. "Now. It gives me great honor to—welcome this omada into our ranks."

The cheers resumed but fewer than before.

"I think you were spot-on with the dickwad thing," Sabrina sighed, holding Mikey's arm.

"Agreed. High Elder Dickwad has a nice ring to it, right?" Marcus chuckled.

The crowd began to disperse as the chatter rose again to deafening levels. Luke went to heal Sabrina, and soon she moved more easily.

He's crazy, but he's good.

The dream team headed for the nearest stone pillar and sat down in its shadow. Before Mikey could even take a breath to process what had happened, Sabrina slapped his arm playfully.

"The big freaking secret move you've been hiding from us is elemental?"

"Yeah, man. How dare you go all Subzero on us in secret. Nah, who am I kidding?" Marcus grinned. "The surprise was worth it!" He gave Mikey a fist bump.

"I will say that was a sight to see," Luke agreed. "I told you it would be interesting to be in your omada."

"Glad I didn't let you down," Mikey laughed.

Chase appeared with congratulations and a few cracks about Mikey's new ability.

"Make sure you are free during the summer so you can keep my beers icy cold!" Chase teased one last time before waving them through the portal. He had to stay and make sure the colosseum was evacuated.

Elder Ryan and Elder Cassandra were standing at the entrance to the TC.

"I want to apologize for what happened back there," Elder Cassandra shook her head. "I never would have thought the council could approve such a thing. You really have them concerned."

"But not you?" Mikey probed.

"No. You have given me no reason to distrust you. And you seem to make Sabrina...happy."

"Excuse me," Elder Ryan cleared his throat. Mikey realized he hadn't used her title. "We are here to tell you that the hunting ceremony will be tomorrow. There are reports of some people going missing an hour north of here. If your team can take on a vampire, I have full confidence it's something we can handle."

"And," Elder Cassandra chimed in, "once you complete this mission, you will be handed your blue pins of Orion and accepted as full Jaecar."

"Be outside the factory at five o'clock tomorrow evening," Elder Ryan instructed.

They all promised to be there, and the elders left them to their celebrations. A very heated debate ensued, but ultimately the dream team agreed to go to Luke's favorite place to celebrate, which turned out to be a nearby miniature golf resort.

"I dunno," Luke shrugged after tapping in his first ball. "It just calms me."

"I guess I can see that," Sabrina agreed.

Mikey had texted Arthur that he'd pick him up to celebrate but Arthur told him he was tired and to spend time with his friends. Viki didn't respond to his calls or texts.

I hope she's okay.

With nothing else he could do, Mikey enjoyed the last night as an acolyte with his friends.

CHAPTER 23

The dream team arrived at the Wonder Bread factory entrance at 4:45 p.m. the following day. Elder Ryan was already there, waiting. He motioned for them to follow, taking them a different route that Mikey wasn't familiar with. After a ways, Mikey saw it ended in a small parking garage. The Elder strolled up to an unmarked white van and beeped it unlocked.

"Get in," he instructed. "Like I mentioned yesterday, it'll be a one-hour drive."

They hopped in, and Marcus took the front seat. It became apparent during the drive that no one had considered how weird it would be to drive in a car with Elder Ryan. That feeling of being closer to equals had yet to quite kick in.

What made it worse was Elder Ryan showed no interest in talking either.

Maybe he feels the same way?

The hour that followed was the most awkwardly silent hour of Mikey's life.

It finally ended when Elder Ryan stopped outside a small rural rest area. "This is the place."

"YES," Marcus cheered, jumping out of the car like a sailor lost at sea who had finally found land.

They were all grateful for the opportunity to stretch their legs and do some scouting. They were at a small rest area off a two-lane highway. The pull-off from the main road was only big enough to fit a few cars. There were no buildings. Just some garbage cans and picnic tables.

"There are reports of people being taken late at night from here," Elder Ryan said.

"Wait," Marcus groaned. "Late at night? That means we'll have to stay here for hours together...."

"Have patience, young one," Sabrina advised in her best old-sage voice.

"It is better to scout the area in the daylight so you know your surroundings at night," Elder Ryan informed. "Nightfall isn't for another hour."

Giving advice had turned out to be the icebreaker they needed as the team began asking the elder practical questions about their hunt. Thankfully, that made the time pass less horribly than the drive.

Around midnight, an inhuman growl echoed within the woods, drawing their attention. Their conversations ended abruptly, and the forest ahead was eerily silent. Elder Ryan exited the van and opened the trunk before coming around to hand them outdoor flashlights. Mikey declined while activating his vampiric eyes. It was better than seeing in the dark. There were rainbows of color around him. Every living thing had Source within it in some form or another, and the forest was alight.

They entered the woods with Elder Ryan and Mikey in the lead. Luke was in the middle, with Sabrina and Marcus closing the hour-glass formation.

Mikey winced as bright headlights shined behind them. A car must have pulled in next to them at the rest stop.

"Dammit. Let's hope whoever that is stays inside," Sabrina cursed.

But they continued on. Eventually, they came upon a large open area devoid of trees. There was obvious evidence of—monster activity. Half-eaten human bones and shredded clothing were strewn about.

"Stay on alert," Elder Ryan commanded. "I hope this isn't what I think it is."

"Bugbear," Sabrina guessed.

As if on cue, the boulder on the edge of the clearing began to move. The air around it shimmered, revealing a large, bear-like creature. It had a rock the size of a beach ball in its hand, and Mikey's eyes grew wide as the creature cocked its arm back. Mikey didn't know how he hadn't seen the dark-brown glow of the beast's Source.

"Run to the center of the clearing! Get into formation." Elder Ryan ordered. "The trees give it an advantage."

The hunting party moved together, dodging a parade of falling rocks as massive craters formed around them from the impact. Geysers of dirt covered the team as they ran. But their plan worked, and the bugbear followed.

Mikey began to form his heatsink orb.

"If you can freeze parts of its body, Sabrina and I will blast it away," the Elder called out to him.

My thoughts exactly.

Mikey nodded.

"If I can get my decay on them, it should overpower their regeneration," Luke added, obviously feeling left out.

The Elder flinched, "Okay. Please don't...miss."

Mikey could understand not wanting to get hit by Luke's ability.

"Marcus, keep an eye on our bac—" Elder Ryan paused, staring into the woods.

Mikey followed his gaze to see what they all couldn't. Dozens of Wendigos had surrounded them a couple hundred yards off, with more joining by the second; they were advancing.

"We're surrounded. It's a horde of Wendigos," Mikey warned them.

"Shit. Shit. Shit," Marcus swore.

"Stand together," Elder Ryan encouraged them. "Focus on one enemy at a time. We must take out the bugbear quickly before the Wendigos get to us. Remember, you are Jaecar!"

"Right," Mikey took a deep breath to steady himself. "Okay, everyone. I'm going in one, two...." And Mikey blurred towards the beast in a burst of speed. As he got into range to launch the orb, the bugbear lunged for him with surprising agility, reaching out with hands several times larger than his head.

Mikey dropped to his knees, turning the sprint into a slide underneath the creature's tree-trunk-sized legs. He used the momentum to spin and launch the frozen ball at the bugbear's back. Ice exploded out of the creature's midsection.

Elder Ryan and Sabrina launched a barrage of Source projectiles as large pieces of the troll shattered. The bugbear screamed from the onslaught. Its guttural growls rumbled throughout the forest. Luke ran out from the creature's side, slinging several orbs of decay. Elder Ryan launched one final blast of Source at the creature's head, scattering remnants of bugbear everywhere.

"Guys," Marcus pointed to the edge of the clearing as Wendigos filled the tree line around them. "We've got bigger problems than how gross I feel covered in bugbear guts."

"This was a trap," Elder Ryan cursed. "They lured us to the center with the bugbear while the Wendigos surrounded us."

"Who lured us?" Sabrina asked.

"Good question," Elder Ryan's eyes narrowed. "Regardless, the only way out is through. We can do this."

"I can do about ten more decays," Luke offered. "With a good hit, it would take one out."

"We'll try and make an opportunity to use them," Elder Ryan nodded. "Marcus, conserve your shield and use it to protect us from vital blows. Keep them off Luke."

"Will do," he agreed.

Mikey turned to the swath of Wendigos surrounding them. Unlike the vampires, their blue-grey Source seemed to be rising off their skin. Like their bodies couldn't keep it in.

When they were only a few yards away, the creatures paused. Mikey could see their glowing eyes filled with hunger, saliva pouring from their misshapen maws.

He formed another heatsink orb, knowing he had a few more in him before the damage inflicted on his hand would need to heal. When Mikey had gotten to this stage when he practiced, it took about five minutes before he could do another. He could do much more with his void core opened, but that wasn't an option with his friends near.

A deafening screech from one of the creatures seemed to be the signal they needed because the black swarm of Wendigos charged. Mikey roared as he launched the icy blast at the advancing horde. Shrieks rang out as several Wendigos went down. Similar howls sounded around him as Mikey's team tried to keep them at bay.

Mikey switched to the Source claw when the Wendigos had closed the distance. Their circle shrank as the monsters pressed in.

Luke lobbed decay orbs over their heads into the swarm of monsters, grinning at their squeals of pain.

He's all kinds of crazy.

But Luke's flesh-eating Source seemed to do the trick as the pressure closing around them eased a bit. Mikey used the opportunity to go on the offensive, using his Source claw and superior speed. Around him, Wendigos roared before falling back several limbs short. There wasn't much he couldn't cut through.

"I need a little help here!" Marcus called out behind him. Several of the beasts had surrounded him, and the Shielder was barely keeping them at bay.

"Keep your shield up. I'm throwing an ice orb!" Mikey shouted while forming another elemental attack. He launched it, nodding in satisfaction as the mass swarming Marcus shattered into bits of ice and flesh.

"Thanks," Marcus called out.

Mikey had no time to respond when a claw ripped across his chest. He cried out as black, leathery hands reached for him. His right arm came up in a blue flash, and severed hands dropped to the ground. Mikey used the second reprieve to fall back.

Looking around, Mikey knew there were too many. More seemed to come from the forest, and his party was losing steam. The Jaecar weren't built for long, drawn-out battles. Sabrina was holding her own with a whirlwind of kicks, and Elder Ryan kept his side at bay with a barrage of bullets shredding the Wendigos in front of him. But Mikey knew they couldn't hold for much longer.

I have to do something...

He could see that one section of the clearing had fewer Wendigos. Mikey could use his void core without worry if his team could push through there and get a safe distance away.

"Listen!" Mikey called out, pointing to their left. "You need to fight your way through. There are only about eight or so Wendigos in that area. Once you get clear, I can use my void to stop them all."

"On it!" Elder Ryan bellowed. Mikey realized how much the Elder had been conserving his Source because he let loose a barrage that might as well have been cannon blasts. The path quickly opened up in front of them. Sabrina and Marcus kept Luke safe as he healed their wounds from behind. Occasionally Luke would toss out a ball of decay, but they made their way to the opening.

Mikey made sure to cover their retreat as best he could. But there were too many. Just as his friends were clear a, Wendigo managed to grab Mikey's right arm, hurling him forward at his omada. Mikey cried out as his right arm snapped when it hit the ground.

"Protect him!" Elder Ryan yelled. The Jaecar surrounded him, and Luke began mending his arm.

"Sorry that plan went to hell," Mikey moaned. He could feel Luke's Source grab the pieces of his broken arm and pull them together.

"All done," Luke said a minute later.

"Thanks," Mikey nodded, stretching it out. Regaining the use of his arm did nothing about the fact that Mikey didn't know what to do. He could see his friends' Source dimming by the minute, and the Wendigos kept coming.

"I say we stick to your original plan," Elder Ryan called back. "I still only see a few on this side, and they've thrown you clear. Hold them off with your Elemental attacks until we're out of range."

"Will do," he promised. "Go."

Mikey turned to the coming enemy. To the black sea of gnarled limbs, sharp spines, and glowing eyes charging for him. He reached for the power inside; demanded the Source in his right hand be bigger, stronger. The air around him chilled as ice crystals formed on his skin and hair. The cold had burned horribly at first, but soon Mikey felt nothing. He continued pouring Source into it, feeding the heatsink until his whole arm had turned black from the frost.

With a wicked grin, he hurled the attack at the snarling swarm. The heatsink hit several Wendigos head-on, but Mikey wasn't prepared for its devastation. Within fifty feet of the impact, everything had been frozen solid. It was a nightmarish field of ice sculptures. On the outskirts of the blasts, the monsters squealed. Several arms and legs had been trapped in the ice.

We might get out of this.

But Mikey's relief came too soon. His eyes went wide as a guttural growl reverberated from the direction his friends had gone. He turned in horror as two bugbears charged his group, and Luke was quickly struck down. His white-blue Source had dimmed to almost nothing.

The remaining Wendigos, seeing their opportunity, continued to press Mikey.

What do I do? What do I do?

Panic clutched at his chest. His omada couldn't hold out much longer.

"Noooo!" Thomas roared, rushing out of the woods towards the bugbears. "You said you wouldn't hurt them!"

Thomas punched several holes into one of the bugbears' legs, forcing it to the ground.

What is he doing here?

But Mikey didn't have time to think about it. With Thomas there, he hoped they'd be able to hold off a little longer. Not wasting a second more, Mikey opened the doors of his void, gasping as the swirling rainbow of energy washed his body in pleasure. Wounds closed, and Mikey's strength returned.

The Wendigos froze, their eyes wide before falling one by one. The grass at Mikey's feet blackened, then death spiraled out in all directions as the life around him was consumed. It felt so good.

"Yes! More. You need more," the darkness inside of him cried out. Black tendrils came from the depths of his left arm and tried to pry open the mental doors to his void.

"Just let it go. You'll be unstoppable. You can defeat them all," It promised.

Mikey would be a liar if he said he didn't think about giving in. He wouldn't have to hurt or fight anymore. There would be no more worries. He would just feel—good. Forever.

But a scream from Sabrina woke him up from the trance.

That's what I'm fighting for.

He slammed his meridians closed and pushed the beast inside of him away. Mikey's eyes snapped open and scanned his surroundings... *encircled by death in all directions.* The sounds of battle drew his attention back to his friends. One of the bugbears was down, but the other wasn't, and it had a large tree in its hand.

Elder Ryan and Thomas were the only two left standing. Mikey could barely see the brightness of their Source.

With renewed strength, Mikey covered the distance to his companions instantly. He dove into the standing bugbear with his claw arm extended and burst through its chest, the Source blades ripping through like butter.

"Are you okay," Mikey ran over to them.

Thomas managed a scowl before collapsing to the ground.

"I don't have anything left," Elder Ryan fell to his knees, wheezing.

Mikey checked on the group. Thomas was bleeding heavily, and his left arm had been crushed. The rest of the crew hadn't fared much better.

Sabrina and Marcus had taken heavy blows but were, for the most part, okay.

Luke was the most concerning. Blood drained from his ears, and Mikey could see Luke's Healing tendrils were trying to keep his body going, but his Source was fading fast.

"You held on long enough," Mikey thanked his mentor. "I'll handle the rest."

Elder Ryan nodded before he succumbed to exhaustion.

The second bugbear had gotten back to its feet. Mikey rushed towards the monster to draw it away from his friends. They were shieldless, and one slam from the two-foot tree trunk in its hand would be the end.

A deep rumble escaped its throat as the bugbear lifted the club high. Mikey launched another heatsink orb at the creature's exposed armpit. The furry behemoth screeched when its arm broke off at the shoulder, shattering to pieces when it hit the ground.

Mikey dove to the side as the bugbear's other hand slammed into the floor where he'd been a moment before. The earth rumbled from the impact. Not losing momentum, he threw another orb at its leg, and the bugbear collapsed in a roar of outrage. Mikey climbed on top of the downed behemoth, hoping to sever its head, when something hard suddenly slammed into his back.

Mikey's body hurled sideways, snapping several trees in half before hitting the ground with a crunch. He tried to take a breath but choked on the blood pouring into his lungs. One of his eyes wouldn't open, and his arms and legs didn't want to listen either. Mikey opened the doors of his meridians slightly, hoping it wouldn't harm the downed Jaecar nearby.

Without risking more, he absorbed a tiny bit of the Source around him before closing off the void. Thankfully, it was enough. Breathing became a little easier. Mikey realized the bugbear he'd run through had already regenerated. He used the other as a distraction before hitting him with a tree club.

The bugbear lumbered towards him with an expression that Mikey guessed was a smile. Giant, jagged teeth too big for its mouth gleamed in the moonlight.

I guess this is the end...

Mikey knew he could open his void entirely and kill them. But his friends wouldn't make it, and Mikey knew the darkness inside him would win. He'd let go, and that would be the end--of everything.

The bugbear paused, that same ghastly grin on its face. Then to Mikey's horror, it turned in the opposite direction—towards his friends.

"No," Mikey rasped. He screamed for his body to move, but everything was broken. All he could do was watch as the creature made its way to the helpless Jaecar.

"Ouch. They banged you up pretty good," Viki appeared beside him.

"Wha—what are you doing here?" Mikey croaked.

"I'm here to take you away," she whispered.

"Away? No. No. Help them." Mikey coughed up blood. He didn't understand what she was saying. The others were right there.

"That's not... that's not what I'm here for," Viki looked away.

"What are you talking about? They're right there. Your friends."

But Viki wouldn't look.

Then it hit Mikey. This was a setup. All of it. Memories of that horrible night when he was five flashed through his mind.

It was the same.

Viki wasn't his friend. She was only there to watch him. To wait for an opportunity after he'd controlled his powers.

Sabrina was right. I'm so naïve...

But Mikey didn't want to believe it. Those nights they'd spent talking. The hangouts with Viki and the others. Her loneliness. That was real. Viki had to save them.

"No!" Mikey roared, ignoring the pain. "Those are your friends whether you like it or not, Viki! Now save them! I'll do whatever you want. I'll go with you. Just please!" he begged.

Viki looked at him finally, her mask of callousness wavering. "You don't get it," she shook her head. "I'll be—punished. To disobey him...."

"I don't care! Even if you are tortured for a gazillion years. It's better to stand up for what's right. And letting your friends die is wrong," he declared.

Viki grabbed his head and stared into his eyes before looking at the sky. "Tsk, fine! But you better come when I tell you and no fuss. I trust you. Bad things will happen if you don't. Worse than this."

"Yes. I promise. Now please help them!"

Viki vanished, only to appear on top of the bugbear's shoulders. By the time it realized she was there. Viki had used something from her wrists to slice the creature's head clean off. She repeated the same move just as the second bugbear was getting to its feet again.

"Thank you..." Mikey's body drooped. He'd lost a lot of blood.

But Viki's here now. She promis—

Then Mikey passed out.

CHAPTER 24

Mikey awoke to the faint smell of lavender and honey. He jolted upright as the memories of what happened rushed back.

"Whoa. Take it easy," Sabrina came to his side.

"You're all right!" Mikey beamed. "Thank goodness."

"Thanks to you," Sabrina kissed him.

"Is everyone okay?"

His heart sank when Sabrina turned away, bringing her arms to her chest.

No.

"What happened? Who was it?" Mikey's heart raced.

Viki promised she'd save them!

"It's...Elder Neema." Tears streamed down Sabrina's face.

"Elder Neema?" Mikey didn't understand.

"Luke was—he was in bad shape. And Elder Neema...she wouldn't give up. She used all of her Source to save him," Sabrina cried in his arms. "She was like a grandmother to all of us."

Mikey tried to swallow the sudden lump in his throat, but it stayed. He didn't know what to do or who to be angry at. The old Healer had been much the same to him. And Mikey wasn't sure he'd be standing here if she hadn't helped him. And she'd died because of him. It was all a trap to get to him.

Sabrina lifted her head as Mikey went stiff. "What?"

"This was all because of me," Mikey couldn't hold back the tears anymore. "They wanted me and Neema died...."

"It's not your fault," Sabrina said sternly. "That type of thinking won't help anyone. I won't have you turning into Thomas. You didn't send those monsters after us. You did everything you could to protect us. I won't hear any more of that talk." She flicked him on the head.

"No, you don't understand. It's because of me—Ouch!"

Sabrina flicked him harder, then wrapped her arms around him. "I'm so glad you're safe."

"The feeling is mutual," Mikey kissed the top of her head, the tension somehow gone.

They held each other for a while before a knock at the door drew their gazes. Marcus peeked his head in. "Hey, dude. Just wanted to check on you."

"Hey. Glad you are okay. Come in," Mikey smiled.

"How's Luke?" Sabrina asked.

"He'll be okay. Just needs a couple of days to recover."

"Thomas?" Sabrina added.

"He's up. His arm is gonna be out of commission for a week or so. But he'll live."

"What was he doing there?" Mikey wondered.

"I tried to ask him, but he shooed me away and went into the bathroom," Marcus shrugged.

"I remember him saying, "No, you said you wouldn't hurt them," Mikey recalled.

His friends stood there in silence, confirming what they all thought.

"Do you think he was...involved in this?" Sabrina asked.

The group tried to process what that would even mean.

"I was involved in it," Thomas said, appearing in the doorway.

"Really, Tom?" tears welled in Marcus's eyes. "What do you mean you were involved in it? Elder Neema is dead!"

"I know, okay!" Thomas cried out. "You don't get it. You don't know what I've been dealing with!"

"Then tell me!" Marcus pleaded.

"Simon's alive! The vampires have him," Thomas sobbed.

"What—what do you mean Simon's alive?" Marcus froze.

"He's alive, Marcus. They kidnapped him for some...project. They've been using me to—" Thomas looked down, "to spy on the sect."

"And that's why you've been acting so crazy towards Mikey...." Marcus seemed to piece the puzzle together.

"They told me if I said anything, they'd know and kill Simon," Thomas explained. "Then, when Mikey came, they told me to watch him and report back on everything. So, I thought he was here to infiltrate our order. When I failed at the tribunal—I was so angry at everything. I told them about the hunt...but the vampires promised me that they only wanted Mikey and that everyone else would be okay. And now..." Thomas's eyes filled with tears, "Elder Neema is dead."

"How could you?" Sabrina looked horrified.

But Mikey could understand. What choice did Thomas have? Betray your family or betray your order? He'd never want to be in that position dealing with that weight.

"I see how you could," Mikey said somberly. "I would never want to make that choice. Sorry, you had to go through that."

For a brief moment, Thomas looked like he'd been punched in the face. But then, he threw his hands up and shook his head. "Like, I want to hate you so much for so many reasons...but you make it hard," he smirked.

"Thanks..." Mikey trailed off.

I guess that's a compliment?

"Was Viki involved in this?" Sabrina questioned.

"Yeah. When she whispered, 'stay away from Mikey, or your brother's dead,' I kinda figured," Thomas growled.

"She saved all of us," Mikey blurted. "She came to grab me and was going to leave. But she saved you. You were her friends."

"Yeah. AFTER betraying us," Marcus rolled his eyes.

"She was in the same position as Thomas. Scared of someone...she said she'd be punished for not listening," Mikey said.

"Let's just be glad things didn't end worse," Sabrina changed the subject.

They found out later that evening that Elder Neema's funeral would be held in two days. After, they'd have their initiation ceremony into the order of Jaecar.

Mikey had texted Viki asking if she could wait until after Neema's funeral. She hadn't seemed happy about it but finally agreed, warning that 'bad things might happen.' Luke had woken up shortly after, so they checked in to ensure he was okay. Mikey wanted to spend the next few days with his friends and Arthur as much as possible.

After twenty minutes of him talking about how fighting the bugbears had given him an idea to 'speed up the tissue necrosis,' they knew Luke would be fine.

The rest of the night he spent with Sabrina. Mikey had done his best to make her think nothing was wrong.

He spent his last day with Arthur and wanted it to be just like it used to be. They ordered takeout and watched crappy TV. Then Mikey made some Pop-Tarts for dessert, and they headed off to bed.

The following day Mikey met his omada at the Jaecar cemetery. A considerable section of it had been dedicated to Elder Neema. The plot was outlined by a garden of yellow and lavender flowers. Hundreds of people had shown to mourn one of the most significant losses of their order. Mikey wondered how many of these people Elder Neema had taken care of.

Thank you, Elder Neema. For everything...

Mikey's phone vibrated as the final processions were ending.

Need to go now. Meet me on Nelson St.

3 blocks down.

He turned to Sabrina and kissed her, "I'm gonna find a bathroom, be right back."

"Okay," she smiled.

Once Mikey had waded through the crowd, he was at Nelson Street within a few seconds. Viki waved him into an alley close by.

"Wow. You came. You're a man of your word," Viki looked impressed.

"Uh yeah...what made you think—" Mikey paused, seeing the horrified look on Viki's face.

He followed her gaze to a large, tan, beautiful woman standing behind him, blocking the alleyway entrance. The woman was almost a foot taller than Mikey, with solid and lean features.

That's an Amazon if I ever saw one.

"Brittania—what...what are you doing here?" Viki managed a smile, but it looked like she was trembling to Mikey.

Wasn't Brittania one of the Verdaat she was closest to? He didn't understand Viki's reaction.

"You failed. So your father sent me," Brittania grumbled.

"Don't worry. It's not what you think. He's—" Viki tried to explain.

"Silence! Your actions led to this. Do. Not. Interfere," Brittania ordered.

"I think there's been a misunderstanding here—" Mikey started to say, but the woman's hand appeared around his throat. She lifted him up like he was nothing but a ragdoll. Mikey activated his claw, but Brittania's other hand had already clamped around his forearm. The amazon twisted, and it snapped.

Mikey screamed, looking to Viki for help. But she just stood there trembling with her head down.

That was the last thing Mikey saw before it all went black.

"Ugh," Mikey mumbled.

My head is pounding. Where am I?

Mikey opened his eyes but saw nothing. It took him a second to realize his head was covered with a cloth. His hands were held together by...*iron?*

Light rushed into his eyes as the blindfold was suddenly removed. As Mikey's eyes adjusted, he saw a short man in his early thirties standing before him. The man had an olive complexion with long, black hair tied back with a golden bangle.

Even though he looked ordinary, Mikey could tell by his mar-quis-shaped eyes—entirely yellow—that he wasn't human. That's when Mikey noticed Viki kneeling beside the man, shivering. She looked at Mikey from the corner of her eyes. They were filled with desperation and sadness, and his heart wrenched.

Mikey sensed someone was behind him. He turned his neck to see the woman from the alley, Brittania; she was holding his arms in place.

"Ah, Mikey. Welcome home," the man bowed.

"Are you Viki's father?" Mikey's eyes narrowed.

"I'm everyone's father here—in a way," the man laughed, but it never reached his eyes. "I am Lord Magnus. Leader of the Verdaat," he bowed.

Mikey remembered what his parents had whispered that night. What Arthur had said.

It was him. All of this was because of him...

"You killed my parents! You—you took Simon from his family!" Mikey snarled. "You're a monster!" The doors to his void started to itch, and Mikey wanted to give in.

"Me? A monster?" Magnus grinned wickedly. "My dear boy—" the vampire lord vanished, appearing behind Mikey. "You have much to learn," he whispered.

TO EVERYONE,

This journey has been incredible, and I want to thank everyone who read this book, promoted this book, or helped in other ways.

A special thank you to my family. Shout out to my wife, who was instrumental in getting this story out. More is on the way!

Please leave a review if you enjoyed it. I added a QR code to make it easier. The reviews help more than you know.

Much love,

-Jay